Amazon 5/11/2

FAITH AND JUSTICE

Family is the world's greatest masterpiece

Faith and Justice: A Legal Thriller

Tex Hunter 2

Peter O'Mahoney

Copyright © 2019

Published by Roam Free Publishing.

peteromahoney.com

1st edition.

All rights reserved. No part of this publication may be reproduced, stored in a retrieval system, or transmitted, in any form or by any means without the prior permission in writing of the publisher. This is a work of fiction. Any resemblance to any person, living or dead, is purely coincidental.

Cover design by Belu.

https://belu.design

All rights reserved.

ALSO BY PETER O'MAHONEY

In the Tex Hunter series:

Power and Justice

*****

In the Bill Harvey Legal Thriller Series:

Redeeming Justice

Will of Justice

Fire and Justice

A Time for Justice

Truth and Justice

FAITH AND JUSTICE

TEX HUNTER LEGAL THRILLER BOOK 2

PETER O'MAHONEY

CHAPTER 1

THE CHURCH steps were filled with parishioners, smiling in the winter sunshine, their Sunday morning gossip filling the air.

Thirty potential victims, at least.

Criminal attorney Tex Hunter stood at the edge of the street, looking up at the church steeple, in awe of the structure built almost a century ago. When bells began to ring through the still air, he watched the Baptist church members line up to shake the hand of Reverend Noah Darcy. Reverend Darcy was young, fresh-faced and uncomfortable; still coming to terms with the fact that he was now the leader of the congregation at only twenty-nine years old.

Hunter walked up the concrete steps, hands in his coat pockets, his coat collar turned up to the damp air. Tall oak trees lined the street, their long shadows dulling the warmth of the sun, and the steeple of the brick church poked out above them. The stained glass windows looked impressive, almost as impressive as the building itself. There was a sense of history in front of Hunter, of a past fought long and hard. This church had seen many battles, and the latest battle against racism was challenging its people to the core.

"You shouldn't be here." An old lady, half his height, brushed past Hunter, ensuring her elbow connected with his arm. "Nobody wants you here."

"This is a place of worship." Darcy intervened, turning to Hunter when he heard the woman's aggressive tone. "Your murder investigation has no place here."

"You wouldn't return my calls, and I thought I'd find you here on a Sunday morning." Hunter stepped up the final concrete step and stood next to the pastor. "And I've heard you preach that the chance for true forgiveness can only come when we're tested."

"You're certainly testing me, Mr. Hunter." Darcy held his hands out wide as two males came up behind him, both as tall and as broad as Hunter. "I'm sure you can understand why I wouldn't want to interact with you—you're defending the man who murdered our Reverend Dural Green."

Hunter looked to his left, past the faces snarling at him, past the hatred that these people had for him, and spotted a white van on the road. It was moving forward at a crawling pace, despite the road being clear.

Hunter had seen the dented white van circle past the block once already. It wasn't unusual for a twenty-five-year-old van to be driving the streets of Grand Crossing in Chicago; rather, it was new cars that stood out.

The vehicle slowed as it approached a group of children on the sidewalk, almost as if the passengers were staring at the children, focusing on them.

"That's why I was calling you, Reverend." Hunter kept watching the van out of the corner of his eye. "I wanted to hear your opinion on something."

Five children.

No older than ten.

The men behind the African American pastor stepped closer, but Hunter didn't flinch. He'd been in enough fights, and had enough training, to know that he could take them both. One quick left hook, followed by a straight right punch, and the problem would be taken care of.

The van turned around. Slowly edging up the road again.

Closer.

"Mr. Hunter, I don't feel that this is the time or the place for this discussion," Darcy continued. "This is a place of worship, not a place for a controversial law discussion. I've avoided you because, quite simply, I don't want to talk with you. I thought that would have been clear to a man with your intelligence. I don't want to be a newspaper headline."

Hunter didn't respond.

He watched the van, tires rolling forward, then turned his attention to the children, who were clapping their hands together in perfect rhythm.

Closer now.

Something was not right. These were dangerous times for the church. Controversies were as regular as the Sunday service.

There were three girls and two boys on the sidewalk; all dressed in their Sunday best.

Smiling. Innocent. Carefree.

Hunter moved, ignoring the minister and his congregation. He dashed back down the steps.

The van stopped.

"Mr. Hunter?" Darcy called out. "Are you leaving already?"

The tinted window of the van rolled down.

It had stopped under the shade of a tree. Hunter couldn't see inside; there were too many shadows, it was too dark.

It was only a second before Hunter saw the rifle. It was pushed out of the window, resting on the door of the van.

Hunter looked at the children.

So happy. So free.

The grins on their faces, the laughter in their voices.

Their clothes were so pristine, so perfect. The two boys had neatly trimmed hair, the three girls each had their hair pulled back into a ponytail, not a strand out of place. They were in the third grade, starting to find their own voices, starting to discover their individuality. For them, life was still a perfect collection of days spent with friends; learning, laughing, growing. They knew danger was alive in their suburb, they had practiced school shooting drills earlier that week, but it was always an arm's length away.

The gun pushed further out.

The children didn't sense the danger. They were completely unaware of the menace lurking beyond the street.

Hunter ran.

"Move!" He screamed for the children to take cover. "Get down!"

The first gunshot rang out.

It was unmistakable, echoing through the neighborhood.

Muscles clenched. Instincts kicked in.

Hunter raced to protect the children.

He shot past the shocked faces of the adults, past the people stunned with fear. He reached for the youngsters, moving faster than he had in years.

The second shot came quickly after the first.

His arms wrapped around the children, his back to the white van, huddling the children together.

He felt the third shot before he heard it.

It hit his shoulder.

And when the blood from a girl splattered against his face, his world became a blur.

CHAPTER 2

PLEASURE IS nothing without comparison to pain.

Tex Hunter took great comfort in the idea that a person who had felt the deepest sorrow was best able to experience the greatest joy. It had been more than thirty years since he had felt free, more than three decades since he felt a flash of pure delight. Pain was a constant companion, an acquaintance that was always there for him, a reminder of who he was. Despite his past, despite the decades of pain, he had hope for the future, hope that one day he could experience joy again.

He often thought that if he were ever to get a tattoo, it would be the words of poet Ella Wheeler Wilcox: 'Weep, and you weep alone.' But he wasn't a fan of ink, nor did he trust anyone enough to write on his body.

Oak Street Beach, in the neighborhood of the

Gold Coast, Chicago, had the potential to hold great delight, and in his past, it once did. Sitting on the park bench at the edge of the beach, under the branches of a young tree, he listened to the calm waves lap gently against the sand. Only joggers dared to venture to the beach in late February.

Reminiscing about the days when his family drove from their home in Logan Square, he smiled. There was a purity to their life then. The way they threw the Frisbee around, the way they laughed, the way that their love for each other was unmistakable. He remembered his older brother talking to every girl that walked past, his mother reading fiction under an umbrella, and his father teaching him how to throw a baseball. Those days the sand was too rough, the sun too hot, and the beach too busy, but it didn't matter.

Those summer days were special; days that would never be forgotten, as they were the last days before his father was arrested for the murder of eight teenage girls. The events of that summer changed him; he lost his innocence, his youth. He was forced to grow up far beyond his years.

After that summer, he never let his guard down again.

Love, peace, and calm became foreign notions.

"There's nothing more you could've done." Esther

Wright rested one hand on Hunter's right shoulder, the one not covered in bandages under his suit, and handed him a takeaway coffee. "You did everything right. You didn't pull that trigger."

His assistant sat next to him on the park bench, crossed one leg over the other, and looked over Lake Michigan.

"What if I'd moved quicker, Esther? More to the left?" Hunter grimaced as he reached for his drink. "I could've taken more of the bullet. I could've saved her."

"No, Tex." Esther shook her head. "You did everything right. She's still alive, and by all reports, she's a fighter. You gave her a chance. Without you, without the risk that you took, that girl would've been dead. There were no casualties because you stopped them. You did everything right. No one else was brave enough to dive in front of those children."

The paper reported Hunter as a hero, a man who risked his own life to save the innocent, but that was a concept he was uncomfortable with. He reacted on instinct, not heroism. The real heroes, he had always argued, were the people who used their working hours to save others—the firefighters, cops, paramedics. Of course, the paper didn't print that quote; instead, they chose to print an old quote from his father: 'Don't persecute my boy. He'll be a hero one day.'

Hunter hated that quote.

His father had said it from a prison cell when Hunter first graduated from law school, and the media ran photos from his graduation. The law community already hated Tex Hunter, and that quote only further cemented their dislike of him. Many people were the same—although he had nothing to do with his father's actions, and was only ten when his father was arrested, they held him responsible in some way.

Esther Wright gazed out at the view, and a jogger running past winked at her. She smiled as if she was very used to male attention, and then slurped her coffee loudly.

Hunter recoiled, as did the jogger who also shook his head. Esther, Hunter's long-term assistant, was a woman who had been blessed with the gift of splendor—her eyes were a mesmerizing shade of cobalt, her smile melted the coldest of hearts, and her honest demeanor drew most people in. Her sandy-blonde hair rested just beneath her shoulders, even in winter her skin was lightly tanned, and her figure was a healthy feminine shape. She was almost perfect; except nobody had ever taken the time to teach her any manners.

She slurped her coffee again; this time, it was loud enough for a young child, who was twenty yards away, to lean forward in a stroller, and stare at her.

She smiled and waved, oblivious to the disgust of the world around her.

"How did you even know I was here?" Hunter asked as she took the drink away from her lips.

"You weren't in the office at 9 a.m., and you're never late." She gulped a large mouthful of coffee. "And when you need time to process something in the morning, I usually find you here, looking out at the lake."

It was nice for someone to have his back, but Hunter wasn't used to it. He was used to standing on his own, swimming against the tide, without even a life raft in sight, but the longer he spent with Esther, the more he became comfortable with her caring nature.

"Do they have any leads for the church shooting?"

"They haven't got a thing, Esther. The van wasn't registered, there's no CCTV footage around the church, and the witnesses didn't see much other than a white van. Forty people outside the church and they saw nothing of value." He shut his eyes as a gust blew into them, bringing a sprinkling of sand with it. "And all I saw was a rifle poking out of the passenger window. I didn't see any faces in the van."

"It must be tough for the police. They've already got so much racial tension around your case with Amos Anderson murdering the minister, Dural Green, and then something like this happens. They know they have to tread softly here. There's so much hate in the city at the moment, and it's threatening to turn into a riot. I remember studying the LA riots in school, and nobody wants that here."

"That doesn't mean they should stop doing their job and avoid catching a shooter. If the shooter has done it once, then they're going to do it again." He watched as a young biracial couple, one African American and the other Caucasian, walked past hand in hand, snuggling into each other. "There are rumors the White Alliance Coalition is associated with the church shooting, but there's no evidence, and nobody's claiming it. This was more than a random attack. These people are filled with hate."

"I've heard about the White Alliance Coalition—a small group of deadbeats living on the outskirts of the city. I heard the leader on a documentary saying that people of color should be segregated. It's a pity; I thought those sorts of attitudes were left behind in the 1950s."

"People love nostalgia."

"If there was one thing I learned studying history at school, it was that history belongs in the past."

He smiled. "These people don't have the same morals that you and I do. They receive funding from an anonymous source, and they're actively recruiting. They're playing off people's fear and filling the world with hatred. The media is giving them a voice, even though they only represent a tiny portion of the population, because readers respond to them with loathing. That emotion, that drama, sells papers."

Esther forced a smile.

She looked out at the beach and remembered the time, ten years earlier on her twenty-first birthday, when she went skinny-dipping there. It was past one in the morning on a cold spring night, and her friends dared her to do it. Never one to back away from a dare, she stripped down and leaped into the water. She only lasted a few seconds before the chill in the water almost froze her to the bone.

"Once, there was a man in a police interrogation room." She turned to Hunter. "And the man said to the cop, 'I'm not saying anything without my lawyer present.' And the cop said, 'But you're the lawyer.' 'Exactly,' he replied. 'So where's my present?'"

Hunter chuckled.

"What did the pirate say when he turned eighty?"

She waited a few moments, a grin stretched across her face. "Aye matey."

"That's so bad it's funny." Hunter laughed out loud. "But I fail to see how that's relevant."

"It's not." Esther shrugged. "I'm just trying to get your mind off current events for a few moments."

"I only know one joke and it's a blonde joke. So, why are blonde jokes so short?"

"So, men can remember them." She retorted quickly before he could answer.

"Well, that joke took an unexpected turn."

"Not if you'd asked for directions."

He laughed loudly again. They sat for a minute, enjoying the buzz of laughter, taking in their moment of joy. It was a rare reprieve from their stressful lives, but it wasn't long before their thoughts turned back to the inevitable, back to the unavoidable depravity that they encountered every day.

"Come on, we should get to the office. We have a case to prepare for." Hunter stood and drew a deep breath of fresh air, ignoring the sharp stab of pain in his shoulder. "It's going to be a busy month."

Esther waited a moment longer, and then stood next to her boss, looking up to him.

"I guess the question is: are you going to pass on the current case with the faith healer Amos Anderson? You could step away. You've only had the case on your desk for a week. You haven't poured a lot of work into this yet. You don't have to defend the man charged with killing Reverend Green. You'd only be inviting more hate into your world."

"I won't pass on this case. Not now." Hunter buttoned up his coat. "This case was the only reason I was at the church. It's the only reason I was there to save those children. If I was a man of faith, I would say that it was a sign from above."

"You don't have to invite this danger into your world, Tex. You could step back, take it easy for a while. Maybe even take a vacation. Relax a little—go south and get some sunshine."

"Esther, I'm not a person that runs from danger."

"I know," she whispered as he walked towards the parking lot. "That's what I'm afraid of.

CHAPTER 3

CAYLEE JOHNSON ran her finger over the Glock handgun. It felt so cold, so emotionless, but so inviting.

She loved the weight of the gun. The way it rested in her hand.

Her .22 shotgun leaned against the fence post behind her, looking strong in the country breeze. The weapon was a tenth birthday present from her father, her very own shotgun, the best present she had ever received. Her father painted the handle bright pink just for her, although the years had faded the paint. She was so happy that day. It wasn't the first gun that she had fired, but as she entered her second decade on the planet, it was the first one that she owned.

Falling in love with the handgun almost felt like she was cheating on the shotgun, but the heart wants what the heart wants. She reasoned that there were so many guns in the house, most stored in the garage, that she had the right to choose which one suited her best. The Glock had been her favorite since she'd turned twenty, almost a year ago. There was something real about the kickback, the authority. Something raw about the intensity of power.

It was always her father's aim to influence the policymakers. He wanted to be remembered as a game changer, someone who shifted the course of history. The family had enough guns in the shed to arm every member of the White Alliance Coalition and start a riot on the streets of Chicago. They could start a riot big enough to change policy, a riot that could change their city forever.

Her father, Chuck Johnson, talked about the moment when they would reach a turning point, a point when they would have an opportunity to be remembered in the pages of Chicago's history.

Her Uncle Burt believed every word of the speeches, although he was gullible enough to believe anything her father told him. He would do anything for the White Alliance Coalition. Their numbers had dwindled a lot over the years, down to ten people at the last meeting, but Uncle Burt had enough blind passion for twenty men.

"The White Alliance Coalition will rise," her father had said before the meeting. "We will conquer."

The guns gave them power, the feeling of supremacy. Her father often said that they would be nothing without the guns, nothing without the explosives. They didn't have much money, only enough to get by, but the weapons were their treasure trove; their fortune and wealth.

Their home backed onto the Spring Lake Nature Preserve, outside of Barrington, Illinois; a place of tranquil peace and quiet. She had long felt a kinship to this land.

Most of the homes on their road were regal, with the type of entrance that demanded tall swinging gates. Most of the properties were seven-bedroom monstrosities that sat back from the road and had horses, gardeners, and full-time housekeepers.

Not the Johnson's home.

The old metal gate across their driveway was overgrown with weeds, and held two signs: one warning people not to trespass because of the dogs, and the other warning them not to trespass unless they wanted to get shot.

The other residents complained about them often: the constant gunshots, the overgrown weeds, and that their dogs killed the wildlife that dared to venture onto their thirty-acre property.

The property had been in the family for five

generations; passed from one racist Johnson son down to the next. The original residence, little more than a hut, still sat near the road and their current family home; a one level, four-bedroom brick house built in the sixties to replace the previous weatherboard dwelling, sat at the end of a long driveway.

Chuck Johnson had won a payout due to a work accident when he was only twenty and spent most of his life on the property puttering from one thing to the next.

The two-door garage that sat next to the house contained most of their gun collection. There were forty guns at last count. Not to mention the C-4 explosives that Caylee's father had recently gotten his hands on. It amazed her what was available on the black market.

There were four old broken down cars behind the house; two of them being rescued and worked on by her uncle. Cars were the only thing he understood.

Behind the cars were the dogs' cages; four Dobermans, who were often barking loudly.

The police were regulars to their property, but they had visited more frequently over the last month. First, they came to question her father about his whereabouts on February 1st—the night that

Reverend Dural Green was murdered—and then they were back to ask if he was involved in the shooting at the Baptist church last week.

They asked her Uncle Burt questions too, so many that his answers got mixed up. It wasn't hard to confuse Uncle Burt.

The police didn't ask Caylee a single question. Not one.

She had never been good at lying. If they had asked her the right question, she might have collapsed under the pressure. She almost wanted that to happen; to relieve herself of the guilt that she was carrying on her shoulders, to take the choice away.

She was getting to an age where she had to make a decision between her family or her friends.

Her friends didn't know who her father was, who her family was, and they wouldn't like it at all, but family was family. It was all she had.

She held the handgun tightly, pointing it towards the tree.

The slow squeeze of the trigger was what she enjoyed the most; the anticipation of the power that was to come. She smiled, waiting for that moment.

She aimed at the beer can sitting on a log that backed onto the lake. She was never too sure who would be out on the lake, out there having fun. That only added to the intensity of it all.

When she had no margin for error, no chance to flinch, no chance for a misstep, the melody began. It was when her entire body was engulfed in adrenalin, stinging her senses, pulsating fear through her being. One wrong breath, one slight lean of the body, and she would miss her target, sending the bullet on its own path to destruction.

The sound of the six shots resonated around the woods that surrounded their house.

It felt good—that rush, that power.

She smiled again as she looked at her handgun.

She would end this.

All of it.

She wasn't going to let this war go on any longer.

This was her destiny.

CHAPTER 4

THERE WAS a time for force and a time for patience, and knowing the place for each approach was the most effective skill in any interrogation.

Tex Hunter looked to the furthest ledge of the bookshelf in his office; past the law books, past the reference material, even past the five fiction books that he had placed at the end of the row. There sat his temptation; a bottle of rare Pappy Van Winkle's Family Reserve bourbon. It called to him, often the result of the stress that he faced day after day.

The office was large, with the afternoon sun streaming in behind his desk. Space was at a premium off West Jackson Boulevard, and Hunter realized that every year when he received the notice about the increased rent. Even as a defense lawyer, he thought the fees were daylight robbery.

He tapped his finger on the wide desk that sat prominently in the room; it was starting to get on his nerves. Too dark. He wanted something brighter, something more modern, but he couldn't imagine that his clients would be impressed by a light Scandinavian-style desk. His clients wanted to feel a sense of history when they entered his office, a sense of being intimidated by the might of the law.

He knew that Amos Anderson was terrified by his current situation. In their first meeting, Anderson had barely stopped twitching the entire time. When Hunter agreed to take the case to trial, Anderson almost cried with relief.

If Hunter was to extract the information he needed from the man, he needed to tread gently. He needed to use silence rather than force; patience more than power.

To a nervous person like Anderson, a silent response held more potential in an investigation than a threatening one; the intense pressure of silence was more likely to provide the information he needed.

"Your four o'clock, Amos Anderson, has arrived," Esther buzzed through his phone.

"Send him in."

The door to Hunter's office creaked open.

Amos Anderson stepped into the room slowly, deliberately, trying to calm his nerves. He wasn't doing a very good job. Or perhaps he was, and his actual nerves were about to force him to collapse. Hunter had seen pictures of Anderson in the past, in which his smile was vibrant, his skin glowing, and his eyes clear.

He saw none of that now.

Instead, the man who entered his office had slumped shoulders, bags under his eyes, black frizzy hair, wrinkled shirt and trousers, and one of his shoelaces untied.

"Not sleeping well?"

Anderson tried to smile. "I haven't slept well in a month."

They shook hands, but even his handshake was weak and lifeless.

"It's nice to see you again." Anderson sat in the chair offered by Hunter. "Thank you again for taking this on. I hope this meeting is going to provide some good news. I could really do with some good news today."

Anderson crossed his arms and leaned forward slightly; the pose of a man who looked like he was about to be ill.

Hunter was his third lawyer. Anderson had already burnt through the first two. The first was an experienced lawyer but drunk most of the time, although he managed to stay sober enough to secure Anderson bail during the first hearing. The second was a young man fresh out of law school. Anderson didn't have faith in either of those men keeping him out of prison, and they both pushed for him to take a deal. Anderson wanted someone in his corner; someone who was more than willing to fight for him in court.

Amos Anderson had been practicing as a faith healer for three years. Although he studied to become a scientist, he found his calling using energy fields to heal people. Laughed at by his fellow science graduates, his results spoke for themselves. People claimed he had cured them of addictions, mental illness, and physical ailments. His reputation grew quickly, as did his bank account.

His followers almost became parishioners; they had faith in everything he touched.

"I'm afraid not, Amos. Only more questions." Hunter picked up a pen, studying his client's reaction closely. "What do you know about the Baptist church shooting in Grand Crossing?"

A look of confusion washed over Anderson's face as he rocked slightly. "The one where you were hit in the shoulder?"

Hunter didn't offer a response.

When a person is nervous, silence can be almost deafening. The moments of waiting can be like the sound of fingernails on a chalkboard.

"I know nothing more than what I've read in the paper." Anderson looked away. "Are you going to step aside from my case because you got shot in the shoulder? I completely understand if you do. These are dangerous times."

Still, Hunter waited.

"Okay, okay. I don't know anything directly, but I know people that hate the church," Anderson conceded. "The White Alliance Coalition is always contacting me because they've hated the church for years. They're very much about 'taking America back' from people like Reverend Dural Green. They know how much Green hated me, and they wanted to form a bond between us." He looked over his shoulder. "But I don't side with them."

Hunter didn't reply. Anderson felt compelled to keep moving his mouth.

"They would contact me on the phone."

Hunter held his gaze on Anderson.

"The spokesperson for the White Alliance Coalition would also send me emails." Anderson paused and rubbed the tip of his nose. "But I don't understand what this has to do with my case. Shouldn't we be working on my defense?"

Hunter leaned back in his chair, not offering a word.

"They never said anything directly. I hardly talked to them because I didn't want to be associated with them, but I know that they're dangerous. You shouldn't go sniffing around in their business, you know? I'm sure they've hurt people in the past, and they wouldn't hesitate to do it again."

Anderson didn't continue talking right away. He reached out and moved a pen holder slightly on Hunter's desk, dispersing his nervous energy. It was a sure sign that he was avoiding an honest answer.

"I see where you're going with this." Anderson avoided eye contact, squirming to find a comfortable position. "You're suggesting that he caused the pastor's death and not me. I'm not sure that it's a wise decision to blame someone like Chuck Johnson."

That was the information Hunter wanted. He wanted a name, and he got it without pressing for an answer. That was the difference between power and patience.

He wrote the name down on the side of a folder and then turned his attention to the current file, finally breaking his silence.

"Amos, I'm always honest in my approach to the case, and that's because I want you to have realistic expectations of what lies ahead. The evidence the prosecution has for the murder of Reverend Green is strong, and that means that the case is currently in their favor. They have witnesses that saw you together on the street near where his body was found, your blood and DNA on his dead body, and you have a strong motive for his murder. That doesn't mean we can't win, but the current position is that we won't. If you don't take a deal, we may lose this case, and you may go to prison for a very long time. If you want me to continue to defend you, then that risk needs to be very clear to you as we move forward."

"I understand." During their first meeting, Anderson was intimidated by Hunter's presence, and he hoped that Hunter would bring that power to the courtroom.

So far, he hadn't been disappointed.

"The information I have is that Reverend Green's death was caused by three blows to his skull on the night of February 1st after you had an argument with him at a seminar about depression." Hunter opened a file in front of him. "For this case to progress, I'm going to have to paint a very clear picture of what happened that day. I'm going to need to know everything about that seminar and your movements afterward. I want you to tell me the exact words that were exchanged between you and Green, who was at the seminar, and who saw you arguing. I need to know every little detail about what happened, and I want nothing but the truth because if you tell me it was windy, I'll pull the weather report. If you tell me the traffic was bad, I'll search through the traffic data. If you tell me that a man with a blue hat bumped into you, I'll search the CCTV footage to find him. I need to know everything exactly as you remember it. In a case like this, our best chance of winning at trial is to present another suspect to the jury, and that will create doubt around your guilt."

"Isn't it the police's job to look for suspects?"

"In their eyes, they've already found the killer. Their job is completed. And where their job finishes, mine starts. Now, the police have looked at the obvious answer, and found enough evidence for your arrest. They've looked at the big picture and come to the conclusion that you're the murderer. They haven't looked at the small details. And it's in the small details that I'll find the answers. If we only look at the big picture, we'll come to the same conclusion as the police. Your innocence lies in the small details."

"I didn't do it," Anderson whispered, shaking his head, hands together as if he still had handcuffs on. "That's what matters."

"Whether you're guilty or not isn't my concern; you've pleaded not guilty, and this is how we're moving forward." Hunter held his pen ready. "On the night of February 1st, why were you near the entrance to the alley behind 520 South Michigan Avenue? They have witnesses that place you there around the time of the murder. That evidence is hard to dispute."

"That's fairly compelling," Anderson said.

"Because it's so compelling, we'll need to explain it to the court. We'll need to convince them of a legitimate reason why you were there. These are the things that we need to be prepared for if this is going to trial. I'll ask you again, why were you there in the alley behind the Congress Hotel on South Michigan Avenue?"

"I was never actually in the alley. I was at the entrance to the alley, on Ida B. Wells Drive, but I didn't go down there." Anderson looked like he wanted to fall onto the floor and curl into the fetal position. "I was in the area after the seminar about research into depression cures. I've been to many of these seminars before, and that night, I was giving a speech on the effectiveness of faith healing. Green was also there talking about how God was the answer to treating depression. He ambushed me after my speech. Actually, it was even during my speech—he was heckling me at every opportunity. He purposely chose that function to publicly argue with me because he knew that reporters were there."

"But the seminar finished an hour before you were seen near the alley. Why were you still there? Why hadn't you gone home?"

"I spent a long time talking with Lucas Bauer, my business partner, and after that, I wanted to spend some time walking the streets. Cool my jets."

"Cool your jets?"

"Lucas and I had an argument after my confrontation with Green. Lucas wanted to expand the business and bring on fake faith healers because he saw it as a money-making opportunity, but I knew it wouldn't work. His plan was amateurish; it was a money grab. It might've worked for a month, but it wouldn't have worked long term. Money wasn't the reason we started the Faith Healing Project. We started it to make a difference."

"How far did you walk?"

"I walked around a few blocks, sort of aimlessly, but then I was coming back to the Congress Hotel, and that's when I passed the entrance to the alley."

"Did you see Lucas again?"

"Just past the entrance to the alley. We talked; he'd calmed down. We agreed that he wouldn't take action until a business plan was drawn up. I was calm by then too."

"The biggest problem we have at the moment, Amos, is that your blood was found on Green's sleeve, and your DNA under his fingernails."

"Inside the Congress Hotel, he grabbed me by the throat and slammed me against the wall. His fingernails cut my neck, and that's how my blood got on his shirt."

"He must've been holding you hard to cut your skin."

"He was." Anderson leaned forward, trying to calm his nerves, trying to deaden the grumbling in his stomach.

Hunter could sense that Anderson was holding information back, but Anderson's determination to fight the case, to take the charge to trial despite the risk of a longer sentence, meant that he was either innocent, disillusioned, or thought he could beat the system.

"You come across as very intelligent, Amos." Hunter tapped his fingers on the edge of the desk for a few moments. "You're lucky that your reputation precedes you. We may be able to get away with saying that you were 'cooling your jets.' The jury may buy into that."

"Buy into that? Mr. Hunter, you should be aware that I'm not part of the typical urban existence. I'm not the usual defendant that you represent in court." There was now strength in Anderson's voice. "I'm one of the different ones. One of those people who never fits in anywhere. A loner. Eccentric. Peculiar. Strange. Call me what you will, but I do things differently. I don't do things because they've always been done a particular way; I do things because they've never been done that way. I try new ideas. Push boundaries. Think outside the box. And I do that because often the ones who are crazy enough to try something new are the ones who find something that works."

"We will need to present you to the court as normal."

"But that's not me."

"What matters isn't who you are." It was Hunter's turn to lay down the law. "What matters is how much we're able to convince the jury of our version of the truth. And to convince them of the truth, their perception of you matters immensely. If you were a six-foot-eight biker with tattoos all over your body, the jury wouldn't believe that you were walking the streets to 'cool your jets'. But if your reputation is one of a normal, calm person then that's a story they may believe. How the jury members see you is very important. We need to convince them of your story, and that means that everything must fit. If one thing is out of place, whether it's appearance, your personal story, or the likelihood of an event, then they won't believe the whole puzzle. It all must fit together. Every aspect of it."

"I don't see how appearance matters. None of that should matter. None of that is important. I didn't do it. That's the truth, and that's all that should matter. The courtroom has to be about the truth."

"I'm afraid not, Amos. If the truth were all that mattered, then I wouldn't have a job."

CHAPTER 5

ESTHER WRIGHT scrolled through the files on her computer, her eyes scanning over report after report, article after article, stating that there was no scientific evidence that Amos Anderson's skills were legitimate.

She was fascinated by the Faith Healing Project. The fact that Anderson claimed he could simply wave his hands around a person, feel their energy and life force, adjust it, and change their condition, completely went against everything she was ever taught.

Her father was an accountant, and her mother was a school teacher. They were always doing things by the book, doing everything expected of them. They never did anything outlandish, never anything outside of the box. Their world was straight and narrow.

But there was always something inside of Esther that felt different.

Faith healing made sense to her. Although there was no scientific proof that any of it worked, the proof was in the results. People were falling over backward to tell others how much Amos Anderson had changed their lives.

While researching the case, she found out that Tex Hunter's nephew, Max Hunter, was one of those people. He was on a Facebook page dedicated to Anderson, telling the viewer how much Anderson had changed his life by curing his drug addiction, by getting him off the drugs for good. He had kicked his three-year heroin addiction overnight thanks to the powers of Anderson's hands. His voice was convincing, so passionate.

There was video after video of testimonial evidence from others stating that Anderson had changed their lives.

It was almost cult-like.

That amount of faith in a single person had caused discomfort, and sometimes outright disgust, in church communities. They felt threatened by what some called the Devil's work. In particular, Reverend Green of the Baptist church in Grand Crossing took a stand against what he saw as evil, deceiving, and an outright falsehood.

Esther watched a YouTube video of Reverend

Green preaching about how much evil Amos Anderson was spreading. It was brainwashing, he said; a mind trick.

Under Hunter's direction, she had spent the morning going through the comments on the YouTube videos by Reverend Green, particularly the ones where Anderson was mentioned. Although some comments supported Amos Anderson, most were in favor of Reverend Green and in support of his disgust directed at new-age healing.

She could hear Hunter and Anderson discussing the case in the office behind her, and when the door opened, she sat up straighter.

Anderson walked out of Hunter's office looking more confident than when he had walked in. Hunter followed him out and placed three files on the edge of Esther's desk. It was a long reception desk with two monitors on the left-hand side, but Hunter still found a way to fill the rest of it with paper files. Esther constantly argued that he should be saving trees by printing fewer documents, but he never listened. She had even placed two tall indoor plants by the door of the office to force him into thinking about the trees that were being cut down for paper printing.

It didn't work.

"It's nice to meet you, Mr. Anderson." She smiled.

"I've heard a lot about your work with faith healing. One of my friends was healed of her alcohol addiction with your assistance."

"Thank you." Anderson drew a long breath. "In these times of stress, that means a lot."

"I'm interested, Amos." Hunter leaned against Esther's desk. "Can anyone learn the skill of faith healing? Or is it something you're born with?"

"You asked me to be honest…" Anderson sighed as he stood near the door. "It doesn't work."

Hunter squinted. "What doesn't work?"

"The faith healing."

"What do you mean?"

"My hands don't cure anything," Anderson said with an air of complete tranquility, showing them his hands, turning them over to look at his palms. "At least, by itself, it doesn't work. My hands aren't magical."

"You know that your hands don't work?" Hunter asked. "So what you're doing is a complete fraud? You're tricking people. We can't let that come out in court. You can't be seen as a fraud or the jury will convict you on the spot."

"I'm not a fraud."

"What about all the people in your advertisements that claim the faith healing works? Are they paid actors? And Tex's nephew? He claims that you cured his drug addiction? Is that fake or is he being paid as well?" Esther asked.

"They're not paid actors."

"Those people claim you've cured them of their depression, addiction, or physical ailments. They claim they're happier and more complete than they have ever felt. Are you saying they've been brainwashed? Is that what you do?" The anger grew in Hunter.

"Have you ever heard of the placebo effect?" Anderson was calm as he placed his hands in his pockets.

"Of course."

"The placebo effect is reported to have a success rate between twenty-one to forty percent in any standard clinical trial for pain management. The rate has been steady since it was first discovered in 1955. The first study theorized that it had a thirty-two percent effect."

"What's this got to do with the Faith Healing Project?" Hunter asked.

"While I was in Bali meditating, I had a vision. I

had been meditating for three days, and this moment of clarity was special. It washed over me like a deeper understanding of human behavior. I was able to see how the world was pieced together and understand that we were missing parts of the puzzle. While Western society is developing drugs to do wonderful and amazing things, we are not developing our minds. I was deep in meditation when I realized that if any drug had the effectiveness of forty percent, it would be sent off to labs to be further developed. So much money would be poured into that drug to find a way for it to become more effective, but we have ignored the greatest drug we have."

"Our brains?"

"Exactly," Anderson responded with enthusiasm. "And the reason we're not developing it is because Big Pharma, the drug companies, wouldn't be able to make money out of it. So, I decided to develop the placebo effect. I decided to make it more effective. I'm a scientist at heart, that's what I've studied my whole life, and I knew that I could develop this further. But to do it, I needed a convincing story. I needed people to believe in what they were being told, and if I could do that, I knew that I could be convincing enough to persuade the public of its effectiveness."

Hunter scoffed. "And, of course, you've made money doing it."

Esther turned back to scrolling through the information on the computer in front of her; there were so many testimonials of its effectiveness, so many people convinced by the "show". She considered typing something to them, letting them know about the conversation she was having, but she wisely decided against it.

Having information was one thing; using it was another.

"I didn't make money from it at first—I gave the treatments for free when I started. I gave the treatment to around a hundred people and asked them to come back to me after a month to report on the change. But the effectiveness only seemed to be around ten to fifteen percent, less than the standard placebo effect. And that was despite my convincing tales of its quality."

"So, what happened?" Esther was intrigued.

"I met with Lucas Bauer and discussed the idea. The high cost was all Lucas' idea. He said that if you didn't charge ridiculous prices for the product, then people wouldn't be invested in it. To me, that made sense. The more you spend, the more you're personally invested in the effectiveness of the outcome. People had to make a sacrifice to have this product, and it was only then that they would truly believe in its effectiveness. That sacrifice was money.

And by charging a lot, we also only got clients who were willing to do anything to change their current state. They wanted to change, and they believed in the product. Our effectiveness was suddenly close to ninety percent."

"You knowingly advertise a product that doesn't work."

Hunter was scammed by a conman when he was eighteen years old; the man had played on Hunter's need to prove his father's innocence. Hunter lost a lot of money trying to buy evidence that proved his father wasn't guilty, and he had hated cons ever since.

"The Faith Healing Project does work; the practice doesn't."

"Your customers are sold a lie." Hunter took a step forward as a show of dominance over the man.

He highly disapproved of Anderson's methodology.

A scam was a scam. Plain and simple.

"If the treatment works for them, is it a lie? The treatment is effective in relieving the client of their clinical depression or reliving them of their addiction or healing their physical pain. We have clinical diagnoses that prove that. The results are our evidence."

"If it was effective, why would every scientific trial state that the product doesn't work?" Esther shook her head, stunned by the revelation.

She opened a webpage dedicated to stating how much of a fraud Anderson was. There were statements of abuse from evangelical Christians, statements of disbelief from scientists, and words of distrust from the general public. The keyboard warriors expressed their hatred for the next fad, said that it was a complete rip-off, or that Anderson himself was just another con man.

But not one of the people quoted on the webpage had ever been treated by Anderson. Their disbelief was built on distrust of his methods, not the results.

"It doesn't work in scientific trials because the people in the trial don't believe it works. They don't believe in the effects of the treatment. The treatment itself has no effect, but the mind's power is the secret." Anderson tapped his temple. "It didn't have to be my hands that cured them; it could have been anything. I could have told the clients that rubbing mud on their arms made them smarter. It was about believing in an outcome."

"You're saying that addiction and depression are fake?" Esther shook her head in disapproval.

"No. Not at all. No way. Please don't interpret my

evidence as that. My mother suffered depression, and it was a harrowing way to grow up. There was nothing fake about what she went through. It was horrible. The effect on me as a child was devastating. Depression is a chemical imbalance in the mind. That's a fact. That's not to be disputed. Drugs can affect the chemicals in the mind, and that's why they're effective. What I do is convince the mind to create those chemicals itself. I empower the mind to do the work of the drugs, so that the mind can heal itself."

"So, people should be able to cure their depression by thinking about it?" Esther asked.

"It's not that simple. There must be a belief that is so strong that a person's subconscious accepts it. You cannot do that yourself. I remind you that twenty-one to forty percent of all clinical trials have a placebo effect. That means that at least twenty-one percent of everyone that volunteers for a scientific trial are convinced by their own subconscious. It doesn't matter what the trial is testing; our minds trick us into believing the effects."

"But the treatment you sell isn't effective." Esther was almost pleading with him.

"The treatment gets results. That is effective."

Hunter stared at him for a long time.

Deception was fraud, no matter how the results came about, and there was absolutely no way that he could let that come out in court.

That would destroy any creditability that Anderson had.

"I'm all for justice, Amos. I'll do my best to defend you in the courtroom. That's justice." Hunter stood tall. "It's also justice that people aren't being ripped off. It doesn't do our case any good to expose the facts now, but once this case is finished, the real information about this treatment needs to become public."

"Why?"

"It's a con, and I won't be any part of that. People are spending their life savings on a treatment that doesn't work. That's not right. Your hands don't work."

"The treatment works."

"I won't move forward with this case unless we agree that the real information about this treatment becomes public once the case is finished. After this case is finished, you will make a statement acknowledging this treatment doesn't work."

"But why?"

"Because it's a scam. People have spent a fortune

on a product that doesn't work, and I won't let that continue. I won't allow people to lose their life savings for a fake treatment."

"That's a very old-fashioned view, Mr. Hunter." The thoughts ricocheted through Anderson's head. He had already lost two lawyers; he didn't want to lose the only one that had agreed to take the case to trial. "But if you get me off this murder charge, then I'll agree to that deal."

"When we're in court, they will ask Lucas if the product is effective. What do you think his answer will be?"

"He'll say it's effective. It gets better results than any drug on the market. Of course he'll say that it's effective."

"Except that it's not."

Anderson nodded. "Except that it's not."

CHAPTER 6

TEX HUNTER studied the painting titled Nighthawks hanging in the American gallery at the Art Institute of Chicago. The room was dim, and there were barely any people around on a Tuesday morning. The odd tourist wandered past, but none interrupted his view of Edward Hooper's 1942 classic.

He loved this painting—a still moment in time of people in a downtown diner late at night almost snapped like a picture. He had such an affinity with the painting as if it was a snapshot into moments of his life. The three patrons in the painting, seated around the diner's bar, all seemed to be lost in their own thoughts, focused on their worries. For Hunter, the painting perfectly represented the isolation of life in a large city.

Private Investigator Ray Jones came up beside him and ran his gaze over the artwork. He never really understood art, but this he could appreciate. This was something that had emotion, despite the lack of it, and vibrancy, despite the lack of bright colors.

The men shook hands firmly, and Jones patted Hunter on the arm. Standing at six-foot-four, the African American man, dressed in a tight black t-shirt and old jeans, looked out of place next to Hunter, dressed in a fitted Italian suit.

"Good to see you, Ray."

"Always good to see you, Tex. Is the shoulder okay?"

"Getting better. The bullet only grazed it—it's nothing serious. I'm only missing a small chunk of muscle. I'm sure it'll grow back."

The men chatted about their lives as they walked down the stairs to the foyer of the art institute. When they arrived at the café, Hunter ordered coffees for both of them. First, they chatted about the Cubs, then the weather, and lastly, the Bears.

"I haven't been into an art gallery since I was a child in school." Jones smiled and leaned back in the chair. "And that must've been a long time ago because I didn't stay in school very long."

"I love this place, Ray. There are paintings here that predate Columbus's arrival on the shores of America. There's a feeling of history here, a sense that we're only a blip in time." Hunter swirled his coffee;

tilting the cup to one side and then to the other. "But you know, seeing paintings by Picasso, Van Gogh, Matisse, Monet—it really hit me that they were the precursors to Facebook and Instagram."

"Facebook and Instagram? I don't know a lot about art, but I'd say they'd predate social media by at least a hundred years."

"Exactly, and they were the ones that started posting pictures of their food on walls. They all said: 'Look at me, I'm having a bowl of fruit and I'm going to paint it.'" Hunter smirked with his arms outstretched. "And here we are, one hundred years later, and everyone's doing the same thing. Everyone's still posting pictures of food on their walls."

Jones laughed; his deep voice echoed around the gallery space, causing some people to look down their noses at him. The chair almost buckled under his weight as he moved. The chair wasn't big enough for Jones. Most chairs weren't. As a broad, muscular man, Ray Jones filled most things out.

"You look tired, Ray. Been sleeping much?"

"Not really. I've been partying hard the last few weeks. Not for any special occasion though—just for the sake of it. I've met a girl, you see, but she's only in her mid-twenties. Great girl, lots of fun, but man, she loves to party."

"You're partying at our age? You're a brave man."

"I've always thought that life isn't about reaching the finish line in one piece, Tex. It isn't about arriving at death with the perfect skin, the perfect hair, or the perfect body." Jones smiled. "It's about arriving at death's door on your last legs, barely able to walk, messed up and blissed out, lost and happy, and looking back and thinking, 'Yep, that was all worth it.'"

"I've seen you party, and the way you party seems to bring the finish line a lot closer."

"That's what happens when you party with women twenty years younger." Jones laughed again before he leaned forward, rocking the table under the weight of his arms. "So, what have you got for me, boss?"

"I've got someone that I want you to look into." Hunter opened his briefcase and placed two files on the table. "His name is Lucas Bauer. He's of German descent, and he's the business partner of Amos Anderson's healing treatments. He's the money man behind their business, The Faith Healing Project."

"You want me to sniff around Anderson's business dealings? Get the inside word to see if he could snap and kill someone?"

"I'm not sure if Anderson killed Reverend Green. I'm going to have a hard time proving that in court, but he appears to be telling the truth when he says that he didn't do it. That doesn't mean he didn't, but he looks convincing. What I want from you is to have a sniff around the manager, Bauer. He's a former Las Vegas show promoter, so that's a guarantee that there will be a backstory to why he's now in Chicago."

Jones stared at the table, focusing on the instructions from his main employer. As a private investigator, he could rely on Tex Hunter's office to hand across the most interesting cases.

Last week, he spent his time tracking a housewife because the husband thought she was cheating on him. She wasn't. Instead, the woman was spending time with her friends at a coffee shop. Jones understood that need for socializing outside of the home, and after the husband paid him the fee, he slammed him against a wall and told him that he needs to loosen his grip on his wife's life.

Most people listened when Ray Jones gave instructions.

"Have you got the time now to look into this?" Hunter asked.

"For you, I'll make time."

"Nothing else on then?"

"Not a thing. Work's drying up. Most people do their investigations online these days. They can find out more in an hour Googling than I can in a week's worth of tailing someone. They can find out who a person is talking to, what they're looking at, and what they're downloading with a few clicks. Without your office, my job is almost obsolete; all I'm left with are jealous housewives and duped employers."

"Don't worry, Ray. I'll always need you."

"And this is much more exciting than trailing workers' compensation claims."

"Good." Hunter removed another folder from his briefcase and handed it to Jones. "I want you to look into the church shooting as well. It's making me angry that they haven't made an arrest yet. My shoulder's sore, and there's no one to blame. But you need to be aware that this case might go into territory that you're not going to like. Racist territory. A man named Chuck Johnson may be involved, so I understand if you want nothing to do with it."

"I've heard of him, and I'm not scared of him. I'll gather the information, put it in a file for you, and then you can do whatever you like with it." Jones watched a group of petite elderly women walk past their table. The women were so perfectly dressed in matching bright colors that he couldn't take his eyes off them. They were like moving pieces of art.

"What's your play with the murder case?"

"We're going to present a new suspect to the jury. That's going to be our best play. The prosecution has a lot of evidence that places Anderson there, but no witnesses to the actual murder. If we can make it look like Lucas Bauer was also around at the time of death, then we can create doubt about who is guilty."

"And how do you intend to do that?"

"I'm going to push him until I hit a breaking point. That's why I need information on him. The more information I have, the easier it will be for me to get under his skin."

"These Vegas promoters are dangerous people, Tex. I'd rather be in a room full of violent criminals—at least you know how they're going to react. Criminals get angry and throw punches. Show business promoters, well, you have no idea what they're going to do because they're going to do it while your back is turned. They're dirty people. Underhanded. Ruthless. There's no honor to these people. You're inviting danger in by just going there."

"Ray." Hunter grinned, closing the file in front of him. "That's how I like it."

CHAPTER 7

THE HALLWAY was dark enough to fear tripping over an unseen object.

The curtains were black, the lighting was nonexistent, and the space was narrow. The perfect place for a mature stage director to pressure a young star.

Tex Hunter walked through the space, running his hand along the velvet curtain, slowly edging his way to the back of the stage. Three twenty-year-old girls kicked their legs high, spun around, and then wiggled their breasts. The director at the side of the stage clapped and cheered, and Hunter thought that the old guy was creepy enough, but it was the man sitting in the front of the theater that really caught his attention.

One long leg crossed over the other, he was studying the dancing burlesque girls practicing their moves as if he was undressing them with his eyes.

Within two days, Jones was able to build a hefty file on Lucas Bauer. Born to German parents, they moved to Chicago when he was ten and educated him in an international school for foreign speaking children. He graduated high school at the top of his class before the bright lights of Vegas called him west. He spent twenty years as a show business promoter in the glitz of the strip before leaving the city almost bankrupt and destitute, returning to Chicago three years ago.

"Mr. Hunter," the man called out.

The girls stopped dancing, turned, and looked at Hunter. They smiled, then giggled.

Hunter returned the smiles, followed by a small nod.

"Alright, break time," the director shouted and then hustled the girls off the side of the stage. He slapped one of the girls on the behind, and Hunter glared at him. The director noticed the stare and kept his head down, aware that he was one small step away from a sexual harassment charge, or many of them.

Hunter walked down the steps at the side of the stage, and the man in the seats stood.

"Mr. Lucas Bauer."

The man that stood before him was flamboyant;

his clothes were perfectly tailored, his physique was athletic, and he was immaculacy groomed. His suit was navy blue, his shirt checkered pink, his tie bright orange. The style of his thin gold necklace perfectly matched the three rings on his fingers.

A man full of color, flair, and style.

Not exactly what Hunter expected from the promoter of a faith healer.

They shook hands, Tex's dominating Bauer's. He was sure that Bauer wasn't dominated very often, but he had to mark his territory. Hunter kept his grip solid throughout the handshake, using his large hands to tighten the grip more than usual. Hunter held Bauer's stare, and grunted as Bauer let go.

"The famous son of 'The Chicago Hunter'. How does it feel to be the offspring of a serial killer?" Bauer dipped his head.

"Famous son?"

"Everyone knows you, Tex. Can I call you Tex?"

Hunter nodded his response.

"Everyone in Chicago knows your family story. We all watched it on television, and my family was the same as everyone else. We were all glued to the television as we watched your father's trial, and we cried for you as the heartbroken boy that watched as his father was dragged off to prison. You and I were the same age when it all happened, and I used to think about how I would react if that happened to my father. The perfect suburban life torn apart by your father's crimes. It shocked the whole city."

"That's not my story."

"Regardless, nobody's family is perfect, certainly not mine. My father has a lot of secrets in his closet. Some that may hurt me one day." Bauer shrugged. "Although my father didn't kill eight girls."

Hunter didn't respond.

"Please, sit down."

Lucas Bauer sat comfortably in the front row of the theater seats. The seats were cushy, well used, and worn down. As Bauer crossed one leg over the other, his bright green socks were on display. Clearly, he chose those socks as part of his outfit. When Hunter opened his new packet of socks that morning, ordered online the week before, he noticed that they all had small compartments for his toes, like a glove. One of the socks had room for seven toes. That was an odd sock.

"I'm sorry we had to meet here, but my schedule is so busy. At the moment, I'm promoting this burlesque show, and I needed to make sure the girls are up to standard, if you know what I mean." Bauer winked.

Hunter didn't respond in kind.

"This show is one of the only things I have left from my time in Vegas. I have the rights to the name of this show, and I'm trying to get it started in Chicago." Bauer brushed his hands down his tie. "They take almost everything from you, you know? When someone in Vegas decides that you're done, you're done. And any attempt to come back is only met with danger."

"You don't look like a man that runs from danger."

"Usually, I'm the danger that most people face, but there are bigger fish than me in Vegas." Bauer confidently leaned back in his chair, spreading his legs wide. "How is it that I can I help you?"

"As you're aware, I'm defending Amos in the case of the—"

"Do you think he did it?" Bauer interrupted.

"Whether or not he did isn't the problem; it's whether or not we can prove it in a court of law."

Bauer laughed brashly, loud enough for the echo to circulate through the small theater. The acoustics were good.

"That's the way with all you law types. Not worried about the facts, or what actually happened. All you're worried about is what you can prove in accordance with the law."

Hunter ignored the jibe. "What can you tell me about Amos?"

"He's not perfect. You aren't either, and nor am I. But Amos is one of the few people that can make a difference in this world. He's a game-changer. He doesn't think the same as normal folk. His brain seems to operate on a different level than yours and mine. He's a trained scientist, you know? He studied science at The University of Chicago because he thought he could develop something new, something to change the world, but science was too restrictive for him. There were too many boundaries."

"Boundaries are important." Hunter looked around the room. "Tell me, if you think he's innocent, why are you testifying against him?"

"I'm not," Bauer retorted. "I'm testifying for the prosecution about what I saw. I don't want to go against my friend, my business partner, but I saw what I saw. If he did it, if he killed Reverend Green, then he has to go to prison. Do the crime, do the time, so to speak."

"What has the prosecution told you to say?"

"The truth."

"The truth is very subjective."

Bauer scoffed, "Reverend Green was a lot like you—always concerned with doing things the right way and by the book. I'm not like you guys. I'd much prefer to break the rules and get an advantage."

"You knew Reverend Green well?" The surprise was obvious on Hunter's face.

"We talked a lot, Reverend Green and I." Bauer smiled. "And the fact is—he was good for business. The more he hated Amos, the more people heard about us. And the more people heard about us, the more they became intrigued. And the more they became intrigued, the more money I could make."

"How romantic."

"I thought of every argument between Amos and Green as free advertising. The papers were beginning to love the battle between the black church and the white faith healer. It was the perfect contrast." Bauer moved his hands to the armrests. "Green served a purpose for us."

Lucas Bauer had the look of a man who was very comfortable in his own skin. His olive complexion and square jaw wouldn't look out of place on a midday soap opera, and nor would his deep, smooth voice. Bauer cast a shadow over most people; however, that shadow would be a bright and colorful one.

It was clear that he was cunning, and if anybody pushed the right buttons, Bauer wouldn't be able to hold back. His combination of arrogance, success, and testosterone made him a melting pot of emotion.

Not what Hunter needed right now.

"Did you set up potential disagreements between them? Arrange for them to be in the same place at the same time so that they could have a public argument?"

"Whatever was good for business." Bauer shrugged as if everyone should have that perspective in life. "Amos has been my ticket to success for a while now. After things fell apart in Vegas, I came back here looking for new ideas. Amos and I went to school together, and after he told me what he was trying to do, the rest is history. We were the perfect team—at least until he didn't want to expand."

"Why didn't he want to expand?" Hunter was intrigued.

"You should ask him about that. We had massive conference rooms ready to be booked out on a national tour, and people were willing to pay through the roof just to talk to him. Amos was the next big thing; faith healing was the next trend. Everything he did was starting to go viral. Even one of the testimonials went viral on Instagram—a before and after shot of a client with a bad back. I had worked so hard to get the Faith Healing Project to that level of success, and it was time to expand. People were ready to be convinced about the power of faith healing. They wanted to believe."

"Do you?"

"It's not about what I believe." Bauer smiled. "It's about how many patients I can sell it to."

A barely dressed girl ran onto the stage, picked up a towel that she had left on the ground, looked down at Bauer, and winked before she tiptoed away.

He smiled proudly.

"I did have plans to make his name even bigger, although that's going to be very hard to do now, whether he's found innocent of this crime or not. I wanted his name to become synonymous with faith healing. I wanted his name to go down in history. We were in a perfect position; the timing was just right. Amos was ready to be the leader of a new wave of healing. We could've been massive."

"While you took your cut."

"Of course. I'm doing the hard work, and I

deserve my cut of his success. I'll still push ahead with the new wave of healers, even if Amos is locked up for life." He looked around the room to see if anyone else was around, before leaning closer to Hunter. "And I'll tell you this right now: if they put me on the stand, then you can be guaranteed that I'll say anything that's in my best interest. Right now, my best interests are to tell the truth and state that I saw Amos at the end of that alley on February 1st, but I'll change that story if I need to. I'll even blame you for the murder if it's in my best interests. I'll say anything. I'd be happy to lie in court."

"I'll pretend I didn't hear that."

"I don't care about your rules. I don't play your game. I make my living out here, in some of the most dangerous parts of the country. I'm not scared of an oath in court. You should step out into the real world, and find out that most of us have to scrape and fight to survive. It's instinct."

"Your testimony better align with Amos' statement. If not, then you're sending your star directly to prison. If you make a mistake up on the stand, then it'll be Amos that pays the price. I need a guarantee that'll you stick to that story."

"You won't get a guarantee from me; I'll do what's in my best interest."

Men like Lucas Bauer had no regard for truth, justice, or the law; something Hunter never understood. Hunter's respect for the law, even when it betrayed his morals, was insurmountable.

"At least I've still got this show, the burlesque, but it won't make much money." Bauer grinned slyly. "But that's not why I do it, if you know what I mean."

"I don't." Hunter leaned closer to Bauer. "Let's get this straight between us—I'm trying to keep Anderson out of prison and I'm going to do what it takes to make sure that happens."

"Alright, alright." Bauer drew a long breath and threw his hands up. "Amos is a very unusual character—that's why he came to you. You're probably the only lawyer in the city that can handle him. That's why he's willing to buy your services and pay top-dollar. He even downloaded a file about all the lawyers in the state, and you were the top choice. I told him not to go with you because of your family history. I'm sure you understand that, but Amos was determined to get you."

"I'm his third choice."

"No." Bauer looked off into the distance. "You're his last hope."

Hunter knew Anderson's last lawyer, Matthew

Marshall. Although only fresh out of law school, he had already developed a reputation as a very capable lawyer. Diagnosed with an autism spectrum disorder, Marshall had a very low tolerance for anything that wasn't standard. He wore the same black suit every day, drove a nondescript sedan, lived in a standard two-bedroom apartment, and talked in a monotone voice. Defending someone with ideas as crazy as Amos Anderson must have driven him insane.

Hunter lived in a different world than Marshall. He loved the characters of his city. He loved the way they made city life a colorful place. And he always loved a challenge.

"Did Amos have a motive to murder Reverend Green?"

"As much as I loved Green and his arguments, he wanted to run us out of business. It seemed like his life goal was to make us bankrupt. That night, at the seminar, he confronted Amos and I. He said that he had evidence that we knew that the faith healing didn't work and he was going to destroy us unless we stopped practicing right away."

"Why would he want to take your business down?"

"Because he didn't like what we were selling. He thought that we were doing the work of the Devil.

Faith healing wasn't something that he bought into, and when some of his congregation started coming to see us, to heal their problems, he was furious. He hated the fact that we were stealing people away from his church, away from his precious version of faith."

"What you're selling has no scientific proof—naturally that must've infuriated a man who preached about religion."

"Ha!" Bauer laughed. "What I sell changes people's lives. I know that. I don't need an official scientific trial to tell me that I've changed the world for the better. Amos and I listened to our patients, and we've made their lives better. If it didn't change their lives, they wouldn't keep paying so much money for it. That's all the evidence we need to have faith in the treatment. People are our results."

Many people had tried to shut them down before, tried to stop them from advertising, but Bauer was as clever as he was colorful. While some companies would've folded under the sort of pressure they experienced, Bauer's business acumen had kept them out of trouble, and thriving.

"Maxwell Hunter, your nephew, said you were by far and away the best criminal defense attorney in the city. He said to me, 'Tex Hunter is the man you have to talk with. He can work magic.' Apparently, they call you the 'Virtuoso of the Courtroom.'"

"Max believes in the faith healing," Hunter admitted. "He said that it changed his life, and for that, I'm thankful. It got him off the drugs, and back into a day job. He's lucky to have that sort of faith in a product that doesn't work."

"Doesn't work? Are you a naysayer as well?"

"I look for the truth. Your product doesn't have one single piece of scientific evidence to back it up, and Anderson admitted that his hands don't have any healing properties."

"Ask your nephew if he wants scientific evidence to tell him that it doesn't work. This is the only thing that has kept him off the drugs."

Hunter shook his head, but he couldn't argue with that. "I'm going to need a list of all the people that Amos treated. I want to be prepared for anything that the prosecution throws at him."

Another girl ran lightly across the stage, holding her chest, covering her body that was naked from the waist up.

Bauer smiled again.

"We can do that. I'm not sure what you'll find on the list, but I'll get my assistant to email you the names. However…" Lucas turned uncomfortably in his chair. "On that list, you're going to find some characters who are quite compulsive. Nancy Bleathman, for one, is an obsessive, psychotic client of the business."

"Go on."

"To her, we're like a cult." Lucas shifted in his chair again. "At first, that amount of praise was good for my ego, but after a while, she became too obsessive and started stalking us. If she knew that Green was trying to take us down, then she may have put a stop to it. I was talking to her that night at the depression seminar. You see, Amos cured her of her depression, and she latched onto anything he did."

"Interesting. She was with you at the conference?"

"She was there that night." Bauer checked his phone, read a message, and then slipped his phone back into his pocket. "Tell me, if you get Amos off the charges, will the cops come looking for someone else?"

"That depends."

"On what?"

"On how much evidence is available to charge the new suspect."

"Do you have a new suspect?"

"I'm talking to one right now."

"Uh-uh, uh-uh." Bauer waved his index finger in the air. "I know how this works. I can see that you're thinking about framing me in the courtroom, but let me warn you." Bauer stood up abruptly. "I'm a man that loves revenge, and if you try to pin this one on me, then I will make it my life's work to have that vengeance. That, I will guarantee."

CHAPTER 8

WHEN THE front door of the church opened, the wind blew inside, sending a shiver up the spines of the few people that sat there late on a Tuesday evening.

The dimly lit church was well insulated, a much-needed feature for any building that had to withstand a Chicago winter, and the stained glass window stood proudly over the front entrance, highlighted against the darkness outside.

A homeless woman sat in the second row, finding a place to rest, an escape from the violent nature of the streets.

Tex Hunter waited in the last pew of the church, closest to the door, looking down at his hands. He resisted the temptation to look at the emails on his phone as he waited; instead, he chose to stare at his hands uncomfortably. It was not often that he was without some form of mental stimulation. There was always another email to check, another form to approve, or another update to read.

He read once that the intense fear of not being able to access a smartphone even had a term, 'Nomophobia'. He was sure he didn't have it, but the longer he waited, the harder it was to resist looking at his phone.

He had no idea what to do with his hands, let alone his mind, without the constant stimulation.

"Mr. Hunter."

Hunter stood as the minister approached, relieved that he was once again occupied. "Reverend Darcy. Thank you for taking the time to talk with me."

"After what you did to save those children, putting your life on the line, it's the least I can do. We said a prayer for you at mass last Sunday. We thanked the Lord that you were here to save those children. Many people prayed together to thank you for your presence." The minister sat next to Hunter. He sat comfortably on the wooden pew with a very straight back, a lot more comfortable than Hunter felt. "We prayed for your soul."

Hunter didn't know how to react; the commendation had caught him off-guard.

"I imagine that my name went down like a lead

balloon," he joked, trying to cover his emotions.

"You still saved the children's lives. Without you, they would've been dead. There's no doubt about that."

Darcy was of African descent—his father was born in Nigeria and his mother in South Africa. They moved to Chicago shortly before he was born, and after he read part of his father's Bible in elementary school, he found his calling early in life. He led the predominately African American parish with passion, as a man with a loud, convincing voice.

"But you're still defending the man that was charged with killing our parish minister. Even after what you did to save those children, I wouldn't say that you're popular in this community. How's your shoulder?"

"It's fine—nothing a few stitches couldn't fix."

"It was certainly a terrible event, and like I said, we were thankful that you were here." Darcy paused for a few moments. "And we must always look at the positives—events like this can bring people together. After the shooting, there have been a lot more people coming to me for support and a lot more attending the Sunday service. A tragedy is the most effective way to bring people together. A tragedy bonds a community."

"That's not the point of view I expected from you." Hunter rubbed his shoulder. "I'm not sure that's the way I would think about a shooting."

"It's the truth. Nothing brings people together like a tragedy, and we've seen that so many times through history. In this modern world, when everyone is becoming so disconnected, we need something to bring people together. I've seen communities in need of tragedy. I've seen communities that need something to link them together. Communities have become so disconnected, and people have forgotten how to even talk with each other. People need each other—that's what makes us human." Darcy moved in the seat, unable to control the emotions bubbling inside of him. "And it's my job to bring people together. It's my job to bring people to the Lord."

"That's an interesting point of view, and one that goes beyond your role as a minister."

"I see my role as very different from Reverend Green's. He wanted to fight a very public fight to achieve peace. He wanted to change the ideas of those filled with hate by giving them more reason to hate. That's not the way I will approach change. My job isn't to fight against the tide; my job is to warm the hearts of those that hate us and fill their empty hearts with love. My work is to achieve moralistic outcomes for everyone."

"Religion doesn't equal morality. They're very separate notions."

"As are law and morality," Darcy snapped. "Your laws in a courtroom don't equal morality. The laws of this city are only as good as the politicians that create them, and the majority of politicians aren't the most moralistic people in the world. They want power."

"And organized religion was created by men who wanted power. No matter what you believe, whether you believe in God, or multiple gods, you have to admit that every religious organization is still run by a person. Its rules are still created by mere mortals."

"Our basis is faith. Faith in the word of God. Faith in the beauty of our Lord. Faith in our scripture."

"And the laws of this city are based on justice. Justice, fairness, and impartiality. That's moralistic."

"We do our best," Darcy conceded. "That's virtuous. Your purpose is in a courtroom, chasing a politician's version of justice; mine is here, in this church, bringing people to their better understanding of the Lord and His work."

Hunter drew a long breath and looked around the church. It was taking all his energy not to argue with Darcy, but he didn't come to the church to have an ideological discussion with a minister; he was there for information. He ran his fingers through his dark hair and then turned to him.

"I've read that you attended the seminar the night Reverend Green was murdered. What time did you leave?"

"Around 10 p.m." Darcy bit his bottom lip. "I caught a cab back to my place."

"How did you pay for the cab? Credit card?"

"No, cash."

"Did you get a receipt? Or can anyone verify what time you arrived home?"

"I don't often get receipts for cab rides." He shook his head. "And I live alone, so there's nobody to verify when I arrived."

Hunter paused, the thoughts tracking through his head.

He looked around the church and imagined it full of people; full of voices. He hadn't attended church since he was ten years old, but he could imagine the power behind it on a Sunday morning service. He figured it would be wonderful—seeing all those people singing their praises for a higher power.

"You said that people have started coming back to the church?"

"They have. Our congregation has almost doubled since the unfortunate passing of Reverend Green. That's what I mean about tragedies. They bring people together." He paused for a moment before continuing. "It's a beautiful thing to see the church filled on a Sunday morning. I always said that I could bring people back here; I always knew I could do it. People like Mrs. Nelson, rejected by Green, and told to leave the church, have started to come back to the services."

"Why was she rejected?"

"She started to see Amos Anderson to heal her decades of back pain, but Green, as you well know, saw that as the Devil's work. He told her she had to choose between the church or the faith healing, and she chose the faith healing. But she has since returned to our flock—returned to help our community."

"That's lovely to hear." Hunter made a mental note of her name. He looked at the names on the walls, of the parish ministers of past years. "Did you always want to be a parish minister?"

"Leading a congregation was my calling in life; it was what I was born to do. This is where I grew up, where I found the beauty of the Lord, and where I had the pleasure of spending my formative years. I always felt like this church, this building, was my home."

"But you would've waited a very long time if you wanted to lead this congregation. Reverend Green was decades away from retiring."

Hunter waited, but Darcy didn't respond. The minister scanned the pew in front of him, running his upper teeth over his bottom lip.

"But with Reverend Green gone," Hunter continued, "you're now able to lead this church. You're now able to fulfill your calling."

Still, Darcy didn't respond. His brow creased, and he blinked frequently, almost looking like he was holding back tears.

"How is your congregation handling the change in leadership?" Hunter pressed.

"People were leaving the church in droves, Mr. Hunter. We were losing the community. Do you know what that's like? Having something that you love so much, and watching as people walk away from it?" Darcy shook his head and looked up to the altar at the front of the church. "It was horrible to watch as every week we had more and more empty seats in the church. Horrible. Reverend Green blamed people like Amos Anderson for taking people away from the church, but he was wrong; people were leaving because the church didn't change with the times. The church, this congregation, was stuck in the past." He opened his hands wide. "And where were they going? Nowhere. Nothing was replacing the community, the love, or the guidance of the church. And that's where society is failing. We've lost our way. We've never been more lost as a community than we are now. Communities need the church. We need each other."

"It's more complex than that." Hunter was stunned by the aggression of the man next to him. "Society is more complex than that. Our knowledge has grown, and science is answering many of the questions that religion couldn't. Religion has been stuck in tradition, stuck in the past, and still refuses to accept science. That has been the church's problem—and not only your church, not only your religion, but religions all over the world. I agree that the church has been the centerpiece of our communities for centuries, our place to share a common bond and that we've lost our way, but that responsibility must rest with the institution that has been stuck in the past. The responsibility must rest with the institution that has been plagued by scandal after scandal."

"No!" Darcy picked up the Bible next to him and slammed it onto the wooden pew. The sound echoed through the almost empty church, the acoustics increasing the aggressive noise. "We're more than our scandals. We must rise above our past, forgive it, and move on. We must move with the times!"

"Reverend Green didn't think so. He wanted to fight it."

Darcy stood up abruptly and walked away from Hunter to the end of the pew before turning back to him and raising his finger.

"People need the church, Mr. Hunter. And I will bring them back to it! I will bring people back to the word of the Lord!"

Hunter didn't respond.

He had come to the church looking for clues about the case, looking for answers about who had the motive to kill Reverend Dural Green and he expected to be pushed in the direction of Lucas Bauer, or perhaps the White Alliance Coalition.

But instead, he walked out of the church with a new direction to follow.

CHAPTER 9

AMOS ANDERSON fidgeted with his hands as he sat on the sofa in his living room, waiting for the arrival of his lawyer. He had a lot to hide, and he knew that the lawyer would uncover secrets from his past.

He just wasn't sure which one.

When the loud knock on his front door echoed through the house, he jumped. He checked the peephole and took three deep breaths before he opened the door.

"You weren't telling me the truth, Amos." Hunter was blunt as he came through the front door of Anderson's home in the neighborhood of Bucktown. Bauer had forwarded the client file from the Faith Healing Project, and it was only a day before a name jumped out at Hunter. "And I don't like lies. They annoy me. I'm your lawyer. Your link to freedom. Your last chance. If you don't play by my rules, then you'll spend the next twenty-five years behind bars."

"I'm not sure what you're talking about." Anderson's answer was honest—but only because he had too many lies to hold back.

Hunter walked into the living room at the front of the house. It had a south facing angle, which allowed the late winter sun to flood in through the windows with enough heat to take the edge off the cold. Built in the 1960s, the home was a suburban refuge from the most populated city in the Midwest, with Downtown Chicago only twenty minutes away by train. The pace in the suburb of Bucktown was relaxed; it was a community that huddled together, watching out for neighbors when the cold nights hit.

A narrow two-story home, the house had a small back yard and an even smaller front yard. The green grass was only a small strip between the metal fence and the red brick home, and the roof was steep enough to keep the snow off during winter. It was tucked next to an almost identical house with the American flag out front on one side, and another red brick home with squarer angles on the other.

"You didn't tell me that you treated a man named Charles Johnson."

"Charles Johnson?"

"Better known as Chuck."

"Oh." Anderson paused. "We're still covered by the attorney-client agreement, aren't we?"

Hunter nodded slowly, not taking his eyes off Anderson.

"Please, come in and have a seat."

Anderson scratched his head and sat back down on the sofa, waiting for Hunter to do the same. Hunter sat in the fabric armchair, old enough to have seen the turn of the century, and waited for Anderson to continue.

"Chuck was one of the early patients we had, not long after Lucas came onboard the business. So I guess that'll be two years ago. Lucas drove me to his house a number of times because he wanted to be healed from his cancer. Lung cancer, if I remember correctly. Or perhaps it was emphysema. I don't know, it was a long time ago, and I've seen many patients since then. I do remember that he coughed a lot. Chuck was participating reluctantly, and he didn't really believe in the treatment. That's why it didn't work. He didn't believe. And I knew who Chuck was, and I didn't like what he stood for. Lucas said that we were doing it as a favor, so Chuck didn't pay a cent for the treatment, and to be honest, I was relieved when Lucas said we didn't have to go there anymore."

"Why would Lucas offer to do it for free?"

"I don't know." Anderson rubbed his wrists. "All I know is that we arrived at Lucas' insistence, and Chuck was very reluctant during the two sessions that we had. The treatment didn't work."

"We need honesty, Amos. You didn't tell me that you attempted to treat Chuck for his ailments. I would hate the prosecution to paint you as a sympathizer with the White Alliance Coalition. That would only strengthen their case, as they could paint you as a racist murderer. That wouldn't be good for anyone."

"If they don't think finding my past clients is important, then, why do you?"

"The truth is important to me, Amos. To proceed with a case, I need to have a full picture of what happened. I need to know every single little piece of that picture, and your past is a very important part of that. This case is already against us; the last thing we need in court is a surprise. I need to cover all the bases and have answers to everything that's coming our way. That means I need no more surprises from you."

"Look, I… I don't know what else to say."

Hunter sighed, leaning back in the comfortable armchair. There was a coffee stain on the left armrest, a loose strand of thread on the right. Although

Anderson earned a lot of money from the Faith Healing Project, money wasn't important to him. It didn't drive him. Buying items for the sake of buying them seemed useless to him. He would rather keep his old, well-loved armchair, than spend money on a new one.

"It must've hurt you to treat him, Amos. You spend your time working to help people, to make their lives better, and that man, Chuck Johnson, is spreading hatred and violence through the world. That must hurt you on some level."

"We're all the sum of our experiences."

"Meaning?"

"If every time I saw a fish, it bit me, then I would be scared of fish. If every time I saw a cop, and he chased me, I would be scared of cops. If my father told me something every day while growing up, then I would believe it. It's our experiences that form our opinions."

"And Chuck's experiences?"

"I spoke to his daughter once about their family while I was at the house. Chuck had a racist father, and every time he saw an African American person, his father told him to be careful. Every experience he had with African Americans was negative. Then his house was broken into by an African American, and the burglar shot his wife and daughter. His wife died, but the daughter survived. That experience only solidified Chuck's opinion. His racist viewpoint was caused by his life experience."

"That doesn't make it right."

"Fear. Isolation. Being scared. They're all factors in his opinions. If all your experiences with one thing were hurtful, you would hate that one thing."

"It sounds like you're defending him. I didn't pick you for a racist, Amos."

"I'm not defending his racism; I'm explaining it to you so that you have a better understanding." Anderson looked towards the window. It was starting to fog up, the inside warmth opposing the cold air outside. "It's the next generation that I feel sorry for. Caylee Johnson, Chuck's daughter. She was different. She was very intelligent, and you could sense that she wanted a different life. I wanted to save her, teach her that we're all equal, but she was so protected by Chuck that nobody had a chance to teach her any common sense."

Hunter took out a small notepad and a pen from his coat pocket, flicked the notepad open and searched through the scribbled pages. He much preferred his handwritten notes over computer files any day. Better for his eyes.

The pen hovered over the pad, stuck as the thoughts raced through his head.

"Amos, I need you to think hard about your options here. The further we get into this case; the more Chuck seems to be involved. The more Chuck gets involved, the more this case is going to escalate in the media. I'm going to have to think long and hard about our options. But in the meantime, I need you to stay away from Chuck. Understood?"

"Of course, but like I said—I haven't talked to him in years."

"Good." Hunter wrote a note on a page. "Now that I'm here, I'm going to ask some questions to get them out of the way. It'll save us from having to do it later. Were you smoking drugs that afternoon?"

"No, sir."

Hunter struck a line through one of his notes.

"Were you high at all?"

"No."

Another line.

"Drinking? Did you consume any drinks that night at the dinner?"

"No. I never drink."

"Were you under the influence of anything?"

"Nothing."

"Is there anything that could be perceived as taking you out of a lucid state? For example, a blackout?"

"No."

"Was there any way that your drink could've been spiked?"

"I don't think so."

"You remember the whole night?"

"I do."

"Good." Hunter flipped the page on his notepad. "The next problem we have is that your DNA was found under Reverend Green's fingernails. That's a big piece of evidence that the prosecution will be pushing. They're saying that you struggled with Green in the alley before you killed him."

"Like I said, when we were at the dinner function, Green grabbed me by the neck and pushed me against the wall. For a minister, he had a lot of unresolved anger. He needed to let go of that anger and find peace. When he gripped my neck tightly, his long fingernails scratched my neck. Everybody saw that."

"When he pushed you against the wall, what did you do?"

"Nothing. Violence is never the answer. Violence—"

"Violence can be the answer, but we will agree to disagree. When did you see him next?"

"He confronted me again on the street after the seminar, as I was trying to calm down. I had left the function one hour earlier, and he was leaving at the time I was walking past the building again." Anderson lurched forward and held his stomach. His bowels had not been kind to him since the case started. Consumed by nerves, he could barely eat, and when he did, the food didn't agree with his digestive system. "As I walked past the event hotel again, Green was leaving. I was on the other side of the street, but he ran across the traffic to confront me again. He shouted at me, and he went to push me against the wall of the building next to us. He had a look in his eyes that I hadn't seen before. This was real hatred, anger, and fear. I was scared of what he was going to do next, so I pushed him back, but only to defend myself."

"You pushed him back?" Hunter's tone was disappointment mixed with irritation. "I thought you were against violence?"

"It was self-defense."

"And this was after the function?"

"Yes."

"Where exactly was this?"

"Outside the parking lot on Ida B. Wells Drive. It was near the back entrance of where the seminar was held."

"Which is also next to the alley where his body was found only a few hours later." Hunter drew a breath. "Why did he attack you a second time?"

"For some reason, I seem to get under particular people's skin. My usual calmness infuriates some people, but that's a reflection of them and not me. It's their highly-stressed lives that mean they cannot relax."

Hunter laughed. "We live in one of the world's busiest cities. Everyone here is stressed."

"We don't have to be," Anderson replied calmly.

"Again, we'll agree to disagree. What did he say to you?"

"He didn't say a lot. He said that he didn't want to meet with me again, and I told him I had no idea what he was talking about. He looked confused."

"What happened next?"

"He walked away from me—down the alley where his body was found, talking loudly to himself. I don't think he wanted anyone to see him outside the seminar. It must have been tiring for him, always arguing with people. I walked back to the entrance of the Congress Hotel and caught a cab back my apartment. I got into the cab around 10:15 p.m."

"The prosecution has witnesses who saw you together around the time of the second altercation. They haven't stated that they saw you push the minister, which is good for us. We will need to disprove their statements. We can do that. Now, the real strength of the prosecution's case is the motive. Obviously, Green was a major objector to your work. He didn't like it at all. In fact, he was about to release evidence that says your product doesn't work at all, and that you know the product doesn't work. The release has been delayed after Green's death; however, the prosecution will know about this report, and they will present that to the court."

"I didn't know that."

"Did you know that Lucas Bauer wanted you out of the business?"

The statement came as a revelation to Anderson. He had suspected it, but he hadn't pieced the clues together.

He looked at his hands, his leg twitching as he took in the information. The past month had been a roller coaster full of emotional distress, and he wasn't sure how much more information he could take in.

"I… I knew he was looking to expand." He fumbled his words. "But I didn't know he wanted me out of the business. I didn't know that he wanted to push me aside. Are you sure?"

"We've got word that he has thirty faith healers ready to take your position and expand the brand across the country. The only thing standing in his way was you."

"I didn't know that." Anderson looked away. "I didn't know that's what he was going to do."

"Well, now, you do." Hunter was softer in his approach. He crossed another line through his notes and turned to the next page. "Tell me about Nancy Bleathman."

"She's got a good heart, and she means well."

"But?"

"But she's a little… how can I say…" He pondered for a moment. "She's a little obsessive. She'll defend us to the ends of the Earth."

"Dangerous?"

Anderson looked away. "I don't know."

Hunter knew this was going to be hard, he knew he was going to have to work for his money, but he didn't expect to be fighting against lies from his client.

"We're done for now, but I don't want any more lies. When I ask you a question, you need to be fully upfront."

"Yes, sir." Anderson bowed his head like a schoolboy after getting into trouble. "When will I hear from you again?"

"Within the week. Sit tight. Esther will call you and set up a time to meet. But remember: try to stay away from public gatherings. We don't want you to become an even larger media story than you already are."

After Anderson closed the front door of the house, Hunter walked out into the cold air, reflecting on the case.

Reverend Green had many enemies, people who hated his outspoken ways, and none more than Chuck Johnson.

And no matter how dangerous, that was the direction Hunter had to head in.

CHAPTER 10

CAYLEE JOHNSON ran her cloth up the barrel of the shotgun as she leaned against the Ford sedan in front of her family's house. The Ford was twenty years old but still newer than the other vehicles on the property. Her father had sprayed the car a fresh green color for her birthday. It didn't look professional, but she liked the hue and appreciated his effort.

She looked down the barrel of the gun, made sure it was straight and gave it a little kiss.

She enjoyed this life—although her university studies in geology gave her hope for the future. It was this life, the quiet one, where she enjoyed herself the most.

The property was out of the way, the entrance discreet, and they had the constant chirp of birds in the background. The afternoon sun was low in the sky, and there was not even a hint of wind. She looked to the trees, and the leaves didn't move. It felt strange to her—that stillness, that calm.

Calmness was something that she hadn't experienced a lot in life.

Her life was always about pushing boundaries. Always living on the edge. Always filled with hate.

"You still studying those stupid books?" Burt Johnson walked out of the house and came up behind his niece. While Caylee was blessed with intelligence from the gene pool, Uncle Burt was blessed with height and strength.

So much strength that there remained little room for intelligence.

"You know I'm still studying, Uncle Burt. You know how I love books."

"The only thing you should worry about is getting married. That's what your dad says too. You need to find yourself a good man, have kids, and settle down." He grunted as he leaned against the car. He rubbed his hands—the days as a laborer were starting to take a toll on his fingers. It was his third job that year. Even at fifty-one, he struggled to control his anger, and that usually meant that he was shown the door very quickly whenever he started a new job.

"You don't have to believe everything that my dad says." She looked down the barrel of the gun again.

"You must have your own thoughts up there in your big head."

"Nah, your dad's always right." He folded his arms. "Thinking hurts my head too much, and your dad sure is right about you needing to find a good man. He says that you could give up studying then. You could focus on having babies. Lots of them."

"Now, Uncle Burt, why would I want babies?" She loved her uncle, despite his overt sexism.

"I don't get why girls study at all. You're never going to use all that knowledge. You need to find yourself a good man to marry, and he'll work to support you."

Caylee shook her head.

Sometimes living with her family frustrated her. Their attitudes were stuck in a bygone era, and she had to fight just to be heard. She was attending Northeastern Illinois University, forty minutes away by car, and when she stepped onto campus, it seemed like she was entering a different century, a world full of different ideas.

It was a different life, and one she had come to love. She accepted the new ideas, the open attitudes to the world. Ideas that her family would hate.

But she also loved her father and uncle, and they

loved her. There was a comfort in family, a comfort in her past, a comfort in everything she had been taught.

She limped around the back of the car, hobbling like she always did.

She didn't remember much about the night she was shot in the leg—she was only four at the time—but she did remember her mother screaming, and those terrified shrieks have never left her. She still heard them every night when she closed her eyes.

"Uncle Burt, I hope you realize that the world is more complex than that. There's more to life than getting married, and I thought you would've figured that out after marriage number three."

Burt had moved in with his brother and niece after his third marriage collapsed two years ago, due to his many infidelities and gambling issues, and had been living in the spare bedroom.

He had been to prison twice, had the tattoos, and the scars to prove it.

Although strong, he was out-witted easily. His older brother, Chuck, had spent most of his life bailing Burt out of one situation or another, but Chuck promised his mother that he would look after his younger sibling. When she was on her death bed, her final wish, her final whisper into Chuck's ear, was to look after "that dumb sack of potatoes."

Dumb as a log, and as heavy as one, Burt Johnson had two kids that didn't talk to him, three ex-wives that hated him, and no friends to speak of.

The Johnson family and the White Alliance Coalition were all he had.

"What's more important to a woman than marriage and babies? How could you achieve anything in life without a man?"

"Uncle Burt." Caylee's voice was flat. She'd had this conversation more times than she cared to count. "Women have an opportunity to change the world. We have the chance to do something great. Just because Dad says something doesn't mean it has to be done that way." She smiled. "We can change the course of history, make the world a better place."

Burt started to say something in response, but he heard the gate at the end of their 200-yard driveway open.

"Now what's a fancy car like that doing out here?" Burt stood up straight. "It'd better not be one of those church folk, or I'll take care of them."

Even at that distance, they knew it wasn't a car they recognized.

"Shut the garage door, Burt. Cover up that van."

Burt moved quickly, and Caylee hobbled back to the front of her car, the shotgun slung over her right shoulder, watching as the man in a nice suit shut their gate, and started to drive his shiny BMW up the gravel driveway.

CHAPTER 11

"QUITE THE welcoming party," Tex Hunter mumbled under his breath as his car moved up the driveway, the pebbles crunching under the tires. The girl with a shotgun on her shoulder watched him closely as a large male quickly closed the garage door.

Hunter parked his sedan back from the girl, and turned the car around, facing the gate. That made it easier for a quick escape.

He texted Ray Jones his location and said that if Ray didn't hear from him in two hours, he should come for a drive. He took a deep breath, checked that the girl in the rearview mirror wasn't advancing towards him, then exited the car.

As soon as he opened the door, dogs started barking.

An older man stepped out the front door of the house, looked at the man standing near the garage door, and then said something to the girl. The girl looked angry with him but did as directed; first, taking the shotgun off her shoulder and then walking in the front door of the one-story house.

The brick house was bland in color but long enough to fit six bedrooms. The area around the house was what Hunter expected—overgrown grass, unkempt yard, and way too many run-down cars. Exactly what he thought the home of a racist should look like.

The older man had grease stains on his shirt, and his jeans were torn at the knees. He stood just under five-foot-nine, but if he stood up straight and didn't slouch, then he might gain an extra inch. His thin gray hair was frizzy, and his skin had seen too many hours in the sun, but it was the smoking that had clearly taken its toll.

As had the cancer.

And the emphysema.

If there was ever an advertisement for why kids shouldn't start smoking, Chuck Johnson was it.

"Who are you?" The man's question was blunt, followed by a deep cough.

"My name is Tex Hunter. I'm a defense attorney. I'm here to talk with Chuck Johnson."

The man spat on the ground, a mixture of phlegm

and blood. "We don't get many strangers up here, especially ones dressed in nice suits."

"You must be Mr. Johnson." Hunter held out his hand, but the man ignored it. "Lucas Bauer mentioned you were friends."

"Lucas said that? I don't believe you." Chuck raised his eyebrows.

"Why not?"

"Because Lucas doesn't want people to know we're friends. It wouldn't be good for his business." Chuck spat on the ground again and stepped closer. "You've lied to me, and that's not a good start to this conversation."

"You and Reverend Green weren't friends. I know that's the truth."

"We don't call him 'Reverend' up here. He was no priest. He didn't spread the word of the Lord. He was a dark-skinned troublemaker. He didn't like me, and I didn't like him." The man pointed at Hunter. "And I don't like you either."

Chuck looked over his shoulder at his brother, Burt, leaning against the garage door, ready to pounce the moment that Chuck needed any physical backup. Chuck dipped his head towards his brother, and Hunter watched as Burt walked around the side of the house.

"I'll get to the point." Hunter stepped closer, staring down at Chuck. "I need your help in the case of the murder of Reverend Green. I'm defending the man charged with his murder. I'm sure that you would like to help that man."

"As much as I'm happy that the faith healer murdered Green, I'm not going to help him. He's not my family, and he doesn't believe what I believe. I want nothing to do with him."

"Perhaps we can discuss this further inside?" Hunter pressed.

"No chance." Chuck laughed. "I don't trust lawyers as a general rule, and in your case, I'm not going to make an exception."

"What I came here to ask, Chuck, is where were you on the night of February 1st?"

Chuck stiffened but smiled when he looked over his shoulder.

Burt Johnson walked from the side of the garage, holding two black barking Doberman dogs by the leash. Despite his strength, Burt struggled to keep them from charging at Hunter, leaning backward as he pulled on the leash.

"You'd better not be thinking of framing me,

lawyer boy, because I'll warn you—I can be very dangerous."

"I'm not framing anyone; I'm asking questions."

The dogs came closer to Hunter. They snarled, drool dripping from their mouths. They were hungry. That was clear. Burt yanked one back, but it only made the dog angrier.

"And I'm not answering any more questions." Chuck crossed his arms. "So, unless you want to become dinner for my dogs, it's time for you to leave."

The dogs pulled Burt closer.

The smell of wet dog hung in the air.

They were within inches.

But Hunter didn't budge.

He took a step closer to Chuck, closer to the threat of the dogs. "This case is pointing me in your direction, and I'm going to be looking into your past."

The dogs snarled again.

Hunter saw Caylee walk out the front door, but his focus was on Chuck.

"I don't care about your laws, lawyer boy. We live by the laws of the White Alliance Coalition." Chuck spat on the ground for the third time, right next to Hunter's shoes.

"If I find out that you had anything to do with the murder of Reverend Green, or the Baptist church shooting, I'm going to bring this whole house down on top of you." Hunter stepped within inches of Chuck's face. "Watch your step, Chuck."

"Back off! Get back!"

A shotgun was pointed in Hunter's face.

"Back off! I'll shoot you!" The anger in the girl's voice was clear.

Hunter stared at Caylee Johnson holding the shotgun barrel only a foot away from his face. The gun was steady.

"Back off! I'll shoot you!" she repeated.

"That's my girl." Chuck smiled. "Full of hate for boys like you. You see, we don't like city boys. Now, get off my property, lawyer boy. I don't want to have to bury a lawyer up here."

Hunter held the stare.

The shotgun moved closer.

The dogs continued to snarl.

"I'm coming for you, Chuck." Hunter turned and

walked back to the safety of his car.

Danger was very close.

And so was the solution.

CHAPTER 12

THE LUNCHTIME sun snuck through a small gap in the blinds, trying to poke its way in to wake up the hardy souls who had been drinking since the place opened.

Tex Hunter gazed into his whiskey, the thoughts of the case forcing his mind to travel to places it hadn't in a long time. The deeper he dug into the case, the deeper he went into the family dramas, the deeper he dug into his own hurt.

He didn't like that. Not one bit.

But as he did with all his strong emotions, he was trying to dull them with the taste of whiskey.

His life hadn't been easy—he knew that. From the day the handcuffs went on his father's wrists, Hunter's life was a constant struggle—his relationships, his work, his reputation. Most people ran once they found out who he was related to.

That was his lot in life, and as he approached his mid-forties, he understood that he had to do the best with what he had been blessed with. And he had been blessed—he had a great career, a comfortable life, many of the luxuries that the modern world had to offer.

But love was something that eluded him.

He sipped his whiskey, disappearing deeper into his thoughts.

Why is love so hard? Why is it so hard to be vulnerable? Why is it so hard to let the stone wall down?

It was only the soft touch of Esther's hand on his shoulder that brought him back to reality.

"Are you ready?" she asked.

He drew a long breath. "I think so."

He stood tall and buttoned up his suit. He reached across and finished his drink, his second. Together, they walked out of the dive bar and onto the main road, then towards the Comer Children's Hospital.

"Come on, big guy." Esther playfully punched him on the arm. "You saved this girl's life. There's nothing to worry about here."

"That's not what I'm worried about."

"What are you worried about then?"

"My family's reputation."

Esther didn't respond. She didn't even know where to start.

For Hunter, it was a train of thought that didn't have a station to stop at. He knew how to fix most things, he knew how to solve most problems, but there was one thing he couldn't fix, one thing that was beyond his capabilities.

His father's convictions.

That was the reason why he wasn't driven to have a family of his own; all he knew was the pain from his late childhood.

"The young girl, Eva, seeing her at ten years old, having her innocence taken away, reminded me of my past and how much it affected me. She's the same age as I was when everything changed." Hunter put his hands in his pockets as they walked across the street. "And the further I go into this case, the more I think about my family. The more I find out about these people, the more these questions continue to bubble away in my mind. I hate it, Esther. I hate it. This is my head, and I should be able to control the thoughts in there. But with my father, I can't. I can't switch it off."

"And so you thought you would suppress those thoughts with whiskey?"

"That usually works."

"It's not healthy, Tex. You have to face your emotions. You have to acknowledge what they are and face them head-on. Otherwise, they'll just keep coming back, worse and worse each time. It's time for you to face these feelings. If you don't have someone to talk to, then I know a really good psychologist that you could contact. He'll help you process these demons."

"We all have a past—even Reverend Green hated people." Hunter shrugged.

"Don't change the subject, Tex." Esther rolled her eyes. "This is about you, not Reverend Green. You can't keep focusing on work."

"Yes, I can."

They walked into the busy hospital foyer. Hunter hated that smell; the mixture of disinfectant, ammonia, and fresh flowers made him nauseous.

"Okay then. This should calm your nerves. I saw footage of Reverend Green trying to reach out to the White Alliance Coalition. There was footage on YouTube of Green talking to the daughter, Caylee Johnson, that was posted a year ago. He offered his hand in peace when he found her outside a local shop."

"Interesting. Was it heated?"

"Not until Chuck Johnson came along. It was a very calm discussion, and the daughter really seemed to listen to Green, but then Chuck came to his daughter's 'defense'." Esther used her hands to indicate the quotation marks. "Chuck pushed Green and told him to stay away from his daughter. So I think that maybe Caylee Johnson is a soft spot, a way to get some evidence about Chuck. She might be more open to a conversation."

"Caylee isn't weak." He stated. "But if Chuck is protective of her, then it may be the leverage that we need."

After Esther spoke with the receptionist in the hospital's foyer, Hunter stopped to buy a bouquet of yellow daisies, but even they smelled like they were grown in a hospital. With the flowers in hand, he walked in silence along a corridor, moving past people rushing to save lives, past people comforting each other, and into the elevator.

"Want to hear a joke?" Esther smiled as she tried to lighten Hunter's mood.

"Is it really tasteless, really dirty, or just really bad?"

"I'll tell the joke, and you can make up your own mind." Esther hoped to elicit a smile. The elevator doors closed, and Hunter pressed the button for the 4th floor. "My friend was a good guy. He was always thinking of others, always giving out gifts. Even when he was on the ground dying from eating peanuts, he managed to give me a present. It seemed really important to him that I got his Epi-pen."

Hunter managed a grin as they walked out of the elevator and down another corridor.

"That almost worked, so how about some dirty jokes?"

"Go on." Hunter smirked, his dimples visible.

"A man came into the hospital with burns on eighty percent of his legs, and the nurse helped the EMT transfer him to a hospital bed. The doctor said, 'Give him two Viagra.' The nurse asked, 'Will that help his burns?' 'No, but it'll keep the sheets off his legs!'"

Hunter chuckled.

"A hot blonde orders a double entendre at the bar… and the bartender gives it to her."

He laughed.

"A man was arrested by a female police officer. She started saying, 'Anything you say will be held against you—', and he shouted out, 'Boobs!'"

"Are you sure that you weren't a dirty old drunk man in a past life?"

"That's my whole family history. We were English drunks before coming here one hundred years ago and trying to sober up." Esther touched Hunter's elbow to lead him into the private room. "Come on."

Hunter was barely a foot in the door of the room before a tall African American man stepped forward.

"What are you doing here?" The man grunted. The stress on his face was clear. He looked like he hadn't slept in weeks.

"I've come to bring Eva flowers." Hunter offered the peace offering. "And to see how she's doing."

Hunter looked to the girl, and his heart broke. The ten-year-old was hooked up to tubes, wires, and multiple machines. Her eyes were closed, and the drugs that were pumping through her veins kept them that way. The machines beeped, whirled, and hummed, drowning out any thoughts.

She had a Cubs signed jersey draped over the end of her bed; her favorite team had rallied once they heard of her plight. The whole city had. The room was filled with cards, flowers, and gifts. While school shootings were becoming the norm, nobody wanted to hear of a young girl shot as she played outside a church.

Despite Hunter's best efforts to save her, Eva West received the brunt of the bullet shot into her chest on the day of the Baptist church shooting. She couldn't breathe by herself and had spent the last month in an induced coma.

"Get out. You're not welcome here. You're the son of a serial killer who defends other killers. You're not welcome anywhere near my daughter." The man pointed his finger at Hunter. "This is your fault!"

"Dwight, please." A woman, Eva's mother, stepped around the bed. "This man saved our daughter's life. Without him, she would've taken the whole bullet."

Hunter presented the bouquet of flowers to the mother. "I pray that she pulls through."

"You wouldn't know how to pray." The father turned his back to the visitors. "You wouldn't know the first thing about the Lord!"

The mother offered Hunter and Esther half a smile, and Hunter returned the same. This was not the time for him to press forward.

Hunter turned and walked back down the hospital corridor, Esther following a step behind.

His pace was quick, and Esther struggled to keep up.

"Sorry, Tex, I was wrong," Esther said as they stepped back into the elevator. "I thought they would've embraced you."

"Hatred is a powerful emotion, Esther. One of the strongest."

They rode the elevator in silence; Hunter trying to keep his sadness at bay while Esther gave him the space to do that. Without a word between them, they walked out of the elevator, through the corridors, and back past the reception desk.

When they stepped out of the hospital foyer into the cold air, Esther looked to her boss. "What can I do?"

"There's not much you can do at the moment."

"Come on, Tex." She brushed a strand of hair away from her face. "There must be something I can help with. Let me help you. I really want to."

He drew a long breath and looked back at the hospital, up at the windows of level four. "If you really want, you can look into Chuck's family. Do a little bit of digging around, but don't get close to them. They're dangerous, so don't confront them at all. The daughter may be a chance to push Chuck's buttons, and get the leverage we need. She's twenty-one, and if she showed some interest in what Green was saying, then she might be our chance to get some information. Ask around, search the Internet, that sort of thing. I want to find out how she spends her days, who she's close to, where her income comes from, how she supports herself."

"I'm on it, boss."

"But be careful. Don't get too close to the fire."

"Yes, boss," she replied with a cheeky grin. "It seems like you're feeling emotional, and that means you're going to do one of two things right now—either go back to the bar or go back to work."

"You know me too well, Esther. I'm going to see if I can meet with Nancy Bleathman, and find out what she knows."

"What will she know?"

"I'm not sure, but I'm sure that Anderson isn't a killer. Even if he hasn't been completely honest with us, he doesn't have the look of a murderer. He was in the wrong place at the wrong time, but the list of people that had a motive to kill Green is long. We have so many potential suspects."

"What does your gut say?"

"Lucas Bauer. After I chat with Bleathman, I'm

going to follow him. See what he's about. Bauer may be the key to the case, and possibly the church shooting. I have to get close enough to him to find out what he knows, and who he knows."

"You promise you'll be careful as well, Tex." The joy was erased from Esther's face. Her serious side had returned. "They've hurt people before, and they won't hesitate to do it again. These men are dangerous and full of hate. Promise me you'll be careful."

Hunter smiled again, his heart rate increasing. "Yes, boss."

CHAPTER 13

THE LATE afternoon sun was shining, warming people enough to ditch their coats, bringing out smiles that hadn't been seen since November. Caylee Johnson was full of laughter, sitting on an outdoor bench, planning her next summer trip with her friends. The Northeastern Illinois University campus was abuzz with students outdoors, trying to soak in every bit of vitamin D that they could.

"On our last trip, you met that boy in Miami! He couldn't get enough of you!"

Caylee laughed as her friend, Maria, scrolled through the photos of their last adventure—of the nights where they were drunk and wild, of the memories that would last a lifetime. "He followed you on Instagram, didn't he?"

"He might've been a bit crazy, but he was really toned. I loved his abs. I think he was more interested in you though. He loved that stunning city girl look.

Most boys do. I only get the ones that you reject."

"Stop it." Maria playfully slapped her friend's arm. "You could get any boy you want, redneck or not."

"Funny." Caylee scoffed. "So where to next summer?"

"Maybe Cancun?"

"Maybe." Caylee shrugged. Her father didn't like the idea of her owning a passport. "I think I'd rather stay in the US. I don't think I'm ready to travel abroad yet."

"Come on. You're twenty-one now. It's time to spread your wings and see the world. Me—I would love to go to Africa. I would love to see it all—the safaris, the coastlines, the cultures. It would be mind-blowing." Maria looked longingly into the distance. "Where would you go abroad, if money wasn't a factor?"

"I'm not sure." Caylee looked down, and the next words slipped out her mouth without a second thought: "My family wouldn't like it if I went abroad."

"You'll have to introduce me to this family of yours one day. Perhaps they can come around for dinner with my parents?"

"No." Caylee was blunt, and it caught her friend off-guard.

"Okay, okay. I get it. You're embarrassed by your family. We all are. But I do find it strange that nobody on campus has met your family, and you've never posted anything about them on social media. We're all a little bit embarrassed about our families, but it's like you wish yours didn't exist."

"I just…"

Caylee tried to invent a new excuse. For the last three years, she had made a deliberate choice not to mention her family on campus. But her university friends were the closest friends she had ever had, and it was a subject that she couldn't keep avoiding. She covered her tracks online, and used her mother's maiden name, Smith, on her university enrollment, so nobody could connect her back to her father and his organization.

"My family is complicated."

"It's okay." Maria rubbed her arm. She could see the tears welling up in Caylee's eyes. "I understand. In time, I'm sure I'll meet them."

"Thanks for the afternoon hit of caffeine." Caylee shook the half-empty takeaway coffee cup. "We'll plan more about the trip tomorrow, but I have to get to class. I've got a geology lecture now with David Stone."

Caylee hugged Maria, said goodbye, and then

began the walk across the yard towards the science building. She enjoyed studying Earth Sciences, and majoring in geology, but it was the people she met on campus that she valued more.

When she first came to the campus, she was stunned by the variety of people that she interacted with. She had never even known there were that many different races on the planet, let alone in her own city. Slowly, she came to realize what a sheltered life she had led tucked away from the real world.

Walking across the campus grounds, she noticed a tall blonde woman watching her from under a tree. She was too well dressed, and her makeup was too perfect to be a student.

Never one to take a backward step, Caylee immediately confronted the woman. She walked across the grass, ignoring the wetness underfoot. "Can I help you?"

The woman walked closer to Caylee, leaning down to make a statement. "That girl you just hugged; she's African American."

"And?"

Esther Wright looked around the campus, making sure they were out of earshot of anyone else. "I don't think your father would be very happy to hear that."

Caylee's eyes widened, and she took a step forward. She never thought she would meet a White Alliance Coalition supporter on campus grounds. She wasn't prepared. "I don't know who you are, lady, but my family is my business. No one around here knows who my family is."

"They don't recognize the Johnson surname?"

"That's none of your business."

Esther could see the fire in the girl's eyes, could feel the power in her voice. "How do you think your father would react if he found out? Perhaps if he saw a photo of you hugging her?"

Esther waved her phone at Caylee.

Caylee was quick to think on her feet. It was a skill she had learned when it became clear she could easily manipulate her father and uncle into believing anything she told them. A nicely placed word and a tear could get the men to do anything. She was the only connection her father had to his wife, and Caylee knew how to exploit that.

"I'm planning something at the campus. That's what my father knows. He knows how far I'll go. I need you not to say anything to the people on campus. They trust me. I need that to happen if I'm going to do it." Caylee looked around, then lowered her tone. She touched the woman's elbow, making sure her voice couldn't be heard any further than their conversation. "If you know my father, then you know he doesn't have long left. The doctors say the cancer means he only has a few months, maybe a year. When he..." She paused. "When he goes, the world will change, but I need you to promise that you won't say anything, for the sake of the White Alliance Coalition."

Esther was confused but she agreed. "I won't say anything."

Caylee went to walk away, but then stopped and turned back to Esther. "Aren't you too old to be on campus?"

"Thanks." Esther took the comment as a jibe. "I only just turned thirty."

"Still too old for around here. And you're too pretty to be an active member of the White Alliance Coalition. It's usually smelly old men at the meetings. No one like you. Who are you?"

"I'm a friend," Esther lied. "I won't say anything. I'll keep your secret safe from your father."

Caylee turned, unsure if it was the truth, and then walked away. The time for a decision was coming. She knew that.

But that didn't make it any easier.

CHAPTER 14

NANCY BLEATHMAN placed the new book on her large bookshelf.

Everything was perfectly in order; first, the author's surname, then if the author had more than one title, the title of the book. The colors of the books ranged from bright orange to dark black, but she liked that. She liked that there was no order to the colors. A little bit of chaos amongst the strict order.

Despite the fact that there were over three hundred books on the wall-sized bookshelf in the living room of her downtown apartment, there were only two fiction books; The Alchemist by Paulo Coelho and The Monk Who Sold His Ferrari by Robin Sharma. The others were self-help, psychology, and human behavior books.

She bought all the books not because she wanted to understand other people, she couldn't care less about them, but because she wanted to understand herself. She wanted to know what made herself tick, why she got up in the mornings, and why she chose the career path in statistics. She wanted to know why she ate pancakes every morning, why she was addicted to coffee, and why she found solace in alcohol. Why was she single and childless at fifty? Why did she have no long-term friends? And why did she still hate her parents?

She wanted to understand herself deeply.

She thought she could find answers in the books. She thought that if she could understand human behavior, then she could understand herself. From philosophers to scientists, from motivational speakers to self-help gurus—she thought that she could find the answers to her questions about her life in the knowledge of others.

And she knew a lot. Decades of knowledge had seeped into her mind. She knew so much about life.

Everything, except how to enjoy it.

Nancy dusted her coffee table and waited for the buzz of the intercom. She knew what she was going to say to the lawyer, she'd spent the last twenty minutes rehearsing her answers in the mirror, as she did before most social interactions.

The lawyer had said that he would be there at 6 p.m. and it was now four minutes' past. She didn't like it when people were late. When the intercom finally buzzed, two minutes later, she sighed. She had almost given up on the fact that he was coming.

She buzzed him into her apartment and welcomed him at the apartment door. She offered him a cup of coffee, to which he said "yes." She was impressed by him; his good looks, easy charm, and the dimples in his cheeks. His charisma was disarming.

"This is a lovely place, Ms. Bleathman," Tex Hunter said as he looked around the living room, then out to the view of Lake Michigan. The floor-to-ceiling windows highlighted a spectacular vista. "The Gold Coast is a lovely part of Chicago."

"It is," she agreed. Nancy wished, like she did about many things, that she could enjoy the view more, but it had become part of her everyday background. "I'm very blessed."

She said 'blessed' without a hint of feeling because she didn't really feel that way at all. She had only just finished reading Gratitude Is Attitude, a self-help book, which stated that she should repeatedly say that she was blessed for everything she had, but she didn't feel it. Perhaps, if she kept saying it every day for a month, then it might work.

"As you're aware…" Hunter sat down on the white leather couch. It felt new, but the style was at least ten years old. "I'm defending Amos Anderson against the murder charge."

"I'm not sure I should be talking to you. I read that anyone that's involved in a trial shouldn't say more than necessary."

"I can assure you that I want the best for Amos. Anything that you can tell me about your relationship with him may help."

She smiled, leaning forward with her hands cupped around her coffee cup. "Lucas and Amos saved my life, and I don't say that lightly. I had…" She thought about what she had rehearsed. "I had become addicted to painkillers. Codeine. It was destroying me from the inside out. I tried to kick the habit, but nothing worked. I would be good for a while—clean—but I would always fall back into the cycle of addiction."

Hunter looked at the bookshelf and saw many books on how to overcome addiction. "And that's when you met Amos?"

"I found his website online, and I thought, why not? Nothing I was doing was working. I would do something for a week, and it would work, but then I would fall back down—straight back into the habit. When the addiction started to affect my work, I called Amos."

"And what did he do?"

"He cured me. Just like that." She snapped her fingers. "I paid him a large sum of money, and then he waved his hands around. I felt a force surge through me. I'd read about faith healing before, I have three books on it, but this was the first time I had used it. There's no doubt—the Faith Healing Project saved my life."

Hunter looked back at the bookshelf—not at the books, but at the bookshelf itself. Despite its bright white color, he couldn't see a spot of dirt on it, not even some dust.

"If called to the stand in a trial as a character witness, what would you say about Amos Anderson?"

"That he's a wonderful man, and that I would be sad when he's convicted to life in prison."

"Pardon?" Hunter coughed.

"He killed a man. A Baptist minister, no less. He deserves to go to prison, and probably hell after that, if one exists." Her voice was emotionless. "I'm not going to save the skin of a killer."

"But what about the faith healing?"

"Lucas has told me that he has thirty other healers ready to take Amos' place. It'll be better for me with all those others, and it would be so much cheaper. It's a very expensive healing process."

Hunter was shocked. That was not what he expected. He narrowed his eyes. "Nancy, where were you on February 1st?"

"I was there at the Congress Hotel." She looked away. She knew he would ask that question and had prepared her answer accordingly. "I try to go to all of Amos' speeches; he's so impressive, and there's always non-believers at those sorts of things. I like arguing with them, telling them that it worked for me. I think people are shocked when I tell them because I don't look like a person that would believe in that New Age talk. I look like a professional, and that surprises people."

"Did you talk to Amos that night?"

"I talked to him, and I talked to Lucas as well. I was there from the start of the speeches until the end, and I talked to them after the speeches had finished."

"And then what did you do?"

"What do you want me to say?"

"The truth."

She sipped her coffee as if the truth was an easy concept for her to change. "Since Amos has been arrested, I've done a lot of thinking. Amos deserves to be locked up. He's a killer. I'll say what needs to be said to send him to prison."

He stared at her. "How did you get home that night?"

"Is that why you're here? To try and get me to confess to killing Reverend Green?" Her blue eyes and intense stare made Hunter uneasy. "You're going to have to work harder than that, Mr. Hunter. I've read about you. You have a reputation for drawing confessions out on the stand. But I must warn you—I'm ready for you. I even bought two new books about the psychology of the courtroom."

"I'm searching for the truth." Hunter placed his cup down.

"I wanted Reverend Green out of the picture. His attacks on the Faith Healing Project were destroying the business." She looked away again. Everything she said was going according to her script. "Lucas told me that Green was going to present a piece of evidence to the public that would absolutely destroy the company. Lucas couldn't let that happen."

"Where did you go after you left the conference?"

"I walked home."

"You walked?"

"It was only forty to fifty minutes away, and it wasn't too cold that night. It wasn't even an hour's walk, and after all the appetizers that I ate, I needed the exercise. That's not unusual; I walk a lot. I'd prefer that to talking to people. I took stock of the weather, the suburbs I would be walking through, and the shoes I was wearing before I made the decision to walk. It was a good judgment call to exercise at that time. Most people are so lazy that they don't even exercise good judgment." There wasn't a hint of humor in her voice.

"Can anyone verify where you were walking during that time?"

"I wouldn't say so. I didn't see anyone I knew."

"What time did you arrive back here that night?"

"I don't know."

Hunter stood and slowly walked to the bookshelf. He studied the books again for a moment before realizing it was the most ordered bookshelf he had ever seen outside of a library.

"I assume that this building has security footage?"

"Yes."

"Then I'm going to need to check that."

"You have my permission to do that. I'm sure you'll find I arrived that night alone." She stood. "Will you need me to be a witness?"

Hunter didn't respond, casting his eyes once more over the books.

"I've never been to court before. If you want me to testify, you'll have to take me through what to do that day."

Hunter turned back to her. He needed time to think, time to mull over what she had stated. "My assistant will be in contact if we need you. Thank you for your time, Nancy."

He picked up his briefcase and walked out of the apartment, but he was leaving with more questions than answers.

A lot more.

CHAPTER 15

LUCAS BAUER walked out of his apartment at 8 p.m.

He looked like the wealthy man he was. Although once broke, he had hit the jackpot with the Faith Healing Project. He had a Rolex watch, Armani suit, and Ferragamo shoes. He walked with his head held high, full of poise and audacity. He didn't have far to go. The black Mercedes, perfectly matching his outfit, was parked by the sidewalk near his house.

Despite the obvious trimmings of excess wealth, Lucas Bauer had a record. Fraud, in one case. Extortion in another.

Apart from his criminal record, Tex Hunter didn't have much to go on. Most people wouldn't talk about Lucas Bauer. It was clear that he wasn't liked, but it was becoming clearer that he was dangerous. There was no easy method for gathering information on him. Phone calls didn't work. Checking criminal records didn't reveal much. There was barely a mention of him on social media.

Finding information about him involved old-fashioned investigative work. The hard yards.

Hunter followed the Mercedes as it drove for twenty minutes, staying two to three cars behind.

The Mercedes stopped on the Magnificent Mile, and double-parked outside one of the new bars. After a quick Google search on his phone about the establishment, Hunter found it was the sort of place where rich men buy drinks for beautiful young women, and beautiful young women get paid for their time.

Hunter found a spot further down the street to park his sedan and made his way back to the bar. He had no idea what he was going to find. More than likely, Bauer was looking to have his ego boosted by an attractive, young woman. Still, it was worth a shot to see the sort of circles that Bauer floated in.

The bar was full, the crowd mingling freely, making it hard to spot Bauer.

He looked through the crowd from inside the door, and couldn't see Bauer on the first pass.

Looking back down at his phone, he sat on one of the stools near the entrance. The server asked if he wanted a drink, but Hunter waved him away. When he gazed up from his phone, he caught sight of Bauer seated at the opposite end of the bar.

He was discreetly talking to someone.

Hunter moved between two women in red cocktail dresses to get a better vantage point.

He moved to his left to get a better angle.

Moving smoothly, he shot another glance at the end of the bar.

What?

He looked again.

Hunter's heart kicked into overdrive. He couldn't believe it.

Maybe it was the lighting. Maybe he was mistaken.

He looked again, holding the stare.

Dim lighting, and crowded or not, there was no mistake.

Lucas Bauer was handing an envelope to a detective, followed by a brown paper bag.

And it was a detective Hunter knew very well.

CHAPTER 16

"DETECTIVE BROWNE," Hunter mumbled under his breath.

He worked his way through the crowd, past the throng of people desperate to get noticed, and stepped out into the sudden cold, shocking his body.

He pulled his collar up. The questions buzzed through his head.

Hunter saw an envelope change hands, and then a brown paper bag. He would bet that it was money in the envelope, but he had no idea what was in the bag.

Was Browne an inside man for Bauer, screwing the force? Screwing justice?

Hunter walked back to his car in a fog of thoughts, sat in the driver's seat, and drew a long deep breath. Was this why no charges had been filed in the Baptist church shooting? Was there a dirty cop protecting them all?

It was the biggest public shooting of the year, and the Chicago PD hadn't even made an arrest. They didn't even have a lead. It was the lead story in most of the papers for a week, and that usually meant an arrest. Not this time. There was nothing, not even a hint that an arrest was going to be made.

Something wasn't right about the case.

Hunter had known Browne for decades. He was the same cop that arrested his father. Hunter remembered the man that dragged his father off in handcuffs as a man with rippling muscles and a scowl on his face. The years had added more weight, perhaps doubling his size, but the scowl on his face remained the same. The smoking and alcohol abuse had wrinkled his skin, too, and his hair was long gone.

Browne was old school, though he was even considered that when he started in the force almost forty years ago. His attitude about policing would have been more suited to the times of prohibition— when a cop could take money for looking the other way. Browne never had a problem with taking money; he thought of it as a bonus for the times he risked his life. He thought the city was indebted to him, and money was the best way to show that gratitude.

If there was one thing that Hunter knew about Browne, it was that he was dirty.

There was a rumor that he was about to be kicked off the force before his retirement. People had been pushing for it to happen for years, but it never came together. Browne always found a way to avoid what was coming for him. His ability to blackmail people, even those in his department, had made people cautious.

Despite Hunter's respect for the men and women in blue, most of the force hated him. That was understandable. His job was to make arrests look invalid, evidence look shoddy, and paperwork look incomplete. While they risked their lives to protect justice for a small income, he argued in a courtroom for a nice hefty wage. He understood their resentment.

But Browne was different.

Hunter always knew he was dirty.

And now he had a chance to prove it.

CHAPTER 17

AS HUNTER walked to his apartment building in River North, he saw a man with a hood watching his every step.

It was late on a Saturday afternoon, and Hunter had spent the last six hours at the office, but it wasn't unusual for him to work weekends. The streets around his apartment complex were mostly safe; a place where tourists could comfortably walk the streets without the threat of gun violence. River North was mostly harmless, especially in the afternoon on a weekend.

The man stood under a tree on the edge of the street, sheltered from sunshine, and he watched Hunter's steps.

Hunter was ready to fight.

He knew that most people, even left-handers, shot a gun with their right hand. If he had to move quickly, he would stay at the man's left. He tilted his head slightly, keeping the man in his peripheral vision.

As Hunter got closer to his door, the hooded man stepped out of the shadows.

Hunter's shoulders tightened.

It was clear the man was coming for him.

Hunter turned and faced him. Attack was the best form of defense.

He stepped closer.

The man removed his hood.

"Max." Hunter exhaled, his shoulders dropping from their height of tension. "Max, you shouldn't hide in the shadows like that."

"I'm sorry, Uncle T. It's the way I do things now."

"It's good to see you." Hunter patted his nephew on the shoulder and drew him into an awkward hug. "Looks like you're putting some muscle on."

"I've been hitting the gym. There's a cheap gym next door to where I'm working."

"Where are you working now?"

"On one of the tourist boats. It's only a cleaning job, I get to scrub the decks, but it's a start. It's something to keep money coming in."

Hunter drew him back into another hug. After a battle with drug addiction, Max was getting back on his feet.

At fourteen, Max found a white powder that provided him with relief from the stresses of life, a powder that took him away from reality. When he was offered a hit of heroin from some of the older kids at school, Max found his escape; his haven. He thought it was so cool, so rebellious, but rarely does a person escape the grip of heroin without addiction. He became a slave to the powers of the powder, addicted to a world that wasn't real.

Throughout his school years, he was always known as the grandson of a serial killer, the kid from the killer family, and he had to uphold his reputation.

Drugs made him cool.

But quickly, like most people, drugs also made him a mess.

"You could've called." Hunter smiled.

"I don't have your number."

At twenty-one, Maxwell Hunter was starting to rebuild his life. He had finally kicked the drugs, landed a job, and was now working hard. He was finally able to afford a shared room in an apartment, new clothes, and a phone.

He always knew that he could call his father, or Uncle Tex, for monetary support, but that would take away something he was not willing to give up—his pride.

"Come up to my apartment, Max. I'll make you a coffee."

Max shook his head. "Not today, Uncle T. I've got to get back so I can sleep before work tomorrow. Early morning start."

"Have you spoken to your father yet?"

"On the phone." He looked away. "It's all I'm ready for. I haven't seen him in person yet."

"Then how can I help you, Max? What are you doing here, hiding in the shadows?"

"I've heard that you're defending Amos Anderson."

Hunter sighed. The first time he heard the name Amos Anderson was when his nephew told him that the faith healer had cured him of his drug addiction. "That's true. I'm defending him against a murder charge."

"He cured me, Uncle T. He was the only reason I was able to get off the drugs." Max scratched his arm. "About a year ago, I saw this guy struggling to change a tire on his car, so I helped him. I didn't want anything from him; I just wanted to help him change his tire. He could tell I was an addict and then asked me if I wanted to kick the habit. Of course, I said yes, and then he said that I needed to pay him all my money. I did it because all I wanted, more than anything, was to stop taking drugs. I was willing to try anything."

"He cured you with his hands?"

"I gave him all the money I had, and then he drove me back to his house, fed me, gave me clothes, told me to lie down on the floor, and then waved his hands over me. It was like I was hypnotized. And after that, I've never wanted to touch drugs again. Not once. Not even the smallest craving. I still go to see Amos once every few months to help me stay off the drugs. He heals me, and makes sure I don't go back to that life."

"And you pay him?"

"I'd pay anything to stay off the drugs, but we have a deal. I pay him twenty percent of my wage. That's our deal. Usually, he charges people thousands of dollars just to meet him, but he did the deal for me. He says that after two years on his course of faith healing, I'll be cured for life. I believe in him, and I need him to stay out of prison. Without him, I don't know if I can stay off the drugs."

Hunter wiped his brow and almost told Max that it was all a fraud, an act, and the cure was all in his mind. But this was neither the time or the place to make that statement.

"You have to keep him out of prison, Uncle T."

Hunter watched his nephew closely. He looked so much like his mother—the soft eyes, that gentle and vulnerable look. He was tall, but he also weighed a lot less than a man his height should.

"I know that you can't talk about the case, Uncle T. I don't want you to either. But I want you to know that you have to get Amos off this charge. He would never kill anyone. I know that. I know that in my heart. He helps people; he doesn't kill them. And that should be enough for you to get him off."

"The law isn't that simple."

"That man changed my life. I can't lose him. Without his sessions, I feel like I could fall back into the darkness. I could never live like that again. I couldn't do it. I can never go back to the darkness." His eyes were jumpy, never quite focusing on one thing.

"I'm sure that you can find another faith healer elsewhere. Someone else will help you. That's how business works. If there's a gap in the market, someone else will fill it, and I'm sure that Lucas Bauer will help you find the right healer."

"I don't want to take that risk, Uncle T. The ability is very rare, and Amos has this specialized skill; it's a movement of faith healing that works for drug addicts. I know that Amos' movements work and I don't want to risk losing them. You can't let me go back to the drugs," Max pleaded with his uncle. "You can't let him go behind bars. That man makes my life worth living. Promise me that you will get him off the charges."

"You know I can't promise that."

"There will be so many people impacted if he doesn't get off the charges. Nancy is saying that he'll get life in prison if he's convicted, but you can't let that happen. He does more good in the world than bad."

"You know Nancy Bleathman?"

"I do."

"How passionate is Nancy about the Faith Healing Project? Would you say that she would do anything to make sure the business is protected?"

"Nancy is one of the backers for the business. She's one of the silent business partners. She's as passionate about faith healing as anyone. I met her after I started going to sessions with Amos, and we've stayed in contact."

Hunter looked up at his apartment building, the revelation pounding through his head.

"What if I look into this case and find that Amos is guilty?"

Max took a moment and then shrugged. "Don't tell me that you have grown a conscience, Uncle T? You'd be the first one in our family to do that."

"Maybe." Hunter stepped closer to his nephew and rested a consoling hand on his shoulder. "I'll do my best, but I can't promise anything because I don't make promises that I can't keep."

"Thanks for listening, Uncle T. It's good to see you," Max said softly before he began to walk away, pulling the hood back over his head before stepping back into the shadows. "Get Amos off for me," he added over his shoulder.

Hunter ran his fingers through his hair.

He would do almost anything for his nephew, but a scam was a scam, and at the right time, the truth had to be revealed.

He couldn't be a part of the lie.

No matter the cost.

CHAPTER 18

CAYLEE SAT on the hill looking out at the sunset.

She loved watching a winter sunset, the day slowly turning into night, the colors gradually changing in the sky. She found calm in the slow-moving clouds, tranquility in the soft glow of colors. Watching the sunset provided her time for reflection, time to consider everything that was happening.

She understood her father's racism. She understood his hatred for people of color.

He often told her how unsafe they had made the world.

'All the violence in Chicago is their fault,' he told her constantly. 'Without them, Chicago would be heaven on earth.'

But as she grew older, she was beginning to realize that life was more complicated than that.

When her elementary school teacher tried to tell her that human life had originated in Africa, she refused to accept it. Even at eight years old, she had enough fire in her to kick the male teacher in the groin when he wouldn't accept her arguments.

That was the first of her expulsions from different schools.

She learned that hate from her father. The hate her father had for the man that broke into their home and killed her mother was palpable. The day that man was sentenced to life in prison was etched into her memory as one of the clearest memories of her childhood; her father was in the front row of the courtroom, her uncle beside him, shouting racist comments for all to hear.

That crime fueled their hate. It grew and grew until it became an organized group that brought the hatred of others together.

Her father formed the White Alliance Coalition to protect his family. That's what he always said. They needed the segregation for protection. That was his experience.

She was raised in a world of hate, violence, and racism.

Despite the hate that bubbled inside of her, she was a good learner. She studied hard and found her calling in Earth Sciences. There were no lines to blur in geology. The answers were either right or wrong. It was that simple.

No gray in the world of rocks.

Growing up, she was surrounded by white people; all hardworking, all family-orientated, all somewhat racist. Once, when she was eleven, and starting to ask questions about her father's ideology, Chuck got fed up and threw her in the back seat of their pickup truck. He drove for two hours, to the suburb of Englewood, as the night began. The suburb was predominately African American, poor, and violent. He checked that his handgun was loaded, placed it under his sweater, and then took her out of the truck to go for a walk.

They hadn't even made it to the end of the street when the abuse started.

Cars driving past shouted at her, sexualized her, and screamed racist comments as they went past.

By the time that they had reached the end of the residential block of flats, people started coming up to them and demanding that they leave the neighborhood. She couldn't understand some of the words that were said to her father, but it was probably better that she didn't.

She pleaded with her father to leave.

He dragged her another block down the road before he turned back.

The abuse followed them the whole way.

That was her first experience in an African American suburb, and it was her last for many years. Everything that her father told her about them seemed true—in her experience, they were rude, violent, and determined to cause trouble.

And after that day, she had believed every word that came out of her father's mouth for years.

The first time she met an African American girl at college, she was terrified. She sat in the lecture hall scared she was about to get shot the entire time. She wondered where the girl was carrying her gun, constantly keeping an eye on the girl's hands to ensure she wasn't reaching under her sweater for the weapon.

It wasn't until she was paired up with Maria in Geology 101 that Caylee saw her as a person. She was kind, sweet, and fun. It was the beginning of a friendship that grew stronger every day.

Her experience changed her opinion. Suddenly, the group of people that she feared, the people that terrified her, became her friends. She loved that experience.

But she loved her father more; more than anything in the world.

As the sun finished setting over the hill, Caylee smiled.

She had to make a decision: her father, her family, or her friends.

She knew she couldn't have it all.

She had spent a year thinking about the best time to do it. She would have liked to finish college first, but her father's cancer had pushed the decision closer.

Caylee had to decide.

Either way, she would end it.

Once and for all.

CHAPTER 19

"YOU STILL taking those?" Hunter asked, his voice louder than usual. His brother, Patrick Hunter, downed another pill, followed by a large gulp of water.

"It helps with…" Patrick looked down the almost glowing green fairway of the Evanston Golf Club, thought for a moment, and then turned back to his brother. "Well, it helps with everything. Life, really."

Hunter didn't respond.

"What? Do you think I should be drinking whiskey instead?" Patrick turned to play his ball, sitting on the edge of the fairway, 100 yards from the flag. "Would that be better for me?"

Patrick swung smoothly, and they watched the ball land not far from the tee, bouncing twice, rolling past the flag, and stopping before it rolled off the other side of the green.

The grounds looked perfect in the late winter light, almost like the grass was painted by an artist, and there was nowhere else Hunter would rather be. Golf was a byproduct of his need for being outdoors, his need for being surrounded by such greenery. As he went through his forties, he was learning that life was about balance—work hard in the city, but take a moment to breathe in nature. He didn't need the golf, the competitive side of it; all he needed was to walk along the fairways, along the greens, and take in the smell of freshly cut grass.

That did him more good, provided more relaxation than any pill or bottle could do.

"Listen, there has been something that I've wanted to say for a while… I know that our mother was a very emotional person, and she used to speak for the two of us." Patrick drew a long breath as they walked up to the eighteenth hole on the quiet morning. "I know that our mother used to tell us that she loved us, but since she passed, there hasn't been anyone to say it, but I think I should say it."

"You don't have to say it."

Patrick continued looking out to the green, trying to gain the courage to say something important.

It was hard for him.

With their upbringing, it was hard for both of

them. They had developed a toughness; a stoic character designed to never let their guard down.

Being vulnerable was not something they were used to.

"You may know what I'm going to say, but I need to say it to you." Patrick looked at the ground.

They walked in silence for another two minutes.

Patrick struggled to open up, and the uncomfortable quiet was painstaking.

"What are you working on?" Patrick finally asked, breaking the silence, and diverting the conversation away from being vulnerable. He couldn't find the courage to say what he was feeling.

"The faith healer case."

"Of course." Patrick smiled, happy to have avoided the previous conversation. "I talked to Max on the phone, and he couldn't be happier. This faith healer, Amos, cured him of his drug addiction. What an amazing thing. You can have all the help in the world, you can have all the science, but in the end, it all comes down to a mystery art."

"I know how much this means to him."

"It's not just how much it means to him, Tex; it's about how much that guy means to me. I have my son back, Tex. The phone call was only a small step, but he's coming back into my life. I have that beautiful, smart, funny boy back. I can't tell you how happy that makes me. And I haven't heard that light in his voice since his mother died. You know what Max has been through. But ever since he has been talking to the faith healer, his life has changed. Amos Anderson has brought my son back to me. There's nothing more important than that. You have to keep that man out of prison so that magic can keep working."

"Except it isn't magical."

"What do you mean?"

"It's a rip off, Patrick. It's all a lie, a dirty scam."

"The faith healing? How can you doubt it when the evidence is there?" Patrick asked. "I know that I'm the psychiatrist and I'm the one supposed to be defending science, but you can't argue with results. He cured Max of his drug addiction."

"I know it doesn't work because Amos told me it was a lie. He came out and said that it was all a scam. The Faith Healing Project is a fraud."

"Don't tell me it doesn't work, Tex. I've seen the results. It helped Max kick the drugs."

"But it isn't the faith healing, it isn't the hands—

Max was cured because of the placebo effect."

"The placebo effect?"

"Yes, Patrick."

Patrick still looked perplexed.

"Tex, there's a story about war that we're told in psychiatry training about the placebo effect. In the first Gulf War, a group of US soldiers had to march for twenty-four hours to get away from a bad position they were in. They were under all sorts of attack and had suffered multiple hits by bombs, losing some of their team. They had no food, no ammunition, and no communications. They were a twenty-four-hour march away from any help, and it was a twenty-four-hour march through sandy deserts. They had no hope. None. That was until their sergeant told them that he had an experimental drug that was only to be used in an absolute emergency. They were told they needed to take one tiny sip of the liquid every hour, and they could march for days. The sergeant had two bottles of this clear liquid drug in his pack. The boys were scared, vulnerable, and looking death in the face.

"The men had heard about experimental drugs like this being used in war, so they took it. They took a sip every hour, on the hour. When they were starting to physically fall apart, particularly around the eighteenth and nineteenth hour of marching, this liquid drug picked them back up, and they kept going. It was like they were invincible. By the time they made it to camp, almost twenty-four hours later, they felt great. The only person that was struggling was the sergeant. They made a stretcher for him and carried him for the last six hours, but that didn't matter because the drug worked. They felt like they could have kept marching for another twenty-four hours."

Patrick looked out into the distance.

"They felt great, Tex," he continued. "Twenty-four hours through sandy desert and they felt great. Can you believe that? That drug saved their lives."

"What drug was it?"

"That's the thing—it wasn't a drug; it was water. Pure water, nothing but water, and they believed it was a drug. They all believed. The sergeant knew it was only water, but he convinced them that it was an experimental drug. He convinced them that this tiny sip of the drug would get them back to base. It worked because they believed that it would work."

"And the sergeant didn't believe, so it didn't work on him."

"That's right. He saved their lives with a sip of water, a trick of the mind, not a drug. It was their minds that got them through."

"The placebo effect," Hunter said softly.

"Exactly, Tex. It saves lives."

"But that's different than what the Faith Healing Project is doing. Lucas Bauer makes a lot of money selling a treatment that he knows is ineffective. That's not right. They're making money from ripping people off. That's the definition of a scam."

"I know that you've had problems with scams in the past, but this is more than a cheap trick."

"It's ripping people off. It's taking their money and throwing it away. That's not justice. That's a crime. Max is spending a small fortune on this healing, and it's a fake. Amos has agreed that he will make a legal statement at the end of this case stating that he's aware that the treatment doesn't work."

"All I know is that Max's faith in the man has changed my son's life. We have Max back. That's worth more than anything. I would sell everything I own to keep paying for those treatments. As long as Max believes it works, then I will do anything to get him back to those sessions."

"But that's not the truth. And justice relies on the truth."

"It might not be a legal truth, but it's a truth for our Max."

Hunter lined up his putt on the edge of the fairway. He checked the roll of the green, checked his putter and then pushed at the ball, watching it roll smoothly along the green before dropping into the hole.

"It's not a legal truth, and that's something I can't walk away from."

"Truth is subjective." Patrick took his second putt and watched the ball drop into the hole. "The truth is that in laboratory trials, the healing doesn't work. The truth is that there's no magic force in the universe. But Max's truth, his belief, his certainty, is that it does work. It's cured him of his addiction. That's his truth."

"The facts are the facts. There's no disputing them. It doesn't work."

"It does for Max."

Hunter sighed. His brother loved a good argument. As siblings, it was the main way they had bonded.

Hunter took out his scorecard and noted down the numbers.

Patrick looked over his shoulder, eager to watch his brother write the sum of their game. If he got within five strokes of Hunter, he considered it a win.

"You played well today, Patrick." Hunter began packing up his clubs. "Only eight shots off the pace."

"Getting better." Patrick placed his putter back into his golf bag. "You're not stopping for lunch after our game?"

"Not today. I've got too much going on with this case."

"Tex?"

Hunter sighed. "Go on. Say your peace."

"You may have your own sense of justice, but for me, I need you to look after your nephew. I can't lose him again. Not after losing his mother. Max told me that he attempted suicide when his addiction was at its worst. I can't lose him, Tex. If he thinks that man saved his life, then let him think that. Promise me that you will do what's best for him."

Hunter paused and looked back out to the golf course. Not only did Patrick suffer through the trials of their father's killings, but he also lost his wife in a car accident, and then his son to drug addiction. That almost killed him.

"Promise me, Tex."

Hunter paused. "I can't, Patrick. I can't promise that."

Hunter began to walk away, wheeling his golf bag behind him.

"Tex."

Hunter paused again but didn't turn around.

"I love you." Patrick looked at the back of his brother's head. "That's what Mom always said to us, and that's what I wanted to say to you."

"You too, brother," Hunter whispered, but again, he didn't turn around. "You too."

CHAPTER 20

SITTING OUTSIDE the theater at the Loop after midday on a Tuesday, Hunter wasn't concerned with where Lucas Bauer was going.

He was concerned with being seen.

He followed him as he exited the theater, staying three people back as Bauer walked down Dearborn Street, past the Picasso sculpture, through the lunchtime crowd. Hunter kept his head down as the "L" train rumbled overhead, hands in his coat pockets, keeping Bauer in his peripheral vision. He followed him as he walked through the busy mass of people, getting closer as Bauer walked into a Starbucks to loudly order a Grande Latte. Hunter sat quietly inside the café, near the entrance, just visible enough for Bauer to notice him.

As Bauer collected his coffee, Hunter pretended to read his phone.

"You know, if you're going to tail someone, you

should've stayed outside the shop. You haven't even ordered a coffee." Bauer leaned in. "You're not very good at this, are you?"

"Lucas. What a surprise." Hunter's voice was monotone. "I don't know what you're talking about. I wasn't following you."

"You weren't? It was a coincidence that you were walking behind me down the street and then followed me here, where you haven't ordered a coffee?"

"Stranger things have happened."

Bauer shook his head as he walked out of the busy Starbucks, coffee in hand.

It was only ten minutes later that Hunter's phone buzzed. He smiled as he looked at the name on the phone.

"Hello, Detective Browne."

"That's quite formal for an old friend," Browne stated. "Are you free to talk in person?"

Hunter grinned, making sure his smile wasn't big enough for anyone to see. "Yes, Browne, I am."

Twenty minutes later, Hunter was sitting in a café past the entrance of Union Station, Browne's preferred choice. Hunter sipped at the burnt coffee and ordered a serving of bacon and eggs, both of which he was sure would be burnt as well. There weren't many people in the dimly lit diner, but that was expected. The sign out front was dirty, as was the table. The light inconsistently flickered overhead, and it annoyed Hunter every time it did.

When Browne arrived, he ordered a coffee before taking a seat opposite Hunter in the narrow booth. The vinyl seat stuck to his trousers as he struggled to squirm across. With a large stomach, Browne only just squeezed into the booth.

Preemptively, Browne struck first.

"Why were you tailing Lucas Bauer?"

"You tell me. You seem to know my movements quite well."

"I'm a cop. A detective," Browne said with a growl. "And as a cop, I need to know why you met with Bauer."

"I'm a lawyer," Hunter retorted. "And it's my job to know things before the cops do."

Browne exhaled, leaning back in his chair as the waitress placed Hunter's plate of burnt bacon and overcooked scrambled eggs on the table. The bacon smelled like it had spent the last day in a smoker, but Hunter was thankful that it overpowered the smell of Browne's body odor.

As the waitress walked away, Browne commented, "Looks like they didn't burn it as much as usual."

Hunter didn't respond. He much preferred his eggs overcooked, and his bacon extra crispy. He liked the extra crunch.

"I'm not the man you want to mess with." Browne pressed his finger down on the table. "What do you have on Bauer?"

"It's none of your business." Hunter moved his bacon to the edge of the plate with his knife. The light flickered overhead again. "What did Bauer tell you?"

Browne leaned back in the chair. "When?"

"When he gave you that envelope and paper bag in a bar on the Magnificent Mile."

"Is that what Bauer said? Of course, he would say that." Browne's voice rose, and he shrugged, trying to hide his lie. "He's trying to cover his own butt, that's all. It's all misdirection. He's trying to make you think that I've got something to hide."

"You do."

Browne tried the friendly approach: "Tex, old buddy, you—"

"Don't call me your buddy. I'm not your friend."

"You know me. You've known me for years. We're more than colleagues trying to get justice. We're friends. You and me. You know I'm on the straight and narrow now. My life has changed."

"A leopard doesn't change its spots, Browne. Once a dirty cop, always a dirty cop."

Browne sighed, holding out his hands as a sign of surrender.

"I know you're dirty, Browne. I know what was in that envelope," Hunter lied.

"What do you want, Hunter? A piece of it?"

"I want you to know that I'm coming for you."

Fear spread across Browne's face. "Tell me what you want, Hunter. I can help you get whatever you want. Whatever it is, I can help you. Money. Girls. Drugs. Whatever. You name it, and I have the contacts to get it."

The light flickered again, and it took all of Hunter's restraint not to put the dinner knife through it. He looked towards the ceiling and contemplated it for a few moments, then placed his knife back down. His appetite had disappeared.

"You can't get me what I want."

"I can help you," Browne pleaded. It was his

standard procedure—backed into a corner, he would wheel and deal until he could get out. "You and I could be a great team. Tell me what you want."

Hunter pushed his plate away, no longer comfortable with his present company. He left a few bills on the table before choosing his next words very carefully.

"I want justice." He stood. "And you could never give that to me."

"Listen." Browne paused, then stood too. "I know that we aren't friends. I know you hate me. But I'll give you a tip—with this case, be careful who you talk to."

"I always am," Hunter retorted.

But this time, he wasn't so sure.

CHAPTER 21

RAY JONES climbed inside Hunter's sedan to provide a brief update after weeks of investigative work. His long limbs filled the front seat and his knees squashed against the dash, despite the leather seat being as far back as it could be.

Hunter spent extra on the latest BMW sedan model for comfort, knowing he conducted a lot of meetings in it—and that Ray needed legroom. Hunter had the same problem; his knees often hurt after long car journeys.

Parked next to the waterfront, their meeting was held in the comfort of the car's heat, but with the added benefit of the beautiful Lake Michigan in sight. The side windows of the car fogged up quickly, the cold air on the outside contrasting with the artificial warmth. They sat in the parking lot on Northerly Island near the Alder Planetarium, with the late afternoon sun skimming across the horizon.

Jones had parked his truck next to Hunter's car, the big red beast almost shiny enough to be a mirror. A limousine rolled past them, white wedding ribbons tied on the hood, and a 'Happily Married' sign on the back.

"Do you know what the world's most dangerous food for men to eat is?" Jones smiled. "Wedding cake."

"I'll keep that in mind if I ever cross that bridge." Hunter chuckled. "How're things with your new girlfriend?"

"We split up. I couldn't stay with her after what she said to me."

"What did she say?"

"Get out." Jones laughed. "It's fine; we weren't a good match anyway. We were never going to work out."

"She didn't like the gym?"

"Ha." Jones clapped his hands. "In our last argument, she said, 'You're not even listening.' And I thought: that's a funny way to start a conversation."

"That's good." Hunter laughed.

Jones grinned broadly and playfully slapped Hunter on the shoulder. Hunter recoiled.

"Sorry, Tex. How's the shoulder?"

"Still sore, but it's healing. There'll be a scar, but women love scars. At least it's an interesting story to tell them." Hunter turned the stereo in his car down. Piano Man by Billy Joel was playing, a song he loved, but if it was up too loud, he wouldn't be able to resist singing along to it. And nobody needed to hear him sing. "What did you find out about Chuck?"

"I followed him yesterday afternoon—tailed him from when he left the house and watched him arrive at the home of Dennis Comity, a known mafia man, in the northern suburbs. These are dangerous people."

Hunter drew a long breath, humming the tune to the Billy Joel classic. "What else have you got?"

"Chuck's well connected. Really well connected." Jones tapped his fingers on his thigh along to the tune. "I know because he seems to be a step ahead of everyone. After he walked out of the mafia house, the cops arrived only a few minutes later. He obviously knew the cops were coming and when to bail out of there."

"How many cops came to the house?"

"I didn't stick around to find out. I heard the sirens coming, saw the first car arrive, and then got out of there. It wouldn't have looked too good if I was caught there. I checked the reports later—no arrests, but the word is that the cops roughed someone up."

"Any idea who he's connected to?" Hunter asked the question, although he already had some idea of the answer.

Hunter gritted his teeth; he was doing his best not to break out into the last chorus of the song.

"Word on the street is that some detectives in the department want to make a bit of extra money on the side. Buy nice things. You can't do that on a straight cop's wage."

"No names?"

"Not yet." Jones looked out the window as a tourist group on Segways rolled past. He watched them get close to his truck, his fists clenching, ready to explode if one of them brushed it. "But I'll tell you something, Tex. People are scared of this White Alliance Coalition. A lot of people, even my best informants, were reluctant to talk about Johnson and his band of merry racists. I didn't get much information, but what I do know is that these men have hurt people before and won't hesitate to do it again."

"I'm starting to get that impression."

"And if you think you're going to pin the murder case on Johnson, then you better be prepared to be attacked. If anyone goes sniffing in their dirt, they usually end up with a few missing teeth. And the word is that Johnson and his men are on high alert at the moment."

"Sing us a song, you're the piano man!" Hunter sang loudly. He had done his best to resist singing, but he couldn't help belting out the last verse. "Sing us a song tonight."

"Well, we're all in the mood for a melody," Jones quickly joined in. He'd been called many things in his time, but Karaoke King was his favorite title. "And you got us feeling alright."

They smiled, looking out the window as the harmonica finished the song.

In his teenage years, Hunter spent a lot of time alone in his bedroom, with the door locked and the curtains drawn closed. Music was his escape. Listening to his parents' old records helped him disappear from the outside world, and many of the words to the seventies biggest songs were imprinted into his subconscious.

In the comfort of his messy room, with posters of cars and girls on the walls, Billy Joel, Phil Collins, and

Paul Simon became his friends, the people he could turn to when everything else was lost.

"You have Van Gogh's ear for tone, Tex."

"Thanks." Hunter laughed. As much as he enjoyed it, singing was never his thing.

"Do you know who they're connected to on the inside?" Jones asked.

"I tailed Bauer two days ago, and saw him talking to Browne."

"Your old pal, Detective Browne?"

"The very one. They were talking quietly in a bar on the Mile. It was the perfect cover for an off-the-books chat."

"So he's dirty?"

"He's always been dirty; the question is, how dirty? I'm digging around to try and find that out."

"Be very careful where you dig. These men have no issue with violence."

"Justice shouldn't run away from danger."

"But this is next level, Tex. I know you love danger, I know you love a rush, but this is different. This is like going on a theme park ride and not buckling up." Jones turned to face Hunter. "You might get more of a rush, but you might also end up flying into the crowd below. Be careful."

Hunter looked out to the view again, studying the distant horizon. A boat sailed towards the sunset, the glint of reflection shining off the water.

"Tex, I would love nothing better than to take these guys down. The idea that Chuck is spreading hate due to someone's skin color cuts me deeper than you could ever know. I would love nothing more than to beat the weary old man into the ground, but this is about more than that. Your case is taking you close to these guys. They're going to come after you. Hard."

"The girl in the hospital, Eva, she's still in an induced coma, and she deserves justice." Hunter tapped his finger on the steering wheel. "I'm sure that the two incidents are connected—it's the murder of a minister, and then a drive-by of the same community only weeks later. They have to be connected, and I'm sure that Chuck is at the center of it all. I can't trust the PD on this one."

"Just... be careful." There was a level of fear in Jones' voice that Hunter hadn't heard before.

And that alarmed him.

A lot.

CHAPTER 22

THE WALK up the stairs took longer than expected. The elevator was being repaired in the old building, and the stairs were uneven, worn, and slightly sticky. Tex Hunter held onto the handrail tightly, almost expecting to go through one of the steps.

The building was built in the late 1920s when Chicago started to rebuild after the great fire. Its exterior was well maintained, and its interior was kept as close to the original as possible. Over the years, there had been ten murders in the building, earning it the reputation as the "supernatural hub" of Downtown Chicago. There was a chill in the building, and Hunter wasn't sure if it was from the ghosts or the lack of daylight. He didn't want to think about it too much.

When he reached the third floor, Hunter knocked twice on apartment 305 and waited in the dim hallway. The shabby red carpet in the hallway was spooky enough for him. Hunter heard someone check the peephole.

"Hello?" the voice called out. "How can I help you?"

"Mrs. Nelson?"

"Yes."

"My name is Tex Hunter, and I'm a lawyer. I would like to have a word with you about the Baptist church in Grand Crossing."

She unbolted the door, unlocking at least three locks before the door creaked open. In front of him was a short African American woman, but despite her height, she looked tough. She had forearms that most grandchildren would be scared of.

The woman looked over the top of her glasses at Hunter. "You're the killer's son?"

"I'm a lawyer," Hunter replied. "I had nothing to do with my father's actions."

She hesitated. Most people did. He was a physically imposing character with a family history of murder. That usually scared most people.

"You can only come in if you're not going to murder me." She was only half-joking. "I was there on the day of the church shooting. What you did saved those children's lives. Even if you're the son of a killer, you deserve my time."

Inside the apartment was cute. The furnishings looked like they had been there for decades, as had the décor. The room smelled like a fresh breeze hadn't blown through in months, but the scent of the lavender candle was overwhelming any potential mothball smell.

The rooms were tight but homey. There were children's picture books on the bookshelf in the living room, and toys sitting in a red box in the corner, tucked away next to the fabric upholstered couch.

Mrs. Nelson and her apartment weren't hard to find, but then, most people aren't. In the age of the Internet, unless a person has made a deliberate attempt to hide, an address can be located within an hour.

"May I pour you a coffee?" she asked.

"Please." Hunter smiled as she offered him a seat on the sofa that looked like it could be folded out into a bed for guests.

She turned on the coffee pot in the narrow kitchen and then turned back to the lawyer. "How can I help you?"

"I was talking with Reverend Darcy recently, and

he mentioned your name. He said that you're now back within the Baptist church community, but I'm interested as to why you left the church in the first place. I understand that you were quite an active member of that community before you left?"

She sighed and then reached for the coffee machine as it finished brewing. She walked into the living room with two fancy china mugs, the ones she saved for visitors. "You're defending Reverend Green's killer, yes?"

"I am." Hunter brought the mug to his lips and blew on the steaming liquid.

"I loved that community. There are so many churches between here and there, but that was where I grew up. I only moved Downtown fifteen years ago, but I always made an effort to get to Grand Crossing each Sunday. It was my community; it was everything to me. But…" She paused as she sat down. Her body sunk into the cushions, shaped after many years of use. "But Reverend Green didn't like that I was going to see Amos Anderson to heal my back problems. For Reverend Green, it was blasphemous to suggest that faith healing worked. He said it was the work of the Devil and that I had to choose between going to church or going to see the Devil. As you can understand, I wanted my back healed. And Amos did that. He healed decades of pain within a few weeks. It was magic, almost like the work of the Devil, I guess."

"Have you been back often since he passed?"

"Oh yes," she replied quickly. "I've been going to each Sunday service since he passed. I went to Reverend Green's funeral, and I was impressed with the way Reverend Darcy conducted himself. He recognized me and said that I should come back to the church. I'm so glad I did. The church community has been so important to me for so many years. They're my family." She smiled. "Reverend Darcy is much more forward-thinking than his predecessors, and he doesn't mind that I've seen Amos to heal my back. He knows that there are many things in the world that we don't understand, such as the faith healing. He's a lovely man. He's really brought the community back together, especially after Green forced a lot of us away."

Hunter never found it hard to convince an elderly member of the community to talk about a case. Mrs. Nelson was no different—she had almost eighty years of experience, and she longed to share it.

"He forced a lot of people away?" Hunter encouraged her to continue.

"I hate to speak ill of the dead, but Reverend Green was divisive. He was a loud voice against so many things—faith healing, the decay of the community, the lack of religion in schools, and that drove many people away from the church. I could see how that hurt Reverend Darcy." She paused, a sad look across her face. She opened her hands and looked to the ceiling, saying a quiet prayer, before she continued. "Reverend Green asked me directly not to come back to the church, and that hurt so much. I had back problems for many, many years, and it stopped me from doing anything. I couldn't even play with my grandchildren, and when you get to be my age, young man, one of the greatest joys in the world is watching little children play. There were days that I was in so much pain that I could barely walk out the door, and I couldn't keep asking my son to look after me. He had already done enough. And if the elevator broke in this building, which it often does, there was no way I could use the stairs. I was really struggling to find a way to deal with the pain. I had tried everything before then—praying, chiropractors, acupuncture, drugs, doctors, physiotherapists—everything. But then a friend suggested this faith healer, and I had to try it. I had nothing to lose."

"And it worked?"

"Almost instantly. I saw Amos weekly for two months, and the pain was gone. Completely gone. And the amazing thing is that I've never had a problem since. I even ran to catch my grandson last week in the playground. What a beautiful feeling that was. I went from not being able to walk on the bad days, to being pain free and chasing a six-year-old around the playground. I don't know what Amos did, or how he did it, or even how to explain it, but I will tell you that it worked. It was almost magic, and perhaps it was the Devil's work, but I would sell my soul to chase my grandson around."

Hunter sipped his hot coffee. There was no doubt that she believed in the faith healing. There was no doubt that it changed her life.

The pictures of Mrs. Nelson's family sat proudly on the bookshelf, and the black and white pictures of her parents hung proudly above them.

But the most prominent possession on top of the bookshelf was the Bible—well used and well read.

"Did Reverend Darcy ever suggest that he wanted to get rid of Reverend Green?"

She didn't answer immediately.

She stood, walked into the kitchen, and turned on the coffee pot again, even though her cup wasn't even half finished.

She leaned against the bench, looked to the ceiling, said something softly, and then peered back at Hunter.

"A week before Reverend Green's death, I went to

the church and saw Reverend Darcy. I asked what my chances were of coming back to the church. He told me to have faith. He said that he was working on getting Reverend Green out of the community."

"Did he say how?"

"No." Mrs. Nelson shook her head.

She poured her coffee down the sink, washed her cup out with water, and then filled it up again. Once she did that, she walked back into the living room.

"I believe in a lot of things, Mr. Hunter. One, I believe in the scripture. Two, I wholly believe in coincidences. I think they're the Lord's way of telling you that He's looking after you. And it was a coincidence, nothing more. A word from the Lord."

"You hope."

She shot a glare at Hunter.

Hunter averted his eyes, almost feeling like she was about to walk back into the kitchen to retrieve a wooden spoon.

"Did you ever meet Lucas Bauer, the manager and promoter of the Faith Healing Project?"

"Almost everything about the experience with the Faith Healing Project was positive. Amos' office was lovely—he's a lovely man himself, and the results were beyond belief. The only thing that put a dampener on the whole experience was the manager, Lucas Bauer. He was very rude to me, and Amos apologized every time I saw him. I don't know what his problem was, but if I didn't know any better, I would've said that my skin color was the reason he was so rude. When you've been through as much as I have, when you've seen as much racism as I have, you learn a thing or two about a person's reaction to your skin color."

"You're saying that Lucas Bauer is racist?"

"I am." Mrs. Nelson's voice was sure. "Amos told me that Lucas wanted to expand the business to include other faith healers, but Amos didn't agree. Amos wanted the community to stay small. After I was forced out of the church, I volunteered to help Amos' operations because I loved what he did for me, and I had the time to do it. I wanted to spread that love to the world. But volunteering at the office also meant that I had to deal with Lucas Bauer occasionally. He hated that I came to the office, and I was the only black person there. Everyone else was as white as they come. I only lasted a month in his office before I left. I couldn't stand the way that Lucas glared at me."

Hunter looked around the room. "How long ago was this?"

"Around two months ago—that's when I left the organization." She paused, looking glum while she stared into her coffee. "May I ask you a question?"

"Of course."

"Do you believe he's innocent? Do you really believe that Amos is innocent? Because that's what he's saying, isn't he? He's saying he didn't do it."

Her eyes were almost pleading with Hunter.

Hunter sighed, looking at the threadbare carpet, and then gazed back at her.

"Yes, Mrs. Nelson. I do." He stood and placed his mug down gently on the table. "I believe Amos Anderson is innocent."

CHAPTER 23

THE SWEAT started to build under Tex Hunter's shirt.

The more he thought about sweat, the more it built. The sweat was a reaction to walking through the busy halls of the prosecutor's floor; so many people hurried past him, filling the air with tension, desperate to get somewhere, to tell someone something that they obviously thought was critical, maybe even life or death.

The staff moved like they were the only ones wearing the white hat, like they were the only ones that were virtuous. That annoyed Hunter. He knew what their job entailed, he knew how much they sacrificed to bring justice to the community, but he also knew they got things wrong.

That was when he felt like he was wearing the white hat.

The halls were narrow and dimly lit. He could

barely see the people pushing past him, but when he reached the main office, the light flooded in from the tall windows. There were too many office cubicles to count, filled with junior lawyers filing paperwork, and at the end of the floor, the offices of the senior prosecutors.

He walked through the cubicles and was surprised to see the name of the opposing lawyer still on the door. He thought that her life would've fallen apart after he found information about her mother being a murderer.

He had underestimated her strength.

"Mr. Tex Hunter, it's been a while." The prosecutor stood at the door, welcoming him into her spacious office. "And I can't say that I'm happy to see you after what you told me last time we saw each other."

"Michelle Law." He drew a breath. "I must admit that I was surprised to see your name on the file. I didn't think that you would continue practicing law after what happened."

"I've got nothing else, Tex." She shrugged. "I took a four-month sabbatical after the Sulzberger case. I took time out to go and sit in the sun in the Bahamas, but I've never been so bored in my entire life. What a horrible, boring experience. I was sipping Mojitos, but

I had nothing else to do. I ended up researching local cases and sitting in the courthouse. I've been back at work here two months now, and I'm in the swing of things."

"How's your midlife crisis coming along?" Hunter closed the door behind him.

The office was well lit and roomy, but still, it felt suffocating. The desk sat prominently in the middle of the room, a lamp on one side and a computer on the other, while the walls were dark wood paneling with a lone piece of art on the left-hand side. The brown abstract painting did nothing to lighten the mood.

"I've had many, many midlife crises." She smiled as she sat down. "And I had my first at twenty-five, which doesn't really say much about my longevity."

Michelle Law ran her hand over the top of her hair, her black hair pulled back so tightly that it almost gave her a headache. Her black dress also didn't lighten the mood, but that was the way she liked it.

"Do you still steal items from shops?" Hunter asked.

"The only things I steal these days are wins."

Almost six months ago, Hunter uncovered Law's

addiction—stealing small items from convenience stores. She did it for the rush, for the hit of adrenalin. Although she was never caught by the police, Hunter found the information and confronted her about it. Once she knew she was trapped, she committed to taking a leave of absence to sort through her issues.

"Your eyes look very clear," he commented as he placed his briefcase on the floor. "And your skin is almost glowing."

"I'm sober now. 98 days and counting. It's on my calendar at home. I mark off every single day that I make it through, but some days are tougher than others. Mostly I feel great. It… it's hard to describe what life is like without alcohol. I have energy. Clear thoughts. Enthusiasm. It's amazing, Tex. It really is. Giving up alcohol is life changing."

"Don't give me that look."

"All I'm saying is that you should try a month without alcohol. You'll feel fantastic, and you'll never go back. Being sober changes everything. You'll feel…" She struggled to find the right word to convey how much her life had changed. "You'll feel better than ever. I don't even know how to describe the feeling."

"The reason I drink is so I don't feel at all." Hunter's tone was flat. "But congratulations,

Michelle. You should be proud of making it to the edge, and being one of the few that are strong enough to walk back from it. How's your birth mother, Cindy? Do you still talk to her?"

"She's doing the time for the crime. That's what happens when you kill someone. If you do the crime, you've got to do the time. No matter who you are."

"I wish that were true." Hunter smiled. "You and I both know that's not the case."

"Well, lucky for us, your latest client is a prime candidate to do the time for his crime." Law scrolled through the document on the computer screen. She typed quickly, her fingers tapping loudly on the keys. "The remarkable case of the innocent man. DNA, witnesses, and a motive all point to your client killing a popular Baptist minister. But, of course, he didn't do it, did he?"

"That's what he claims."

"Everyone is guilty of something."

"If that's true, then the only real offense is being stupid enough to get caught."

Law laughed and placed a file in front of Hunter. "New evidence. It's only come in today."

"What is it?" Hunter opened the file, read the notes, and looked over the pictures.

"One of our detectives received an anonymous tip-off about Amos Anderson's place. They obtained a warrant, conducted a search, and found a necklace that belonged to Green, right next to Anderson's bed. A little more than a coincidence, don't you think?"

Hunter didn't respond.

He reread the file, flicking between the pages, looking at the photos—no fingerprints, and no DNA on the necklace. That was too convenient.

Law ran her hand over her hair again. "What are your thoughts?"

"It doesn't matter what I think, Michelle; it only matters what the twelve people in the jury box think based on the evidence. That's what we do. Don't tell me that the Caribbean sun has taken that knowledge away from you."

"But you must have an opinion, Tex? You, the famous Tex Hunter, must have an opinion on whether or not your client is guilty."

Hunter closed the file on the new evidence, sat back in the chair, crossed one leg over the other, and rested his hands in his lap. "The evidence is weak. The whole case is weak. You're making a mistake by putting this man on trial. A big mistake. And it isn't going to look very good for your office when you lose, especially with your record. You should admit defeat and walk away now. Drop the charges and be done with it. Let an innocent man walk free."

"And why would we even bother with a fragile case, Tex? The courts are too busy, and the prisons are overcrowded. We only go after the ones we need to." Law made eye contact. Her clear, deep blue eyes were mesmerizing, and Hunter struggled to maintain focus.

"We both know why you're pressing ahead with this case. You're not after my client; you couldn't care less about him. Despite the fact that my client is a great citizen, you want to persecute him for someone else's crime. You want a scapegoat to prevent riots happening all over our city. You took the closest man to the scene and you're willing to sacrifice his future to save face. That's not justice."

"There are people in the city looking for a reason to start a riot. The situation is at a breaking point. It's more than a hundred years since the Chicago race riots of 1919 turned this city upside down, and I don't intend to encourage an anniversary party."

"That doesn't mean you should charge an innocent man."

"We haven't." Law didn't flinch.

When Law saw Tex Hunter's name on the defendant's notes, she was delighted.

Sobriety had been wonderful to her, but she still felt she was missing something in her life. Even after three months, her days were becoming a boring slog of case after case, charge after charge, late night after late night, and without the comfort of alcohol to deaden her loneliness. To go toe to toe with Hunter in the courtroom, considering his reputation, invigorated her desire. It recharged her enthusiasm for the system.

Most charges were settled out of court, settled before the excitement of a trial, but Hunter had a reputation for dragging the impossible before a judge. For this meeting, Law wore her best work dress, one that she only bought the week before and added an extra spray of her best perfume.

It was having the desired effect on her opponent.

"Did you even look at other suspects, Michelle? My client is an innocent bystander, and you're going after the wrong man. Focus your attention on the real criminals. Like you said, you don't have time to chase this case."

"Innocent men don't kill people."

Hunter took a moment to collect his thoughts. The meeting was going exactly as he expected. He would push her to drop the charges, she would refuse, and then, when she was intrigued by his position, he would drop a bombshell on her.

"Tell me about one of the officers in the PD." Hunter leaned back in the chair. "Detective Browne."

"I'm not sure what you're asking?"

"Do you trust him?"

"Of course," she lied.

She hated the man; the last time she talked to him, he called her "baby." She showed impressive restraint not to break his nose.

"Do you think he has any links to the case?"

"Other than the arrest and search? No." Law shook her head.

Even if she did think so, she wouldn't give that information away now, and Hunter knew that. He was testing the waters, checking to see if she flinched under the questions about the integrity of one of the detectives.

She didn't.

"Nothing the Bureau of Internal Affairs would know about?"

"No, Tex. Nothing."

It was the response he anticipated, but what he

had done was planted a seed of doubt, a moment of indecision, in the prosecutor's mind. With the added pressure, she might make a small mistake.

And that was all he needed.

Hunter uncrossed his legs and leaned his elbows on the table.

"How about we drop this case now and save ourselves some time? Go after the big fish. Don't play this game of cat and mouse. Don't put an innocent man behind bars for the sake of avoiding a riot. That's not what we got into law for. We got into law to uphold justice—and this isn't justice."

"This is justice, Tex. Justice for the people of the Grand Crossing Baptist church. Amos Anderson is a killer. He will do time. That's justice. And you know the deals that are on the table. Don't try and convince yourself that your client is innocent. I can guarantee you that he's not. He's not an innocent man. The only reason he spends time helping others is because he makes money from it. If he was truly passionate about this fake magic, if he truly wanted to make a change, then he would do it for free. Just ask your nephew, Maxwell Hunter."

Law had dropped a bomb of her own.

"Pardon?"

"We have very good researchers here, Tex." She smiled. "You're personally invested in this case. I understand why. Your nephew was a dirty drug addict, a part of the scum in the city, and Amos saved him. This is more than a case about an innocent man; this is a case about your family, and we all know what your family is capable of."

His mouth hung open, and for the first time in a long time, he was speechless.

Hunter stood and placed his index finger down firmly on the table. "Don't talk to me about family. Yours isn't much better."

Law grinned, bit her bottom lip, and winked. "I really do like it when you're angry, Tex."

With a grunt, Hunter turned and left the office, disappointed that he had let out such a display of raw emotion.

He needed to get his emotions in check during the trial, or Law would use them against him. The problem was—those entrenched feelings were something that whiskey couldn't fix.

But he was still going to try.

CHAPTER 24

THE FILES were spread out on the table; not neatly, not precisely, but with a sense of order.

The headshots of all the suspects, copies of the witness statements, and files of the evidence sat on the table. Layer upon layer was spread across the boardroom, the whiteboard behind them filled with notes, and a picture of Amos Anderson sat in the middle of the table—the centerpiece of all their work.

"So what do we have?" Ray Jones asked as he circled around the room.

"We have an innocent man that's about to go to prison," Hunter quipped.

The sun was low in the sky, with a slice of light sneaking through the window behind them. Not strong enough to project any warmth, but the temperature in the large boardroom was still warm enough for Hunter to roll up his sleeves.

"Do you really think Anderson is innocent?" Esther questioned. She was sitting at the head of the table and took a loud sip of coffee from her mug.

Hunter and Jones glared at her while she continued to sip her drink.

"It's not—" Hunter began, but Esther sipped loudly from her mug again.

They continued to stare at her, but she was oblivious to their irritation. Once she had finished slurping, she turned back to them. "He could be guilty? He could be the killer, you know. We could be barking up the wrong tree."

"He might be crazy, but he's not a killer." Hunter looked back to the files. "Regardless, it's not our job to determine whether he's the killer or not. Our job is to get the best outcome possible, and the way we do that is to create doubt about his guilt. The best way to do that is to present someone else to the court."

"Is winning from here even possible?" Esther looked at the file and wiped her mouth with the back of her hand. "Look at all this evidence."

"That's the concern. While we have other people to present as possible suspects to the jury, we can't disprove much of the evidence," Hunter stated. "Yes, Anderson's DNA was under Reverend Green's fingernails and his blood was on the shirt. Yes, he argued with Green only hours before his murder and he had a motive. Yes, he was in the area at the time of the murder and Green's necklace was found in his house."

"Sounds pretty closed to me." Jones sat down in one of the leather office chairs surrounding the table. "It looks like Amos is going to prison. It might be best to take a deal. Perhaps ten years for a guilty plea."

"The prosecution isn't going to give us that. If it's anything less than twenty years, there'll be riots in the streets, and they know that. Things are bubbling, waiting to boil over. Green was one of the most vocal African American ministers out there and his followers were as passionate as he is."

"I know. I've listened to his sermons online."

"How many sermons are online?"

"Maybe a hundred. All on YouTube. They've had millions of hits, and they're quite inspiring." Jones clenched one fist and tapped it on his chest. "The speeches inspire hope that there's something beyond racism, something beyond the hate. He often said that he was willing to go through the present pain so that others may benefit from it in the future. He was willing to fight the good fight, even if it turned some people away from the church."

"And now he's a martyr," Hunter stated. "If we get Anderson off the charges without producing another suspect, then you can expect that we'll be targets for that hate. So, we have three options, and we need to focus on one of them—Chuck Johnson, Lucas Bauer, and possibly, Reverend Darcy. We know that both Bauer and Darcy were there that night, and have flimsy alibis after the event."

"A racist, a sly dog, and a nice minister. I know which one I'd be presenting to the jury," Jones said.

"Whichever one we present, we have to go hard, because two of those people will fight back hard against us." Hunter moved a piece of paper across the table. "The best story to present at the moment is Chuck Johnson. He's almost perfect—a racist who hated the church, the Reverend, and the congregation. If we can find out where he was that night, if he was anywhere near the scene, then he's almost perfect."

"But he'll be the one that fights back the hardest," Esther said.

Hunter sat down and swirled his chair around to stare at the whiteboard. "We might also have one other suspect—Nancy Bleathman. She's a fanatic supporter of the Faith Healing Project but seemed unusually content with the idea of getting Anderson out of the picture, and she seemed quite attached to Lucas Bauer."

"Bleathman—I know that name." Esther stood and moved more files across the table. She brushed her long sandy blonde hair behind her ear as she read off a list. "Yes. Bleathman, N. She's one of the people on Bauer's list to begin the faith healing training. One of the expansion healers."

"Interesting. She has a motive, and we know that she was at the seminar that night," Hunter said. "Ray, find out what you can about her. She stated that she walked home after the seminar that night, so if that's true, there must be footage of her walking home from somewhere. If we can tie her to being around the scene of the crime, we might have a chance."

"On it." Jones wrote a note on his phone. "Nancy Bleathman."

Hunter stood back up and tapped his finger on the whiteboard, over Caylee Johnson's name. "How did it go with the girl?"

"It's strange." Esther sighed. "I tailed her and saw her talking to and being friendly with an African American girl at Northeastern Illinois University."

"Really?" Jones interrupted. "Her father wouldn't like that."

"I confronted her about it as she walked to class, and she assumed I must've known her father. I looked in the mirror all night after that. I mean, do I really look like a racist? Do I look like someone that would join the White Alliance Coalition?"

"You don't have enough tattoos." Jones laughed. "And you didn't marry your brother."

"Thanks. I'll take that as a compliment." She smiled. "So she explained that she, 'had something planned for the school and I needed to trust her judgment.'"

"What do you think that means?"

"I hate to think what it means." Esther shook her head. "She didn't give me a time, or what it was, but I was worried. I saw a phone booth on the drive home, and I stopped. I called the police anonymously, but they said they couldn't do anything about it. They said there wasn't enough information for them to take action."

"There was neither a direct threat nor specific information, but you did the right thing by calling them, Esther." Hunter tapped his finger on the table. "She isn't a weak spot, but I imagine that Chuck is protective of her, so she might be leverage to get at him. Look into that."

"Got it. Leverage." Esther wrote a note on her legal pad.

"Burt Johnson, the brother?" Jones suggested,

pointing to the picture on the table. "By all reports, he's as thick as a log. Might be someone that you could pressure into spilling the truth?"

"He's protected. The only way we'll get to talk to him is on the stand, and I'm not calling him to the stand without some evidence."

A hush fell over the boardroom as they all contemplated the case. Hunter inspected the connections on the board, Jones peered down at the table, and Esther's eyes were on her phone. They had options, but the challenge was determining the right choice. They had to make a clear decision about where to guide the case; they needed a clear story to present to the jury.

It was only once Esther slurped her drink, again, that everyone returned from their thoughts.

"What would happen if we get Anderson off the charges without offering up another suspect? People won't like that, will they?"

Hunter looked at the city beyond the window in front of them.

"If that happens, then none of us will be welcomed anywhere in Chicago for a very long time."

CHAPTER 25

CAYLEE JOHNSON smiled as she typed a message on her phone.

She finished the text with a smiley face, mirroring real life.

Her friend replied with a photo—her smile almost as wide as her face, but Caylee had to quickly hide the image.

She deleted it the second she received it.

Sitting around the dinner table, waiting for her father to finish burning the beef sausages for dinner, she couldn't let the men of the house know that she was receiving messages from an African American girl. She hated to think about what they would do—there would be a beating, for sure. Maybe many.

Caylee had received repeated beatings during her youth; it was just a part of her life. The way things were. Every time she stepped out of line, or said something wrong, she could be assured it was followed by a fist. As much as they wanted to protect her, as much as they loved her, the men had asserted their control over her life.

She had no doubt that her father and uncle would do anything for her. No doubt at all. She was their little angel, their precious gift. The day her prom date came to the house, the poor kid was greeted by two men with shotguns at the front gate. Her date barely said a word to her all night.

They ate dinner as a family—burnt sausages with a side of mashed potatoes—before her father broke out into a rant about how America was falling apart. The television was always on at the house, a constant stream of news and drama flowing into their living room, and it usually fueled her father's tirades.

After she finished dinner, Caylee grabbed the men a beer each from the refrigerator and sat with them for a few moments while they screamed the wrong answers at a quiz show on the TV. After every wrong answer—all of which she knew the right response to—they argued with the television about the facts.

When they were engrossed enough in the show, she left and went out to the garage. She opened the many metal cabinets full of guns. She loved the feeling of being surrounded by power.

She had two plans to choose from.

She had thought about them both over the years, each time the thoughts becoming clearer. She had wanted to carry out one of the plans when she was in high school, but the risk was too great. She had wanted to do one of them when she graduated school, but her father was too busy. But now, due to his cancer, she felt the pressure to do it.

This was her time.

This was her chance to make a difference.

Her opportunity.

"What'cha doing, girl?" Her uncle strode into the garage, throwing a beer bottle top across the room.

"Getting ready." She took one of the guns from the rack. She looked down the barrel, checked it was straight, and smiled. There were sixteen shotguns, all lined up next to each other.

"For what?"

"The end."

"The end of what?"

Burt Johnson never claimed to be a smart guy; in fact, smart was an overstatement. When her father told her that Burt never finished high school, Caylee, still only twelve at the time, guided him through the work and tutored him so he could pass the exams. The day he received his graduation certificate was one of the proudest moments of her life.

Burt was a gullible sponge—that was his greatest weakness. He was able to soak up all the hatred that his older brother sprayed upon him, making sure that the hate would continue long after Chuck was gone. Generational racism was alive and well in the hands of Burt Johnson.

"I'm going to make a big move. It's going to be massive." She stepped closer to her uncle and indicated for him to lean down so she could whisper, "It's going to be so big that all this might end."

"Whoa." He snickered and then playfully punched her on the arm. "That's my niece—doing what's right. We're the protectors of the White Alliance Coalition."

"But you can't say anything to Dad. I want it to be a surprise. You've got to promise not to say anything to Dad."

"You got it." He smirked. "We have to look after each other and have each other's back. I'll look after you, Caylee, the same way I'll defend the White Alliance Coalition."

"That's my uncle." She tapped his growing stomach.

"You bet." Burt puffed his chest out proudly. "You wouldn't believe the things I've done to protect the White Alliance Coalition."

Caylee placed the shotgun back in the cabinet, then looked at the four handguns that were sitting on the benches. They would be easy to transport.

It was the dynamite that she was worried about loading into the van.

But she needed that.

She needed it all.

"So when are you going to do it?"

"When the time is right." She smiled and touched the metal crate with the explosives. "And that time is coming soon."

CHAPTER 26

"MR. HUNTER?"

Hunter had barely stepped out of his office building, barely had time to button up his coat, when someone called out to him in the street as he walked towards his regular coffee shop.

That wasn't unusual for him. He was used to the abuse that was screamed from cars, although that had lessened significantly over the decades since his father's imprisonment.

Five years earlier, the abuse had almost stopped. His family's dark past had become a controversy almost erased from the minds of the public. The public was outraged by other events—public shootings, drive-bys at high schools or senseless attacks on the freedoms of Americans.

But a new documentary aired across the country, The Chicago Hunter, detailing his father's crimes with his mother's assistance, and the slayings came back into everyone's focus. The weeks that followed the airing of the show were some of the worst for Hunter.

For his own safety, he was advised by police not to leave the house for a week.

Hunter turned to see a small, familiar woman waving her arms in the air, coming towards him.

"Mr. Hunter," the woman called again.

"How can I help you, Mrs. Nelson?" Hunter asked as the afternoon crowds pushed past them on the street.

"I was coming to the office to see you." She was panting. "I want to stay involved in this case. I'm sure there's something I can help you with. I really want to do everything I can to keep Amos out of prison."

"I'm not sure what else you can do, Mrs. Nelson—unless there's something you haven't told me."

"I've never trusted Lucas." She talked louder as people pushed past. "Maybe I can get information on him for you? He doesn't like me, but I still have the keys to the office. Amos gave them to me. I could go through Lucas' things? Maybe his notes? If he isn't being helpful, then I could get the information for you."

"I wouldn't ask you to do that, Mrs. Nelson."

Hunter was soft in his approach. He held her elbow and moved her to the side of the street, out of the rush.

"I would do anything for Amos. Anything. I owe that man my life," she pleaded. "My life was almost perfect after Reverend Green passed, all except for the threat to Amos' freedom. If you believe that Amos is innocent, then I can't let him go to prison. I have to do everything I can to keep him out of there."

She looked up at Hunter; she was so desperate to help, so desperate to save the man that saved her.

"Mrs. Nelson, this is getting dangerous. I don't want you involved in that," Hunter said. "But I'll give you the number for my investigator, Ray Jones. Tell him what you've told me. It may help him piece together the case."

"The only reason I'm alive is because of Amos." She had tears in her eyes. "And if you think that he's innocent, then I'll do whatever it takes to keep him out of jail."

CHAPTER 27

THE BURKE'S Web Pub in Bucktown was usually quiet on a Thursday afternoon. A few locals, all seemingly named Jeff, sat around the bar, musing about the game of Jeopardy on the television. One man called out an answer, and Anderson looked up from the beer he was cradling in his hand. He knew the answer was wrong, but he didn't have the energy to correct the man. The game show host did that only moments later.

Two blocks from his home, the bar was Anderson's place of refuge. It was his escape from the stresses of the last two months. Here, he could forget about the rocks thrown through his windows, the letters filled with hate, and the abuse spray-painted on his car.

He had never expected that a church community could be filled with so much hate, but he had quickly come to learn that the minister didn't only represent those in the congregation, or those that attended

Sunday mass; Green represented a voice for his people, whether they came to his church or not.

He was a symbol of hope, something greater than just a man.

"Amos." Tex Hunter walked into the dimly lit bar, took off his coat and hung it on a hook. "Are you okay?"

Anderson didn't answer.

"What'll it be?" the female bartender asked Hunter.

"A pint of pale ale." Hunter pointed to the tap.

"We're cash only here."

Hunter threw a few bills on the bar, and the woman quickly filled his pint glass, placing it in front of him.

"They've thrown rocks through my window." Anderson tipped his drink to one side, and then the other. "They've spray painted my car. I've been spat on. I've been pushed. I'm almost too scared to leave my apartment."

"Who threw a rock through your window?"

"Who knows? I guess it's the supporters of the church. I don't know." Amos shook his head. "How did they even find my address?"

"Hate fuels many people in this world, Amos. It can be a great motivator." Hunter sipped his beer as a man started playing a solitary game of darts behind him. "An address is not hard to find. I'll talk to the local police station, see if they can send a few more patrols past your house."

"I don't want this. I don't want any of this." Anderson's hands flailed around, doing as much of the talking as he was. "All I want to do is fill the world with love and make the world a better place. I want to help people, but I can't even leave my house!"

"I understand, and we're going to do everything we can to keep you out of prison." Hunter placed his hand on Anderson's shoulder. "But you have to be prepared."

"For what?"

"For prison," Hunter said firmly. "You have to get your affairs in order before this trial starts. You have to be prepared for that likelihood, because, at this point in time, it's a very real possibility."

The color drained from Anderson's face.

"The prosecution has a new offer—twenty-two years. I'm obligated to bring that offer to you."

"Twenty-two years!" Tears welled up in Amos' eyes. "I'll be more than sixty by the time I get out. Those are the best years of my life—gone." He snapped his fingers. "All for something I didn't do. All for something I had nothing to do with. I didn't want Reverend Green dead."

"Although it's only small, we still have a chance. We haven't lost yet." Hunter patted his shoulder. "We have a chance to win this trial, but it's not in our favor."

One of the customers at the bar came past and rested a consoling hand on Anderson's other shoulder without saying a word. Anderson kept his head down, then put his thumb up as a sign of thanks.

"I've helped ninety drug addicts kick the habit, forty people with depression get back on their feet, and countless clients get over their physical ailments." He turned to Hunter. "I've helped people with back problems, stomach problems, knee pain, ankle issues. You name it, I've cured it. I help people; I don't kill them."

Hunter didn't offer a response.

"All I want to do is improve the lives of others. I don't care about the money. I don't care for the adoration. When you heal someone's ailment, when you help someone break free of their addiction, when you help someone defeat their demons, that—" He looked up. "That's something worth fighting for."

"Then we have only one thing left to do, Amos." Hunter drank his pint. "We have to fight this to the end."

CHAPTER 28

HUNTER HATED this walk.

Despite the fact that he had walked through the entrance to the building more than a hundred times in his life, he hated everything about it—the smell of fear, the frenzied nature of the guards, the pain etched in people's faces. It had been more than a year since he last walked into the Cook County Jail; more than a year since he smelled that overriding scent of fear, testosterone, and body odor all rolled into one distinct mess.

He received a handwritten letter two weeks ago asking to talk. It was two pages long, emotional, and heartfelt.

Not what he usually received from his father.

After the security checks, Tex Hunter greeted the men at the doors and was led down a long hallway. He had intended to come earlier, a week ago, but the Anderson case took up most of his time. Even today, he had only arrived ten minutes before visiting hours finished.

The guards opened the door to the room, and Hunter stepped inside. It was cold, it always was, and the lack of direct sunlight didn't help. The one small window near the roof, covered in bars, provided a glimpse of the blue sky outside but not enough to give a man hope. The paint was fading on the concrete walls, and there were scratches of names that had come and gone.

His father waited on a metal chair, dressed in a white T-shirt and brownish-gray pants, hands fidgeting. A metal table was in front of him, the shine completely gone from it.

Hunter stopped at the door, shocked by what he saw.

Gone was the man he used to know—gone was the life in his eyes, the fire in his heart. He looked weary, skinny, and almost lifeless.

Life, even one contained within these concrete walls, had taken its toll.

"My son." Alfred Hunter stood up from the table, leaning on his right arm for support, and offered Hunter a smile. He opened his left arm to welcome a hug.

Hunter walked to the table, hugged his father gently, afraid that he would crush him, and then moved to the opposite metal chair to sit down.

"I wasn't sure that you'd come, Tex. I've seen you in the news a bit; the trial starts in two days, doesn't it? I didn't think you'd be able to find time to come and meet with your old man." Alfred lowered his body back into the chair, leaning on his right arm for support.

Hunter didn't answer.

"Thanks for taking the time to make an old man happy. I realize how much you love these cases and how hard it is for you to pull away from them."

Alfred scratched his arm. The itching was getting worse. He could take the pain in his joints, he could live with the numbness in his limbs, he could even deal with the constant need to use the toilet, but it was the itching that annoyed him the most. The constant feeling that everything needed to be scratched all the time, no matter how many times he tried to relieve the sensation. His dehydrated skin had cracked often, exposing him to more germs than his body could fight. Infections were an unwanted bonus on top of his pain.

"You're not well," Hunter whispered. "Why didn't you write to me earlier?"

Alfred drew a long breath. He was a tall man, in his mid-seventies, whose cheeks were sunken, neck was thin, and had a clearly visible collarbone due to severe weight loss. On top of that, his once olive skin was tinged yellow, with the wispy gray hairs on his head marking the onset of complete baldness.

"Life is full of ups and downs, sacrifices, and knowledge. I've lived my life the best I can." Alfred's tone was reflective. He'd had a lot of time for contemplation over the past three decades. "I've done what I've had to do."

"What's killing you?" Hunter's voice was low.

"Just about everything." The answer was blunt. "I know my time is coming. I don't have long left, maybe a year, maybe more, who knows? Life is hard behind these bars, and there aren't many men older than me left in here. They took Harry Unger to the hospital yesterday, and I think that leaves me as the oldest male prisoner. What a title, eh? The oldest man in hell."

"Have they taken you to see a doctor?"

"I went to see a doctor once and said that I wanted to live to an old age." Alfred raised a long finger and tried to smile. "He said, 'Don't drink, don't party, don't do any drugs, and don't eat any unhealthy food.' 'Will that make me live longer?' I asked. 'No,' he said. 'But it'll sure make the years feel like a very, very long time.'"

Hunter didn't laugh.

He looked at the table, the words escaping him.

"I don't see the point in continuing past my use-by date, son. When you've spent thirty years back here, time isn't precious. I have nothing left to do, nothing left to achieve, and nothing left to see. There's no use spending taxpayer dollars on keeping me alive, because if my time has come, then my time has come."

Alfred Hunter was once a hard-working family man; a man who took the time to play catch with his boys in the yard after work, taught his kids how to ride a bike, and taught Tex how to throw a fierce left hook when he was being bullied by the older kids at school. On his father's advice, Hunter threw three punches at the kid four years older, flattening him. Despite being called to the principal's office to explain his son's actions; Alfred was proud of his boy.

Alfred Hunter had appeared to love his community—he regularly attended the neighborhood watch meetings, was the school's basketball coach, and often lent his tools to whoever needed them. He smiled at the neighbors, waved to the postman, and chattered to the local shopkeepers. His clothes were always pristine, ironed, and unstained. His shoulders were always back, his head held high, and his walk was filled with confidence.

The picture-perfect life for a picture-perfect man. At least, it appeared that way.

Those who knew him were convinced that he was innocent, none more so than his youngest son, but their voices were quickly drowned out by the collective hate of the whole country. The story captured the nation's attention and they were gripped by the details of his trial—everyone knew someone like Alfred, every neighborhood had one, and they all started to doubt each other.

"Jake Briggs came and found me the other week, told me to say hello to you. He said that you got his sentence reduced from thirty years to ten, said you were a very good lawyer; someone to be proud of."

"Briggs. I remember him. Fraud case, caught red-handed, but we negotiated a lighter sentence for his co-operation. One of the most untrustworthy people I've ever met. How's he doing in here?"

"He's found God." Alfred opened his hands wide and grinned. "He's become a preacher."

"I don't believe that. There must be another reason for him to take that path, an ulterior motive."

"He wouldn't be the first preacher to take up the vocation in search of power." Alfred added the comment flippantly, but it struck a chord with Hunter.

The silence sat in the room for an awkward minute—Alfred scratching his arm, and then his thigh, and Hunter staring at the wall, thinking about the last comment from his father.

"How are you?" Alfred broke the silence. "You haven't been here in over a year."

"I'm well. Busy, but I'm well."

"Married yet? Kids?"

Hunter shook his head.

"In love?"

Hunter shook his head again.

"And Patrick? How is he?"

"He's well."

"Max?"

"Okay."

"I would love to see them again." Alfred's chest heaved up and down. Talking was using up a lot of his energy. "But I understand if they don't want to come."

"Patrick's not keen on talking to you, or even about you." Hunter's jaw clenched. He felt the emotion threatening to break through the hard wall around his heart, and he didn't like the vulnerability that threatened his tough demeanor. "Patrick won't come in here."

"And Natalie? Have you seen her?"

"No." Hunter clenched his fist, pressing his fingernails into his palm. "I haven't seen her in over a decade. I've looked for her, I wanted to know where she was, but I couldn't find her."

"I received a letter from her."

Hunter looked up, shock written across his face.

"She said she was back home. Back in the USA. There was no return address on the envelope, so I had no way to contact her." Alfred scratched his calf. He scratched too hard, and was sure that he was now bleeding under his trousers. "If you ever see her, tell her that it was all worth it."

"What was worth it?" Hunter leaned forward. "What?"

"Life." Alfred offered a half smile. "All of life was worth it. You. Patrick. Natalie. Your mother. My grandson, Max. Every risk we took, every chance, every attempt, it was all worth it. All of it."

"Has this got something to do with why Natalie disappeared? Why she went to Mexico to live?"

"Who knows?" Alfred studied his son's face. "Freedom is one of life's great disappearing acts. It's something that's completely forgotten about until it's taken away. I imagine she wanted to be free of... well, all of this." He opened his hands wide. "I guess she had enough. You could do the same. If nothing is holding you to Chicago, no love, no children, then you should consider starting anew somewhere else, maybe a new country that hasn't heard of our past."

"I don't need your life advice." Hunter started to say the word 'Dad', but it didn't feel right. He hadn't called him that in a long time.

"I can see it in your eyes, Tex. I know that feeling. It's fear. Your deepest fear is that you're unlovable. And I understand it. I understand that you went through so much."

Hunter looked away.

"But it's the light, not the darkness, that's frightening you. Running away from your fear doesn't serve your purpose. There's nothing enlightening about shrinking away so that you won't fail—because you will fail. That's part of the journey. Don't run from your fears. You are lovable, Tex. Everyone is."

Hunter turned to look at his father—half of him was angry that he was receiving life advice from the man that tore his life apart, and the other half wanted nothing more than to listen to his guidance.

"Tex." Alfred leaned forward. "Emotional fear isn't there to tell you not to do something; fear is there to alert you that something is worth pursuing. If you're scared of it, it means that it's worth something to you. When you don't care about the consequences, that's when there's no fear. Don't run from love. Don't block that out because you're afraid."

His advice was interrupted by the loud tapping on the door, followed by the deep voice of the guard. "Visiting time is over."

"Thank you for coming, Tex." Alfred smiled. "I wanted to see you before I—"

"Wait." Hunter held up his hand. "There's one question you've never answered, a question you've always avoided. If your time is coming, then you have to answer that question for me."

"You know I can't answer that question, Tex."

"You have to. I need to know the answer to that question. Did you do it? Did you kill those girls?" Hunter was firm.

"You have to move on from this, Tex."

"I can't. You need to tell me yes or no. After all these years, you can give me that. You owe me that. After all the pain I've been through, all the hate I've faced, I deserve an answer to that question."

The guard tapped the door again.

"Tex, if you want to move on from something, never hate it. Everything that you hate is attached to your heart. If you want to let go of something, if you want to move on, you cannot hate."

"I hate that we lost our family." Hunter stood, leaning over his father. "I need to know. Did you do it? Did you kill those girls?"

"I won't answer that question." Alfred Hunter stood and rested a hand on Hunter's arm. "But Tex, I will tell you this—everything is relative. Even truth."

CHAPTER 29

WEST JACKSON Boulevard buzzed, the constant hum of traffic creating a background of white noise. This was Hunter's part of the world. He felt a part of the action, part of the lifeblood in the city.

His office felt like an extension of his home. His place to think and move through a case. A place to disappear into the words on a file. Despite the years that had passed, every time he walked into his office, it filled him with pride, a testament to the ability to overcome the worst odds that life could throw at him.

Past the reception desk was the door to his separate office, a door that proudly displayed the Hunter family name. There weren't many places that did that. His office was large enough to dance the tango, if he ever felt inclined, but cozy enough to drink in solitude on the leather couch to the left of the room. Law books lined the right wall, and a signed Michael Jordan jersey hung on the other. He had never liked having "stuff" to fill a room; he would much rather sit in an unfilled space than one full of clutter.

As such, his large dark oakwood table looked like it'd barely been used. Esther had left a file in the middle of the table, but apart from his monitor, it was the only object on the long space.

Hunter stopped at the sizable window to take in the view of Downtown Chicago, watching the people walk under the streetlights below, and sat down behind his hefty desk, comfortable in his black leather chair.

He hated the feelings he had to confront every time he met with his father—that rollercoaster of hate, love, and confusion. He would love to see his father free on the streets again, smiling as he watched the birds fly next to Lake Michigan, but he knew that was impossible now.

Driven by the fact that he felt his father was innocent, Hunter made sure that every avenue for appeal was taken on, confronted, and pushed against. Due to the lack of evidence in the court case, his father had avoided the death penalty—still a reality for Chicagoans in the seventies. The case was built on circumstantial evidence at best; misleading at worst.

When DNA evidence became a reality, Hunter thought he had a chance to pull his father and mother out of prison. His mother was convicted as an accomplice to the crimes, despite her pleas of innocence and the lack of evidence, she spent her last years incarcerated. Unable to find DNA evidence that exonerated his parents, Hunter had to watch his mother, a once beautiful kind-hearted woman, wither away in prison until her death.

Hunter opened the file on his desk and scanned over the notes, before walking over to his cabinet and pouring a glass of whiskey. It was the only way he knew how to avoid emotions—alcohol and work.

Some people got their thrills from painting or hitting the gym or learning a new skill.

Not Tex Hunter.

He got his thrills from pushing for justice, and doing the hard yards was a part of that.

Most criminal cases didn't make it to trial. Most criminal cases were dealt with long before they confronted the judge for day one—deals with the prosecution, dismissing evidence, or the guilty party turned over to the police.

But there was a part of Hunter that yearned for the action in the courtroom. He loved the spotlight, standing up in front of the court and the media, and proving all those people wrong.

As he closed a file on his desk, he looked to the clock on the wall. Just past 10 p.m. An early night. He smiled as he switched off the lights in the office and closed the door. He went down the elevator and out onto the street. After the two whiskeys in his office, as he had read the last of the case files, he'd decided not to drive home, walking to the taxi rank a few blocks down.

There were a few people out and about, going places under the dim lighting of the street. He had only walked half a block when the rumbling of the "L" train thundered overhead. It was bone-chilling loud, loud enough to drown out any thoughts as it rattled past.

That distraction, that moment of cover, provided the perfect time for someone to grab him.

Hunter felt the hand on his left shoulder first.

He had spent most of his early adult life under the constant threat of attack and trained hard in boxing gyms across the city. Recently, he had turned his attention to Muay Thai, the art of kickboxing originating from Thailand.

Hunter turned.

The man behind him tried to throw a wild hooking arm, but Hunter blocked it with his forearm, and then pushed the man back with an open hand to the chest.

"Turn around and walk away." Hunter was firm.

The man dressed in a flannel shirt didn't look homeless, nor did he look like he was trying to mug Hunter.

But he did look angry.

He came at Hunter again.

He threw another wild hook, and Hunter almost laughed as he moved back from it. He could see it coming a mile away. The wild hook might have worked in a rough country bar, but not against a trained fighter like Hunter.

The man swung again, and Hunter drove his foot into the man's abdomen, buckling him under the pressure.

A taxi horn honked as it went past.

Hunter didn't see the man behind him.

He was hit with a metal rod across the middle of his back, sending him flying forward towards the first man. That man swung hard again, landing a solid right hook to Hunter's cheekbone.

Hunter buckled. He moved to his right, still on his feet, turning to face the man with the metal rod.

The metal rod swung at Hunter again.

He blocked the bar against his shoulder, the one that took the bullet, and landed a quick hook to the man's chin. The man fell to the ground.

The man with the flannel shirt helped his friend, pulling on his shirt, exposing a tattoo on the man's forearm. A man stood behind Hunter, across the street, and dialed nine-one-one. When the two men saw him on the phone, they scampered away.

Hunter was in no mood to chase them.

"You alright?" The man dressed in a suit approached Hunter. "Do you need an ambulance?"

"I'm good."

"The lady at nine-one-one wants to know if you recognized either of the men?"

"I didn't recognize their faces." Hunter rubbed his shoulder. "But I'd suggest the Nazi tattoo was a giveaway about who he's friends with."

CHAPTER 30

ESTHER ATTACKED her keyboard with intense vigor, punching in notes while they were fresh in her head. Her investigation skills weren't as polished as her boss', but she thrived on the challenge. Being involved in the cases, being part of the action, let her know that she was alive, pumping adrenalin through her veins.

She barely stopped punching the keyboard as Hunter strode into his office, his morning coffee in his left hand, his expensive briefcase in his right.

When she did look up, she saw his swollen lip and lightly bruised cheek.

"Oh my gosh." She gasped. "What happened? Are you okay?"

"I had a chat with the wrong people." He grunted. "Did you see anyone follow you last night when you left the office?"

"Me?" She thought back to the previous night. "No. Nothing. Do you think it was a targeted hit last night?"

"They didn't reach for my wallet, and they didn't try to take my briefcase." Hunter stood up straight, despite the pain surging through his back. "The man that attacked me had a Nazi tattoo on his left arm."

"You think it's the White Alliance Coalition making a statement?"

"Anderson's trial starts tomorrow, and the cops don't have a public lead for the church shooting. The pressure is mounting on everyone." Hunter's phone buzzed in his pocket. "And the media are getting desperate. They want a lead. They want something on this story. This story is selling papers, people are hungry for an answer, and every day they're getting closer to making the link between the White Alliance Coalition and the church shooting. It's not a good look for the police department when they have a shooting at a Sunday mass, and they have no one to give to the public. The media want a suspect, so they're creating one themselves. The pressure is building, and they'll continue to get front-page news every day this isn't solved."

"But why attack you? You aren't the one making accusations."

"I've stepped close to them, and they're protecting something." Hunter slowly removed the phone from his pocket. "Or someone."

His phone buzzed again.

He unlocked the screen.

Two photos, nothing more.

No text. No words.

"But you think one of them is involved in the church shooting?"

"I'm not sure…" Hunter's focus had turned to the message.

He stared at the picture on his phone—a color photo of their office front door, and a photo of the door to his apartment.

Clear. Bright.

Recent.

Slowly, he turned around and looked at the door.

"What does the message say?" Esther asked.

"Nothing. It's only a photo."

"Of?"

"Our office front door."

"And that's it? No message?"

He called the number.

Nothing.

It had already been disconnected.

Esther reached across, grabbed Hunter's phone, and Googled the phone number. "There's nothing on file about the number. It must be a burner phone."

He turned to look at the front door. "Esther, you need to be very careful over the coming days. If you're in the office alone, I want you to lock the door. Make our clients buzz in. Don't work late. Don't be here after dark. If you don't feel comfortable at any time, call me. I'm going to talk to building security and make sure they're extra vigilant."

"What's going on?"

"Do you understand me?" Hunter's stare was unflinching. "I want you to be safe."

"Okay." She nodded apprehensively. "Do you think that photo is about this case?"

"Esther, it'll be better if you take a few days off while the trial is on. Don't come into the office at all."

"No," she argued. "I know the risk, I know what can happen, and I want to come to the trial. I want to help with this case."

"No." He shook his head while thoughts raced through it. "I won't let you get attacked again, not after what happened in the Sulzberger case."

"I promise I'll be careful, Tex. I won't leave late. I'll lock the office door. I promise."

He looked at her, his eyes narrowing as he stared down at the person who knew him the best. "Only if you stay safe. Only work during daylight hours. I'm not going to let you get hurt again."

But the way the case was building, he wasn't sure if that was true.

CHAPTER 31

THE DARK wood paneling in the courthouse was the perfect foil to dampen the enthusiasm. It provided a somber mood to contrast Tex Hunter's exhilaration, a sedative for his eagerness.

As he walked past the empty rows of wooden benches, which looked like they were borrowed from a church, he took three long deep breaths. His heart was pounding in his chest, his jaw was clamped shut, and his fist clenched the briefcase tightly.

It was an hour before the case was due to begin, but the junior prosecutors were already at their table, eagerly awaiting the arrival of their lead, Michelle Law. The two young lawyers, who looked like they were fresh out of law school, smiled at Hunter as he placed his briefcase on the defense table.

Amos Anderson followed him into the courtroom moments later, his eyes darting around the room as he tried to take it all in. This was the place where his fate would be decided. This was the room where his future was on the line. He looked up at the empty jurors' box, separated from the rest of the courtroom by a long wooden barrier that sat hip height, and he wondered what it would be like to sit in those seats. What would it feel like to judge someone's guilt? How much pressure would a person feel knowing that they had the power to take a man's freedom away?

Anderson shook Hunter's hand and pulled out the chair where he was to sit. He took one deep breath before he sat down, looking to the windows with the blinds drawn, not allowing any sun to stream in or any sense of hope to escape.

Anderson's brother and sister-in-law arrived first. They were the type of people that arrived for the train twenty minutes early and were stressed if they weren't going to be on time. They patted Anderson on the back before sitting behind him in the gallery. Then came his friends and supporters.

Michelle Law entered the courtroom next, and she was surprised to see such an audience. However, she walked to the desk with her head held high, her back straight, and her vision focused.

Over the next hour, the rest of the court pews began to fill. Anderson's quiet family and supporters on one side, looking timid in their fear, and the loud, proud, and angry supporters of Reverend Green on the other side of the court. If Hunter didn't know any better, he would have thought he had walked in on a court case in the South during the times of segregation.

The reporters came last—fewer than Hunter expected. However, there had been another school shooting the day before in Wicker Park, and that had taken the media's attention away from the first days of the high-profile trial.

"Five minutes," the bailiff called out, alerting everyone to the fact that the spectacle was about to begin, and Judge David Lockett was to enter the courtroom.

Hunter looked over his opening statement one last time, then rested his hand on Anderson's shoulder.

Anderson nodded his response, too nervous to speak. His fate lay in the files on the table, his future in the hands of someone else. Anderson made sure the wastepaper basket under the table wasn't far away, in close enough reach if he needed to vomit.

"All rise. The Court is now in session, the Honorable Judge Lockett presiding."

The slight and wearied figure of Judge Lockett edged through the courtroom, his eyes down until he sat behind the judge's bench. He moved files to the left, checked that his pen was working, huffed, and then raised his eyes to look at the full courtroom before him.

After Judge Lockett had announced the procedure for the audience and defendant, he talked to the bailiff, who then welcomed the members of the jury to the courtroom. Awkwardly, they walked to their places, a few stumbling on the seats. The eyes of the courtroom were on them as they silently sat down; some were nervous, others thrived in the environment.

Juror eleven certainly did the latter. His chest was puffed out, his shoulders back, and his chin up. He was wearing his best checkered shirt, which was at least ten years old, his best jeans, and his best boots. He had cut his hair the night before, had his eyebrows trimmed, and his ear hairs clipped.

The *voir dire*, the juror selection process, was arduous for both the prosecution and the defense. Both sides dismissed so many potential candidates that it should've been referred to as a deselection process. With the murder case headlining news for weeks, it was hard to find people who hadn't been influenced, commented on, or sympathized with the events.

Under Formal Opinion 466, the ethical guidelines provided by the American Bar Association, Esther Wright used her skills to scour the publicly available social media posts of the potential jurors. That search eliminated five potential jurors—having already voiced opinions on the murder of Reverend Green or the guilt of Amos Anderson.

Neither side wanted sympathizers with the defendant or the victim—Hunter used his seven peremptory challenges before they had reached nine jurors, and Law had used hers quickly after. The challenge for cause, used by the judge to reject a juror, was used for every second person that was brought in front of them.

Hunter rejected all the possible supporters of Reverend Green and the Baptist church, and Law rejected all the people who could have been offended by one of Reverend Green's speeches. Despite statistics stating that over 30 percent of the Chicago population was black, only two sat on the jury of twelve. That alone infuriated Reverend Green's supporters.

Although Hunter felt the jury was leaning in his favor, there was one person on the jury that could cause him a problem.

Juror twelve was tall, broad-shouldered, and intelligent. A retired African American doctor who had worked his way up from the projects to a successful life, he claimed he had never heard of Reverend Green's name, and had been traveling on a cruise ship in Alaska for the past three months. Hunter argued that the juror must have known the name due to all the media coverage, so it was almost impossible to avoid. However, the judge sided with the prosecution, turning Hunter's luck on its head.

Juror twelve had a healthy glow, and a very nice suit, but more than his looks, he had respect as a doctor. Both Hunter and Law knew that it would be a long deliberation regardless of evidence, regardless of the strength of either case. Juror eleven and twelve both looked argumentative and stubborn, and would naturally choose the opposing sides of a dispute.

Despite the jurors' potential for arguments, the true facts of the case were indisputable.

Reverend Dural Green was beaten in an alley behind the Congress Hotel on February 1st, and he died as a result of the wounds he sustained.

That was fact.

But there were no direct witnesses or any direct evidence of Anderson's involvement, and that left the door slightly open for Hunter to argue there was reasonable doubt.

With one week scheduled for the prosecution's case and three days for the defense, the jurors were anticipating a lot of evidence to come their way. After Judge Lockett informed the jury of their duty and read the instructions to them, Law was ready to lay all her cards out on the table.

She opened her statement sitting behind her desk, but when she got into her speech, she stood to emphasize her point.

*****

"On February 1st of this year, Reverend Dural Green, of the Grand Crossing Baptist Church, attended a function at the Congress Hotel to deliver a speech on the effect that faith and the church community has on the treatment of depression. He often did this sort of thing. He had argued that finding the good Lord was the first step to curing depression.

Also at the function was Amos Anderson, the man sitting at the defense table.

He also gave a speech that day and stated that faith healing was the way to cure depression. You see, Mr. Anderson is a faith healer. He 'heals' people through the movement of hands, the air, and possibly, the wind. Who knows? There's certainly no scientific evidence that supports Mr. Anderson's claims of healing.

Reverend Green called this form of healing a fraud, a scam, or worse yet, the Devil's work. Reverend Green was a very loud opponent of Mr. Anderson's claims.

At around 8.45 p.m. on February 1st, Mr. Anderson argued with Reverend Green, and that argument became physical. Two men of supposed 'peace' became violent, and Reverend Green was seen grabbing Mr. Anderson by the neck.

Only two hours later, Reverend Green was dead.

Beaten to death in the alley behind the Congress Hotel.

A minister, a man of peace, was beaten to death in an alley.

His parish was devastated.

My name is Michelle Law, and with my team, we will present an astonishing amount of evidence that will leave you with no choice but to convict Mr. Anderson for the first-degree murder of Reverend Dural Green. My opening statement is to provide you with a roadmap, if you will, of the prosecution's case against Mr. Anderson, as anything I say now is not considered evidence.

Fed up by the constant attacks on his profession, Mr. Anderson intended to murder Reverend Green that night. He intended to murder the minister. He invited Reverend Green into the alley to discuss their differences further. Of course, Mr. Anderson had no interest in a discussion.

You will hear from witnesses who will state that they saw Mr. Anderson standing near the alley only moments before the murder took place.

You will hear from witnesses who will state that they saw Mr. Anderson get into a physical altercation with Reverend Green that night.

You will hear from witnesses who will talk about the hatred that Mr. Anderson had for Reverend Green.

But more importantly, you will also hear from expert witnesses throughout this case who will provide details about the evidence taken from the scene of the crime.

One such expert witness will explain the DNA evidence that was under Reverend Green's fingernails. Another expert witness will provide details about the blood that was found on the sleeve of Reverend Green and its match to Mr. Anderson's DNA. And a third expert witness will detail what sort of blow caused this heinous crime.

You will also hear the testimonies of the Chicago Police Department detectives that were at the scene of the crime, the detectives who made the arrest, and the members of the department that executed the search warrant of Mr. Anderson's apartment.

They will detail what they found at the crime scene and present photos to you. You will hear from Detective Browne who will give evidence and state that he found Reverend Green's necklace at the home of Mr. Anderson. Reverend Green was seen wearing that necklace on the night he died; however, it was not found at the crime scene.

You will hear from the Cook County Medical Examiner's office as they detail the cause of death.

You will hear from the arresting officer who will state that Mr. Anderson seemed nervous when they arrested him the next morning.

Without the intervention of the hard-working police officers of the Chicago Police Department, Mr. Anderson would be back out on the streets. Without the intervention of the police, a killer would still be on the loose on the streets of Chicago. Out on the street where they could attack vulnerable people. Attacking the defenseless people of this city.

Causing chaos on the streets.

Causing violence, crime, and pain to our great city.

That's what murderers do.

And to take that killer off the streets is a win for our city. A win for all of us.

But, I must say, it's only half the battle.

The other half of the battle is to convict killers, which happens in here, within these walls, in this courtroom.

This week, you have an opportunity to make our city safer. Safer for you, and safer for families.

Don't be swayed by the entertaining show that the defense will present. Don't focus on what might have been. Don't think about possibilities.

Focus on the facts. That's your job. That's why you're here.

And if you look at the facts, if you look only at the evidence, then it will lead you to only one possible conclusion.

Only one.

Amos Anderson murdered Reverend Dural Green.

He must be found 'Guilty' of murder in the first degree.

Listen to the evidence, listen to the witnesses, and make your decision based on the facts.

Thank you very much for your duty to this great city."

*****

The jury was transfixed by Law's speech. They couldn't take their eyes off her as she delivered the speech with passion and fire. Hunter was the same; he appreciated her great performance.

After only one speech, one statement, Law already had the jury in her soft hands. To them, she was the voice of authority, the voice of justice. They were all on the side of the good guys.

In contrast, Hunter's speech wasn't about to reject the facts, or dispute the prosecution's evidence; it would focus on the technicalities of the law.

He knew that his client's personality wouldn't win this case. He knew that he couldn't win based on his client's appearance. The only hope he had for the case was to present the facts as they were, focus on the missing pieces, and then create reasonable doubt in the mind of at least one juror.

The reasonable doubt of one person.

That was all he needed.

*****

"May it please the court, Miss Law, her team, and members of the jury. My name is Tex Hunter, and with my team, we will present the reasons why you cannot convict Mr. Amos Anderson of this crime.

On February 1st, Reverend Dural Green died. That's the fact as presented by a police report.

Indisputable fact, and we are not here to dispute that.

As the prosecution has informed you, your job as a member of this jury is to reach a verdict based on the evidence.

Not assumptions, not expectations, not

probabilities—but evidence.

Not potentials, not likelihoods, not chances—but evidence.

You must be clear on that.

You cannot fill in the gaps yourself. You cannot make up theories based on your bias. You cannot convict a man based on your assumptions.

An assumption is defined as something that's accepted without proof.

Without proof.

I make this clear to you because there will be gaps in the case, there will be holes in the prosecution's case. And it's in those gaps, in those questions, that you will find reasonable doubt.

Let's be clear—there's no direct evidence, none, that states Mr. Anderson murdered Reverend Green. None. There are no witnesses to the event, no witness that saw them in the alley together, and no surveillance footage that shows the event.

It's here that you will find doubt.

It's here that you will find uncertainty.

In a court of law, you cannot convict a man based on assumptions. You simply cannot do that. You need to make a decision based on the facts. The evidence.

By now, your question should be: What is reasonable doubt?

It's doubt that still exists upon reason and common sense, after careful and impartial consideration of all the evidence.

You will find that you have that reasonable doubt at the end of this case. Even after all the pieces of evidence are presented in this case, you will have reasonable doubt based purely on common sense.

I'm here to explain to you the undeniable fact that, right now, Amos Anderson is presumed innocent.

That's the way our system works.

Time and time again in this case, you're going to hear about the presumption of innocence. That means right now, Amos Anderson starts this court case with a blank page. The presumption of innocence means that suspicion, bias, prejudgment, and assumptions have no place in your thoughts.

That's your responsibility.

And it's a big responsibility.

Together, we're going on a journey. On that journey, I will tell you where the police, and the department's laboratory and apparent 'experts', have ignored obvious evidence, used false science, performed untidy fieldwork, and rushed to a very wrong and early judgment.

That's why we have a justice system. That's why police themselves don't decide the guilt or sentencing of the people they arrest.

We're here, together, as a safeguard, as the thoughtful and considered end point to the process.

You will hear from experts who will show you where the gaps exist in the police work. You will hear from specialists that will show you where the prosecution has made assumptions and not based their case on the facts.

And you will hear from people who will state that their lives have been saved by the work of Mr. Anderson.

That's right.

Mr. Anderson saves lives; he doesn't take them.

I will help you in this process, and together, we will find Amos Anderson 'Not Guilty' based on the reasonable doubt that lies within the prosecution's assumptions.

Judge Lockett will remind you throughout our journey not to make up your minds until the journey is done, because it may be in the last moment of the trial that you discover the reasonable doubt in the final piece of evidence.

There's no evidence, no evidence, that will reasonably convict Amos Anderson of this crime. You will have reasonable doubt at the end of this case, therefore, you can only make one decision.

When our journey comes to a close, I will stand before you and ask you for a verdict of Not Guilty.

Thank you for your time, and thank you for listening. I wish you well."

CHAPTER 32

THE PROSECUTION started their witness list with the coroner and his report, the worker who found the body early in the morning, and the paramedic that declared Reverend Green deceased at the scene of the crime.

They were all solid witnesses, people who gave an-in-depth picture of the scene, but nothing game-changing, and certainly, nothing that would convict Anderson of the crime.

"The prosecution calls Rosa Santiago to the stand."

And there she was—the main witness that placed Anderson at the scene. Law wanted to end day one with a bang, a chance for the jurors to walk away from the first day with Anderson's guilt in their minds.

Rosa Santiago was unsteady in her walk to the stand. Her shoulders were slumped forward, her eyes focused on the floor, and her hands fidgeting. Her clothes were too big, and her glasses were equally oversized. Her timid demeanor was matched by her stick-thin body shape.

"Please state your name and vocation for the court." Law was gentle in her approach with the witness. She had softened her voice, seeking to calm Rosa's nerves.

"Rosa Jasmine Santiago. I work as an administration manager for a large stock market firm." Her voice was shaky as she sat in the witness box. Public speaking wasn't her strength.

"How long have you worked in that company?"

"Yes," she replied awkwardly. "I mean, five years, ever since I graduated from college."

"What did you study at college?"

"I did." She played with her glasses. She didn't want this pressure; she didn't want to be a witness. She was merely a person in the wrong place at the wrong time. "Sorry. I'm so sorry. I mean, I studied accounting and economics at a community college."

Her confused answers were going to annoy the jury very quickly. It was time for Law to encourage more direct answers from Rosa Santiago.

"Can you please tell the court where you were on

February 1st?"

"I had attended a seminar on depression at the Grand Congress Hotel. I've suffered from bouts of nerves and depression my whole life and I like attending these types of seminars."

Law looked at her laptop and waited for more to come from the witness, as they had practiced, but she was silent. Law looked up, smiled nicely, and continued to encourage her.

"Where did you go after the seminar had finished?"

"I had drinks with Mary Gravely, who I went to the seminar with, and I also work with. She's also an administration manager. We were in the hotel bar for over an hour before we decided to leave. We had two cocktails, then we hugged goodbye. She left in a cab, and I began the walk back to the train, to catch a ride home to Logan Square. I walked along Ida B. Wells Drive to get to the station."

"On your walk from the Congress Hotel to the train station, along Ida B. Wells Drive, did you see the alley at the back of the Congress Hotel?"

"Yes."

Again, Law waited for more to come, but Rosa had stopped. The nerves were eating her alive.

Law and her team had spent hours preparing each witness; taking them through their questions, confirming what they had said in their witness statement was correct, and preparing them for anything that might come from the defense. Law personally spent time preparing Rosa Santiago as she knew that her knowledge—of the time that she saw Reverend Green and then Amos Anderson—was a solid start to the eyewitnesses' testimony.

But none of that preparation mattered now.

The nerves were winning.

"Did you see anyone before you passed the alley?"

"I saw Reverend Green standing next to the side entrance of the Congress Hotel."

Again, Law waited for more to come, but Santiago had forgotten everything they prepared.

"Did you see anyone else standing at the end of that alleyway?"

"I saw Mr. Amos Anderson at the end of the alley." She pointed to the defense table. "The same man that's sitting there."

"Let the court records show that Miss Santiago has pointed to the defendant." Law paused, allowing time for Rosa to perform a number of loud breathing exercises. When she finished, Law continued. "How did you know it was Mr. Anderson?"

"He gave one of the speeches that night at the seminar. I remembered him because he was very interesting and engaging and his picture was on the brochure. He was the first faith healer I had met, and I remembered his face."

"Did you talk with Mr. Anderson?"

"No."

"And what was Mr. Anderson doing?"

"Apparently, he was waiting for—"

"Objection," Hunter calmly called out. Rosa looked like she wanted to run and hide. "Speculation. The case needs to stick to the facts. No sentence in a testimony should start with the word 'apparently'."

"Sustained. Miss Santiago, please stick to the information that you know."

"Yes, sir. Your Honor, sir. Yes. Yes, sir."

Law waited for Santiago to continue again, but her body was completely still. She didn't even seem to take a breath.

"Was Mr. Anderson alone?" Law was still soft in her approach.

"Yes."

"And what time were you walking to the "L" train?"

"10:30 to 10:35." Rosa took a deep breath. "I caught the 10:45 train home, and it was ten minutes before then. I always arrive at the station five minutes before the train is due. I hate missing the train."

"Thank you, Rosa. No further questions."

Hunter leaned back in his chair and stared at Rosa Santiago before deciding to stand and ask his questions. She quivered under his stare, avoiding all eye contact. Hunter felt uneasy about intimidating her, but it was what the case called for. The freedom of an innocent man lay, in part, on his ability to discredit her.

"Hello, Miss Santiago. Thank you for taking the time to talk with us today."

"Good," she responded. "I mean, yes. Okay."

"How many drinks did you have that night, Miss Santiago?"

"I had two cocktails."

"Two?" Hunter's face expressed surprise. "You're not a large woman, Miss Santiago. Did two drinks affect you very much?"

"A little." She fumbled her words. "I was slightly

tipsy when I left the seminar, and I was quite wobbly on the train. I don't drink often, but the cocktails at the bar were half-price for anyone who attended the seminar."

"At the seminar, did you talk to Mr. Anderson in person?"

"No."

Hunter tapped his finger on the table. He really didn't enjoy discrediting people, but it was what his job called for. "They're very nice glasses that you are wearing, Miss Santiago. How well can you see without them?"

"Not very well at all."

"No?" Hunter paused and wandered around the courtroom. "They also look like they're new glasses. Are they a recent purchase?"

"Yes. They're one month old."

"Only one month old? They look very stylish."

Rosa blushed from the compliment. "I like them."

"Did you receive those new stylish glasses after you claimed to have seen Mr. Anderson that night?"

"Yes." Rosa smiled. She was taken in by Hunter's good looks. "About one or two weeks later. I bought them in the middle of February."

"Can you please tell the court if you made this Facebook post on January 15: 'Dropped my glasses. Need new ones.'"

"Um, yes. I think that was me. That sounds like me."

"Is this the photo you posted of the glasses that you dropped?"

Hunter presented a photo of scratched glasses to the court, and he could feel Law's disappointment behind him.

Although her team prepared Santiago thoroughly, they didn't conduct enough research on her. The easiest way to create doubt in an eyewitness statement was to discredit their vision, and Santiago's details were easily found via her public social media profiles.

"And would it be fair to say that you were wearing those scratched glasses on the day that you attended the seminar?"

"I guess that's right. I needed to save up to buy new ones. New glasses can be quite expensive, and I'm also saving to buy a new car." Rosa looked at Hunter. The prosecution lawyers had warned her that the defense would ask about her vision, but all the preparation in the world wouldn't have eased her nerves.

"Did you walk directly past Mr. Anderson that night?"

"No, I was on the other side of the street."

"On the other side of the street?" Hunter feigned surprise. "So perhaps twenty yards away when you saw him at the entrance to the dark alley?"

"I suppose." She looked like she wanted to cry. "I suppose it was twenty yards or so."

Hunter sighed. He hated doing this. She looked so innocent on the stand, so terrified, and all he wanted to do was protect the woman and give her a hug.

But he had to do what was required.

"Let me get this straight, Miss Santiago." His voice rose. "Late at night, in the dark, in winter, you claim to have identified a man twenty yards away. A man that you've never met in person before. A man that you've never talked to. And all while you were drunk and wearing glasses that were scratched and needed replacement?"

"Um." She held back the tears. "I suppose."

"You suppose?"

"I… I thought it was Mr. Anderson."

"You thought it was Mr. Anderson? Now, under oath, you're unsure if you saw Mr. Anderson that night?"

"It looked like him."

"Looked like him? You were drunk, it was dark, and you were wearing glasses that needed replacement, yet you claim to identify a man that you've never met. This is a court of law, Miss Santiago, and you need to be certain, have no doubt, that it was him. Your testimony may convict a man of murder." Hunter focused his glare on her. "I will ask you again—are you certain that it was Mr. Anderson that you saw that night?"

"No, I'm not." She shook her head, blinking rapidly, avoiding eye contact with anyone. "I'm not certain."

"Could it have been someone else that you saw, Miss Santiago?"

"Um, yes. Yes, it could've been someone else."

One of the jurors scoffed at the answer, another let out a disapproving sigh, and many were shaking their heads.

Michelle Law resisted doing the same.

"No further questions." Hunter shook his head.

Hunter had done what was needed—created doubt in the minds of the jurors. The perfect end to his day.

CHAPTER 33

THE CROWD was packed in for day two, thanks in part to the page three article that ran in the Chicago Tribune that detailed the case, complete with a picture of Anderson looking angry and arguing with a reporter. Although the picture was from two months earlier, it was the photo of Anderson that the paper wheeled out when they wanted to invoke emotion from the reader.

By the noise of the crowd on day two, it had certainly worked.

Three more witnesses came to the stand and claimed that they saw Anderson near the alley that night—claimed that in the dark, in the middle of winter, they identified a man they had never met in person. It was easy for Hunter to discredit their eyesight, their story, or their memory; however, the prosecution was building their evidence in the weight of numbers.

The more people that claimed they saw Anderson at the entrance to the alley that night, the more the jury became convinced. Even if every single one of the witness statements were incorrect, the numbers pushed the evidence in the prosecution's favor.

By the close of day two, the defense was fighting an uphill battle.

Day three of the case saw the prosecution's next witness, DNA identification specialist and forensic scientist, Dr. Stephen Phillips, walk to the stand. While some people found passion in activities such as sports, fitness, or reading, Dr. Phillips' passion was researching DNA. His business website had a banner that declared DNA was "the last unexplored section of the human body." He spent his life exploring DNA, often putting in eighty-hour weeks in the lab, much to the detriment of his family.

Passion was one thing; obsession was another.

Law spent the first hour and a half of the morning laboriously discussing the finer details of DNA evidence, trying to establish there was no doubt that it was Anderson's skin found under the fingernails of Reverend Green. She harped on the same points repeatedly, Hunter objecting where he could, but it became clear that in the mind of Dr. Phillips, there was little doubt about where the skin came from, and that it was there for only a few hours before the murder.

However, without an admission from Anderson, Hunter had a chance to discredit the details. He had a chance to throw doubt over their evidence.

Dr. Phillips wore a fitted black suit, presenting the image of a respectable person. It was a good look for the jury, and Hunter was surprised that he wasn't wearing a lab coat with a stethoscope around his neck—just to emphasize the point.

"Thank you for your time, Dr. Phillips," Hunter began.

"My pleasure," Dr. Phillips replied in a soft tone.

"Dr. Phillips, you've provided a lot of evidence about the DNA that was found at the crime scene. Fifty pages of evidence. In fact, it might even be more evidence than necessary. I guess the real question is, the one we all want to know the answer to; in your expert opinion, does the DNA prove that Mr. Anderson murdered Reverend Dural Green?"

"No," he scoffed. "The evidence is—"

"Thank you, Dr. Phillips." Hunter interrupted. "The information that you've included in your detailed report, is it exact?"

"I'm sorry, I'm not sure which part of the report you're referring to."

"In your summary of the report, you've stated that the likelihood of a DNA match to be incorrect is an 'estimate' of one in ten billion. Is that number exact?"

"It's an estimate." He scoffed again. "But there are only seven billion people alive, Mr. Hunter."

"As stated in page fourteen of your report," Hunter opened the report to the highlighted section. "This estimate that you've provided, this one in ten billion, is it a mathematical calculation?"

"It is."

"In your expert opinion, do you believe that the accused should be sent to prison on the basis of a mathematical equation?"

"Objection." Law stood up. "Relevance. This is merely wordplay by the defense."

"Your Honor, this witness is here to provide their expert opinion on the DNA evidence. I believe it's important that the jury understands what this evidence represents and they don't take the evidence on face value alone."

"I'm inclined to agree with the defense here. The objection is overruled. Please answer the question."

Hunter knew that there was growing doubt in the minds of the public when it came to DNA evidence. After the jury was formed, Hunter's team had studied the publicly available social media posts of the jurors and found that two jurors had expressed their anger when a murder conviction was recently overturned by the court due to incorrect DNA testing. In the eyes of the public, DNA testing was no longer the infallible answer, no longer the magic bullet, and he needed to emphasize that point.

"I'm here to testify whether the DNA samples found at the crime scene matched the accused. That's all I can comment on. I can't comment on when it got there, how it got there, or why it was there. The data doesn't give us the answers to those questions."

Hunter nodded, as did some of the jury.

"Are you certain that the DNA belonged to Mr. Anderson? Are you certain that the DNA sample you found matched Mr. Anderson's DNA sample?"

"There's a one in ten billion chance that the DNA extracted from under the fingernails of the deceased didn't belong to the sample that was provided by Mr. Amos Anderson. With the information we had, with the processes that exist for DNA analysis, that's the best we could've hoped for. The way the analysis works is that the result is one in ten billion, to the exclusion of all others. That's referred to as the probability of accuracy."

"The probability of accuracy? But, Mr. Phillips,

we're not here to deal with probabilities, nor are we here to deal with mathematics. We are here, in this court, to deal with the truth." Hunter stood, placing his hand down to press onto the table. "Is there doubt in your DNA evidence that the match belonged to Mr. Anderson?"

"Objection," Law intervened. "Asked and answered. It has already been established that the DNA test is not one hundred percent certain."

"Sustained. Move on, Mr. Hunter," Judge Lockett stated.

"In layman's terms, so the court can understand DNA testing without decades of studying, do you and your colleagues know everything there is to know about DNA?"

Dr. Phillips sighed and shook his head. "In the field of DNA analysis, there are still known unknowns, and there are unknown unknowns. There's still a lot that we don't understand, comprehend, or appreciate about DNA. It's a very complex field."

Hunter paused, ran his fingers through his hair, and turned the pages over in the file. He read over his notes, and then looked to the jury.

"The sample of blood found on the shirt of Reverend Green, what did it match?"

"We matched the DNA drawn from that blood sample to Mr. Anderson's DNA sample, which was taken after his arrest."

"And, of course, you're absolutely one hundred percent certain that it matched, aren't you?"

"No."

"No?" Hunter acted surprised. "You're telling this court, this jury, that you're not one hundred percent certain of the bloodstain match to Mr. Anderson?"

"That's correct." Dr. Phillips wasn't being drawn into playing games. Instead, he sat still on the witness stand, giving straight answers based on his scientific knowledge.

"If it's not one hundred percent certain, what does that magical missing percentage represent then?"

"The very, very tiny percentage represents the amount that we could not match to the exclusion of all others." Dr. Phillips thought about it for a moment, his eyes looking to the right, trying to think of a better term. "An insignificant amount of uncertainty."

"Uncertainty." It was Hunter's turn to scoff. He lifted his hand and then placed his hand back on the table. "Dr. Phillips, is there uncertainty in the DNA results that you've presented to the court?"

"Objection. Misleading. This is another play on words; it does not represent the scientific testing that has to take place." Law had made a last-ditch effort to avoid that answer.

"Overruled." Judge Lockett was quick to respond.

"I'll ask you again," Hunter stated firmly. "Dr. Phillips, is there uncertainty, no matter how small, in the DNA results that you have presented to this court?"

Dr. Phillips squirmed in his chair. Looked to the ceiling.

"Dr. Phillips?"

He looked away.

"Can you please answer the question, Dr. Phillips?"

He sighed. "The testing does have an insignificant amount of uncertainty in the scientific result."

Hunter sat back down. "No further questions."

CHAPTER 34

FOR CHICAGO PD Detective, Daryl Browne, policing wasn't a way to serve his community. It wasn't a way to do good for the people of his city. It wasn't even a way to gain respect.

It was a way to make money.

He wasn't interested in the law as it was written; his rule of law was governed by his lack of moral compass—formed during a hard, abusive childhood with an unemployed single mother. He had lived his life with the foundation that no one stayed in his life for long, no one had his back, and life was meant to cause pain. That pain had become a connection to his past, a way to hold onto his childhood terrors. He self-medicated with alcohol, ignoring the pleas of his ex-wife to see a doctor for his health issues, and his adult children no longer spoke to him—due to the regular beatings they had received growing up.

As the lead detective in the arrest of Amos

Anderson, Browne came to the stand as the prosecution's star witness, a man willing to say what was needed to put another man away.

At least he had put on clean clothes for the appearance.

Tex Hunter and Daryl Browne had clashed many times before, and Hunter was certain he was on the take. When he was a young detective, still fresh on the force, Browne had been the man that put handcuffs on Hunter's father. Age had long since wearied Browne, but somehow, he'd stayed alive and out of trouble long enough to be thinking about retirement.

How he survived that long baffled Hunter. He was sure the truth would catch up to him one day, but then again, "truth" wasn't a part of Browne's vocabulary.

Most people didn't listen to the truth either, jurors included. They heard what they wanted to hear. They saw what they wanted to see. They searched out stories that proved what was already in their subconscious.

That was where Hunter excelled in court. He planted a seed, a well-placed word, a perfect sentence, and let that moment be nurtured into a fully grown thought. He didn't tell people where they needed to search for their truth; he merely gave them the tools to see his point of view.

Detective Browne sat on the witness stand wearing a dark black suit, perhaps the same suit he wore to funerals—of which he attended many. His smile was smug, his arrogance strong, and his patience thin. He had no time for courtroom games or lawyer antics; he would much rather be twisting arms and taking money from people on the street.

"Please state your name and vocation for the court."

"Detective Daryl Browne. I've been a proud member of the Chicago PD for thirty years."

Law's personal dislike for Browne was well-known through the force—his old-school behavior, mostly bordering on sexual harassment, didn't sit well with the feminist. "Were you the detective that arrived at the scene of the deceased Reverend Green?"

"That's correct."

"Can you please explain what happened when you arrived at the scene?"

"I arrived at the scene after 5 a.m. The body was found by Gavin Sutton, a hotel worker, at 4:45 a.m. when he was putting trash out into the alley. He called nine-one-one, and I was nearby with my partner, so we were given the job. We arrived, saw that the body had clearly been beaten, and then checked the deceased's vital signs. Obviously, there weren't any—his lips were blue, and he'd been deceased for many hours. We cordoned off the street to declare the alley a crime scene."

"Is this the scene that you found on that day?" Law presented the crime scene photos to the jury via the monitor at the side of the room.

One of Green's older supporters, sitting near the back of the courtroom, burst into tears as she saw what was on the monitor. A well-dressed male wrapped his arm around her shoulders and escorted her out of the courtroom while she continued to cry.

At the door, the lady turned around. "Burn in hell, murderer!"

"Order!" The gavel was quick to slam. "Remove her from the courtroom."

The well-dressed male whispered something to the elderly woman, and she walked out the doors calmly, under the shadow of two tall security guards.

The judge spoke to the jury, informing them that they had to ignore all statements from the crowd, and instructed Law to continue. She allowed time for the accusation to sit in the minds of the jurors before she returned her focus back to the screen.

"What did you find at the scene?"

"Reverend Green was beaten by someone that night. His face was bruised, his jaw appeared broken, and there was blood on the ground next to his head, as you can see on the photo." Browne pointed at the screen. "It was also clear that there was blood under his fingernails."

"Did the deceased have his possessions with him?"

"It appeared so. His wallet was still in his jacket, his watch was still on his wrist, and his phone was still in his pocket. It didn't appear to be a robbery."

Law read her notes, running her finger over the next lines. "At what point did you make the decision to arrest Mr. Anderson?"

"After we identified the deceased as Reverend Dural Green, we canvassed the area for witnesses and spoke to the people who had interacted with Green the night before. Witnesses stated that Amos Anderson had fought with Green the previous night, and we asked Anderson to come to the station, and then we questioned him. We released him and conducted further interviews with more witnesses, who also identified Mr. Anderson seen nearby the alley. Within two days, we had a match to the DNA that was found under Reverend Green's fingernails, and that match belonged to Mr. Anderson."

"Did you arrest Mr. Anderson?"

"That's correct."

"Is this the arrest warrant?" Law presented the warrant to the court.

"It is."

"Is there anything wrong with this warrant?"

"No, there isn't. It's a valid and lawful arrest warrant."

"Thank you, detective. Can you please explain to the court what happened when you made the arrest?"

"We arrived at Mr. Anderson's residence at 7 a.m. on February 4th and knocked on the door." Browne leaned back in the stand, straightened his shoulders, and flattened the tie down the middle of his shirt. "The door was promptly answered by Mr. Anderson, and at that point, we read his Miranda Rights to him and made the arrest. It was at this point that he asked for a lawyer and exercised his right to remain silent."

"Was there anyone else home at the time?"

"No. Mr. Anderson had informed us earlier that he lived alone."

"Did you search his home at the time of the arrest?"

"Other police officers conducted a search of the home at the time of arrest; however, they did not complete a thorough search."

"Did you conduct any further searches of Mr. Anderson's property?"

"Yes. We had an anonymous call on our tip line, and we conducted a second search of the property three weeks ago." Browne looked at Hunter before he pulled on the lobe of his ear. "And that was when we found the necklace that belonged to Reverend Green in his possession. We found the necklace in the cabinet next to Anderson's bed."

That was a lie.

With his small grooming movements, Browne was dispersing the nervous energy of his falsehood. To a casual observer, that small error might be overlooked as a normal movement, but Tex Hunter wasn't a casual observer.

Anderson started to squirm in his chair, almost like he wanted to explode and yell, "Lies!" to the jury. He leaned forward, twitching his leg nervously under the table. Hunter tapped his pen on a handwritten note on his legal pad, catching Anderson's eye.

'Stay calm.'

Law introduced the video recording of the second

search, and for the next six minutes, the court watched the beginning of the search. Browne called out for any persons present, Anderson answered the door, and they put him in handcuffs. Browne then made his way through the house to ensure there were no other people in the apartment, but when he began to conduct the search, he took off his vest and left the small camera device resting on the kitchen counter.

For the next ten minutes, Browne painstakingly detailed the search that was conducted, with constant questions from the prosecution. Together they presented a detailed diagram of the apartment, where the necklace was found, and anything else that was found in the apartment that might tarnish Anderson's reputation. They detailed the books on the shelves including a copy of 'God is Gone' to emphasize the point, the paintings in the house including the anti-Bible painting in his kitchen, and the medicines in his cupboard including the many packets of prescribed codeine.

Hunter objected where he could, but the prosecution was painting a clear picture of a man who didn't follow the church.

"Was Mr. Anderson at home when the second search was conducted?" Law asked.

"He was. We had obtained a search warrant, and we waited until he arrived home before we entered and conducted the lawful search. Mr. Anderson was out on bail at the time. He answered the door, and that's when we presented the search warrant to him," Browne replied.

"Thank you, detective. No further questions."

A good solid start by the prosecution.

Now it was Hunter's chance to change that.

CHAPTER 35

TESTING BROWNE'S patience, Hunter took time to review his notes. It was a deliberate ploy; he was asserting his authority in the courtroom. This was his place, and Browne had to play by his rules.

"Thank you for your time, Detective Browne," Hunter began after three long minutes of silence. "Did you take video evidence of the search?"

"Yes, that's what we're required to do in the department now."

"Is every detective in the Chicago Police Department required to take video footage of a search?"

Browne rolled his tongue around his mouth before he responded. "Certain detectives are asked to take video footage of a search. It can be for a variety of reasons, and those reasons are not disclosed to us or to anyone."

"And you're one of the detectives that have been asked to take video footage of every search warrant?"

"Yes." Browne was trying his best not to say the wrong thing and fall into the defense's trap.

Hunter knew why they asked him to take footage of every search—his list of false accusations ran about as long as his arm.

"Why did you remove the video recording device from your shoulder and leave it on the kitchen counter?" Hunter played the video for a few moments on the court monitor and then paused the search video.

"When the premises had been secured, I left the device in a place that covered the greatest area for recording. In this case, it was the kitchen counter. You could see the hallway, part of the kitchen, and the living room."

"Is this common practice?"

"No, but I thought it was appropriate for this particular search."

"Were you reprimanded by your superiors for taking off the camera?"

"I was…" Browne squirmed in his chair. "And I was asked not to do it again."

"And is this you in the video?"

The video was then paused on a quick moment of Browne walking down the hallway of the apartment.

"It's a bit blurry, but yes, it appears to be me."

"Are you carrying a brown paper bag as you walk down the hallway—before you enter the bedroom?"

"Ah." Browne didn't expect that question. He thought he kept that bag out of view. "Yes." He stumbled for a moment. "In that bag is the equipment that I needed to conduct the search."

"Such as?"

"Things I needed to check the apartment. Fingerprint dusting tools, torch, screwdrivers… that sort of thing. You never know when you need it. It's my 'goody' bag. Every raid has one, but sometimes they're left in the car and collected once the premises have been secured. I decided to take it with me because I made an assessment about the raid."

"It seems rather a small bag for those supplies. Are you sure all those things fit into that bag?"

"Yes, and I'm not sure what you're implying?"

"It seems strange that you would keep that equipment in a brown paper bag." Hunter looked to the jury. "Would that bag be large enough to fit a necklace?"

"Objection! Leading the witness!" Law called out. "What the defense is suggesting here has no evidence to back it up!"

Hunter was quick to reply. "Withdrawn."

Law marked it down as a win for her, but the damage was done. The jurors were already questioning whether the bag was large enough to have held the evidence.

The seed had been planted.

"You entered the apartment with this bag. Is it usual procedure to enter a perpetrator's premises with such a bag at the time of a raid?"

"Not quite." Browne paused for a few moments, rubbing his thumbs together. "It's not usual procedure, but it's what I needed for that day. I decided to bring the bag with me on this raid after I made an assessment of the situation." He was fumbling for an excuse. "The bag I normally had the equipment in ripped earlier, and that was the only bag I had in the car. It was the only way I could carry those things."

"Hmm..." Hunter ran his fingers over his jawline, pausing again; not because he needed the time to think, but because he wanted to provide the jury a moment to process the evidence. "Was anyone else in the bedroom when you found the necklace?"

"Not when I found the necklace."

"Just you and this paper bag?"

Browne hesitated before answering, "Yes."

"Is it usual police procedure to search a room by yourself?"

"Sometimes we do it, and it's not against the law." He was becoming agitated. "The facts of this case are that we had a tip-off that the necklace was in the apartment, and we had a warrant to search the place. When I searched the main bedroom, I found a suspicious case, and when I opened the case, I found the necklace that was later proven to be Reverend Green's. Those are the facts."

"And, of course, you left the video camera in the kitchen, so there's no video of you in the bedroom before you opened the case?"

"In the old days, it was normal to search a room without recording everything." Browne's annoyance was clear. "We're police officers. We uphold the law."

"You found the necklace when you were in the room by yourself, with the bag?"

"Objection. Asked and answered," Law called out.

"Withdrawn."

Browne glared hard at the prosecution's table. He wasn't prepared for this.

"Did anybody else see the necklace before you found it?"

"No."

"Just you and the bag?"

"Objection!" Law called out again. "Asked and answered! Inflammatory! The witness has clearly answered this question already. This is repetitive!"

"Withdrawn." Hunter looked back down at his notes, and then pressed play on the video again. "Is this you exiting the room, back into the view of the video recorder?"

Hunter pointed back to the screen.

"It is."

"And in your left hand, what is that?"

Browne squinted, as did the judge and the jury. Law refused to even look at the screen. She already knew what was coming.

"I'm not sure."

"Let me help you." Hunter zoomed in on the still

image, focusing on the bag.

Browne shook his head. "I don't know what that is."

"You don't know what was in your hand at that time?"

"I'm a busy man." He continued shaking his head. "I don't know what's in my hands at all times."

Hunter scoffed as Browne was reacting exactly as he expected. "Does it at all, even in the slightest, appear to a crushed brown paper bag, only big enough to fit in the palm of your hand, and with nothing inside it?"

Browne's mouth sat slightly open.

"Detective Browne?" Hunter pressed.

"It could be."

"It could be?" Hunter's voice rose. "If it isn't the same brown paper bag, then can you tell us what else it could be?"

"I guess it must be the paper bag."

"And can you tell us where the contents of the paper bag ended up?"

"I guess I left them in the room."

"Really?" Hunter remarked. "Let's play the rest of the video footage."

The footage ran. The jurors leaned forward to watch.

"And can you tell us when you removed the contents of the paper bag?"

Browne shrugged. "I'm not sure."

"That's extremely careless of you, Detective Browne. For such an experienced police detective, I'm very surprised if that's the case! Did you make that mistake?"

"No one's perfect." He shrugged. "We all make mistakes."

Juror eleven, the older man with the flannel shirt, was particularly intrigued. His body was leaning forward, his eyes squinting, and his mouth partially open.

Juror five, sitting behind him, followed his lead. Juror five was a young man, well studied and well dressed, but small and without a hint of overt masculinity. He protested with feminist rallies, wrote blogs about his feelings online, and didn't like getting dirt under his fingernails, but there was a part of him, a tiny part, that wanted to be the man in front of him—grumpy, stoic, and with forearms as thick as a tree trunk.

Hunter finished playing the video and then brought a picture up on the screen of a different location.

"Detective Browne, can you please tell the court who this is in the picture with you?"

The shock was clearly written on Browne's face. Hunter walked to the bailiff, and handed him a still copy of the photo, and it was passed to the judge and introduced as evidence.

"Detective Browne?" Hunter pressed further. "Can you please tell the court who that is?"

"That appears to be me."

"And?"

"It appears to be Lucas Bauer."

"And how is Mr. Bauer connected to this case?"

"Objection." Law called out. "Immaterial. There's nothing in the picture that can be connected to the case!"

"Overruled. I'm interested to see where this is going. Answer the question, detective," Judge Lockett stated.

"Mr. Bauer is the manager of Mr. Anderson's

business. Together, they operate the Faith Healing Project."

"Can you tell us what Mr. Bauer is giving you here?"

Browne squinted at the next picture. He shook his head. "It appears to be a paper bag and an envelope."

"Is it the same brown paper bag that you took into the apartment when you conducted the search?"

"No." He scoffed. He knew that Hunter didn't have more evidence than the picture, or he would have introduced it already. "Of course not."

"So then, please tell the court what was in this paper bag, the one that Lucas Bauer gave you?"

"Objection." Law slammed her fist down onto the table. "Immaterial! There simply isn't enough of an established connection to this case!"

"I would argue that there clearly is a connection." Hunter put forward his case to the judge. "We have a prosecution witness exchanging an envelope with the lead detective. That, in the very least, is worth exploring."

"I'm inclined to agree with the defense on this one. The objection is overruled," Judge Lockett said.

"It was simply a letter thanking me for my service,

and in the paper bag was a bunch of home-made cookies that Mr. Bauer's wife had made for me," Browne lied. "Nothing to do with this case."

"And where is that letter now? I don't think I saw it in the evidence."

"It was nothing to do with this case, so I threw it out." He looked to the jury and laughed. They didn't join him. "No offense to Mr. Bauer, of course."

Hunter tapped his pen on the edge of his notepad.

"Detective Browne, did Mr. Anderson say anything when you presented the necklace to him?"

"Yes."

"And what did he say?"

Browne groaned. "That he was innocent."

"Anything else?"

"Yes."

"And what was that?"

Browne paused and sighed, adjusting his tie. "He said that it was a setup. He said that he had never seen the necklace before."

"Did he make a statement about who the necklace belonged to?"

Browne frowned and drew a long breath. "He claimed that I must've planted the necklace."

"Did he? Why would he say that?"

His voice rose with anger. "A lot of criminals say that. We hear it all the time!"

"When you presented the evidence to Mr. Anderson, he stated directly that he had never seen the necklace before, and it was a setup. Is that correct?"

"That's what he said." He looked away.

"That's very interesting, Detective Browne." Hunter wrote more notes on his pad. He paused until juror eleven, and then juror five, nodded. "No further questions."

CHAPTER 36

AFTER A long afternoon of expert scientific witness after expert scientific witness, the jury looked like they wanted to run out of the courtroom and never return. Law may have had impressive moments, moments to convince the jury, but they were almost lost amongst the sea of boredom.

The last witness of the day, the expert crime scene analyst, painstakingly took the court through the details of his report seemingly word by word, and even Anderson looked like he was struggling to stay awake.

"How'd we do?" Anderson was desperate for good news. He had waited until the prosecution team exited the court, with his supporters not far behind them. "Tell me we did well. I felt like we did well. I thought you did well out there."

"We're doing fine." Hunter's answer was cold as he packed up his briefcase. Esther waited by the door, as did Hunter's investigator, Ray Jones.

"Fine? What does that mean? Are we in front? Do you think that the jury knows I'm innocent yet?" Anderson tugged on Hunter's sleeve. "I need more information than 'fine'. I need to know that in five days' time, I'm going to be found innocent."

Hunter turned slowly and looked at Anderson, staring at the other man's hand. Anderson let go of the suit sleeve, and then patted it down, ensuring it wasn't crinkled.

"All this courtroom drama is over my head. It's all about the law, whether this or that matches what's written in a book; it's not about whether I'm actually innocent." Amos was frantic. "You seem more concerned with the way something is written on a piece of paper than whether or not I committed the murder."

"Amos—"

"You don't understand, Tex. I help people out here. It's my life's purpose. I can make a difference in many people's lives. Out here, I'm somebody's angel. They look to me to save them. In prison, I'll be another criminal, just another felon, and I don't know if I can make it through. I wouldn't even know what to do. I can't fight. I can't save myself."

"Then let's hope the jury loves you."

"How strange this feeling is." Anderson rubbed his hair repeatedly. "I have all this emotion, all this fear, all these worries inside me, but to you, it just comes out as words. All you hear are sentences because I can't tell you how much this hurts." He wiped his eyes with the back of his wrist. "What are we going to do?"

"You should focus on getting some rest," Hunter said. "I've got work to do to prepare for tomorrow."

Hunter looked down at his notes and studied them for a while before closing his briefcase. Amos hadn't left. He couldn't. He needed more information.

"Tex." Esther tapped him on the shoulder. "I was given this on the way out. There's a new witness that has just agreed to testify, and the prosecution is going to apply to add him to the list tomorrow morning. Here's their witness statement, and you're going to need to look at this."

She handed him a piece of paper, and he read the first line.

His head went back, and he stared at the ceiling.

"What's wrong?" Anderson pleaded.

"Lucas Bauer is on the stand first thing tomorrow morning, and Reverend Darcy is the third on the list."

"But we knew that."

"We did," Hunter agreed. "But it's the new witness, the second witness of the day, that's going to cause us trouble."

"We could call for an extension, more time to prepare for this witness?" Esther suggested, the files held tightly against her chest. "You could argue that it's too late to add them to the list."

"I don't think that'll help. This witness will change his story at any time to suit himself."

Anderson squinted, and then looked at the piece of paper that Hunter put on the table. "But what could they know about the case?"

"I don't think that's the right question."

"What is then?"

"The right question is: What have they been caught doing?" Jones walked up to them. "I've had a word with an informant on the phone. Word is that they've agreed to testify against Anderson in exchange for a deal with the prosecution. They were found yesterday and arrested."

Hunter turned around. "What for?"

"Weapons charges. They were caught with unsecured weapons in their vans in a routine traffic stop." Jones stepped through the bar, the gate separating the public gallery from the courtroom well, and leaned against the prosecution's table, ignoring the stare of the bailiff.

"But what could they possibly say?" Amos questioned. "What are they going to testify about?"

"He wants a soapbox." Hunter closed his briefcase. "Chuck Johnson will say anything that will help his cause."

CHAPTER 37

HUNTER HAD barely stepped out of his office, into the winter wind, when he saw the man charging towards him. There was anger in the man's movements; his tight shoulders, the scowl on his face, his clenched fists.

Hunter wasn't worried. He was big enough and skilled enough to take out most people. And he knew that his investigator, Ray Jones, was only a few steps behind him.

Ray could sort most things out—no matter the size of the opponent.

"Chuck Johnson," Hunter stated as the man stepped up to him. "What a pleasant surprise. I've only just finished reading your witness statement."

"I'll give you a surprise." Chuck waved his fist. "This one. I'll punch you."

"Talking about it ruined the surprise." Hunter

stepped forward, staring down at the man. "And I'd be surprised if you tried to use that fist on me."

Chuck Johnson looked up at Hunter, then stepped back. Chuck was wearing a sweater that had seen more winters than his daughter, and his jeans were loose and covered in oil. On the busy street, ten minutes to 8 p.m., he looked homeless as well-dressed office workers started to make their way home for the day.

People pushed past Chuck, unaware that a racist was in their midst. Some turned their nose up at the smell of the unwashed clothes, others were too immune to that part of city life.

"I won't have to use my fists. My brother will. He'll take you. He's a former state champion boxer."

"I'm sure he is," Hunter responded.

"I've come to warn you, lawyer boy." Chuck pointed his finger at Hunter's chest. "I'm on the stand tomorrow, and you don't get to play your games with me. I don't want any funny business."

"You don't like jokes?"

"Don't patronize me. You don't want to mess with me." Chuck grunted. "I'm a dangerous man. I've got supporters. I can make things happen."

"You're all talk, Chuck." Hunter began to walk

away.

"I mightn't talk your talk." The street lights highlighted Chuck's smile as he walked next to Hunter. "But that lawyer will. She can talk the talk."

The statement caught Hunter off guard. He stopped.

Chuck was too confident. Too poised.

Something wasn't right.

"The prosecutor?"

"You've got no idea, do you?" Chuck laughed, hand on his stomach. He shook his head as if the joke was clear to everyone. "I'm really going to enjoy tomorrow. You'll get what's coming to you."

"What are you talking about?" Hunter stepped forward again. Chuck barely came up to his shoulders, and his eyes were staring at Hunter's broad chest. "What are you planning to say?"

"Whatever I want."

Hunter leaned down, gritting his teeth. "You'll be under oath. If you say something false, you'll be charged with perjury."

The pressure was building, and Hunter wanted to be there when it detonated.

"I don't care about your oath. Those words mean nothing to me. Nothing! I'll be on that stand, and I'll lie through my teeth. I've done it before, and I'll do it again. Your lawyer talk doesn't mean anything to me. I'll say whatever is in my best interest."

"I will pounce on you if your story changes at any point during the testimony. If I even get a sniff that something is wrong or misplaced, then I'll attack you. And Caylee… well, maybe I'll subpoena Caylee to the stand."

"You leave my daughter alone." His voice went soft. It was the first time Hunter saw real fear in Chuck's eyes. "She's an innocent angel."

A cold silence drifted over them.

As soon as he heard that Chuck was going to be on the stand the next day, Hunter had been thinking about the leverage he needed to break him, the information he needed to twist Chuck into telling the truth.

And now he had it.

As he stood over Chuck, he felt a large hand on his shoulder.

"Everything fine here?" Ray Jones stood tall next to his friend.

Chuck Johnson took another step back. It wasn't

the size of the man that shocked him; it was the man's skin color. "He works for you?"

Neither man offered a response.

"Like a slave, I guess."

Jones jumped forward, but Hunter held out his arm.

"Not yet, Ray. We'll get our chance, but it's not now."

Jones stared at Chuck Johnson, whose smile was as infuriating as it was smug. Jones chewed on his gum, not taking his eyes off Chuck, his heart pounding against the walls of his massive chest.

He lived for these moments.

Moments when he could defend his people; moments when he could reject the notion of racism.

"I promise, Ray." Hunter moved between him and Chuck. "I promise that you'll get your chance but beating up a prosecution's witness is not going to look good for anyone."

"My brother could take you, boy." Chuck spat on the sidewalk. "He's a boxer."

Every muscle in Jones' body clenched.

"Not now, Ray. Not today." Hunter had to

physically restrain him.

"Ha!" Chuck Johnson, full of hateful pride, turned and began to walk away, laughing as he went. "Burt would beat you up. He's a boxer!" he called over his shoulder.

The blood pumped through Jones' veins, but he knew this wasn't the time. It wasn't the place to beat up Chuck Johnson.

And he also knew his time would come.

CHAPTER 38

THE WALK from the bar to the train station was short.

And that was the way Ray Jones liked it.

He felt the strong pull to stop for three pints of lager after his "chat" with Chuck Johnson. Even more so than his racism, Chuck had an air of psychotic danger surrounding him. He was as ruthless as he was racist. That made Jones feel uneasy.

Jones had experienced racism a lot in his life.

He grew up in South L.A., where most of his friends became drugs dealers, prostitutes, or addicts; sometimes all three. His father was imprisoned for murder when he was twelve, and his mother died from a drug overdose when he was fifteen. As a teenager, when he should have been focusing on school, he was left to fend for himself. He turned to what most people in his neighborhood did for money—stealing from the rich. He broke into numerous homes during his days on the streets, but he was caught one day before his sixteenth birthday, a bag full of stolen jewelry under his arm.

It was then that his uncle called him and said he had work for him in Chicago, and Jones broke free of that life. Uncle Carl told him that if he wanted a good life, he had to work for it. He sent him back to school to complete his high school certificate, and then took him on as a trainee investigator in his private investigator business.

With the skills he had learned on the streets, and with his considerable height and strength, Ray Jones became the perfect investigator. After ten years, his uncle stepped away from the business, moving to the sunny beaches of Florida, and Jones took the reins.

One moment of luck and one moment of family love saved him from a life on the streets.

Jones was waiting at the lights, slightly drunk, thinking about how far he had come in life, when the pedestrian light changed from red to green.

A timeworn truck rumbled up to the intersection.

"Hey," a voice came from the truck. "You. Boy."

A wave of anger came over Jones. "What did you say?"

"I called you boy. What are you going to do about

it?" Burt Johnson leaped out of the driver's seat of the truck, the engine still running. Chuck Johnson sat in the passenger seat, a smile stretched across his face.

Burt stood as tall as Jones, but Jones still had a good thirty pounds on him.

And years and years of training.

"You. Boy. I'm talking to you."

"Don't call me that." Jones' hands came out of his pockets.

Burt leaped forward but was confronted by two quick left jabs from Jones.

Followed by a powerful straight right.

That was the one that hurt.

Despite all his training, despite the years in a boxing gym, nothing could have prepared Burt for the anger of Ray Jones.

Burt stumbled back, but then he moved forward again. He crouched right, exactly where Jones thought he would move. Jones' left hook, powered by the swing of his hips, connected with Burt's jaw, and he was sent sprawling back onto the hood of the truck.

But Burt had a solid jaw, one that had been trained over many years too—starting from the days he used to take beatings at the hands of his drunk father. Dazed but not beaten, Burt got back onto his feet, ready to keep fighting. A classic boxer's pose.

He jabbed left; Jones deflected it with his forearms.

He jabbed again, and this time Jones moved left.

The powerful straight right came from Burt, but it was sloppy, leaving his ribs exposed.

Jones moved his head out of the direction of the punch and landed two quick hooks to Burt's ribs, followed by another straight right onto Burt's jaw.

Burt never stood a chance.

He fell to the road, dazed and confused.

Jones waited, ready to keep beating the bigoted man.

"Whoa!" Chuck Johnson jumped between them. "Stop that! Get away!"

Burt climbed to his feet, one hand on his truck, coughing and spitting blood onto the road, and began to make his way back towards Jones.

"No, Burt. Not here!" Chuck pushed him in the ribs. "Get back in the truck!"

"But, Chuck! He hit me!"

"Get back in the truck!" Chuck shouted. "They'll be done tomorrow!"

"You're lucky he's making me go." Burt pointed his finger at Jones, only slightly restrained by his brother. "Or I would've flattened you!"

Chuck ushered his younger brother back into the truck's driver's seat, and then raced around to the passenger side.

Cars honked their horns behind them, but Jones didn't budge.

The engine of the truck revved before Burt rolled down the window and pointed his finger at Jones. "You should watch yourself, boy."

CHAPTER 39

CAYLEE JOHNSON looked around the room.

In the living room was one old sofa, at least twenty years old, and a secondhand armchair they had recently acquired. There were coffee stains on the floor, marks on the walls, and a water stain on the ceiling. The smell was musty, but she liked that smell. It was home. The adjoining kitchen was small, but it did the job. They liked to have the curtains closed during the day; it made it easier to watch television.

It was the same room that she was shot in when she was four years old.

She remembered a lot about that day. Mostly she remembered the pain in her leg, the searing ache of the shotgun wound. She remembered her mother's scream, remembered hearing four gunshots, and then blacking out. She woke up in the hospital, and that was where her father told her that her mother was deceased.

That news was more painful than the gunshot wound on her leg.

The man's face was etched into her memory; his dark features, his piercing eyes, the scar on his left cheek. The African American that broke into their house had watched her father's car drive out of the driveway and thought the house was empty. He thought it would be an easy break and enter on an isolated property, an easy steal.

The next time she saw the man's face was in the courtroom at his trial. Her father was furious that the man pleaded not guilty, pleaded his innocence, even though he admitted to being in the room and firing the weapon. It was an accident, the man complained. Manslaughter, he told them.

That moment was a turning point for her father; the moment that his discontent morphed into pure hatred.

Caylee often thought hatred was too soft a word for the way her father felt. It was a loathing, a revulsion, an absolute disgust for any person of color.

Her father funneled that hate into a group called the White Alliance Coalition, but it never gathered much support. The media groups came to him for sound bites on any race conflict in Chicago, but the White Alliance Coalition never had many members. It was more of a front for her father's hatred than it was a way to motivate the masses. They held regular monthly meetings. At most, they had twenty attendees, but recently, they were struggling to get five people to voice their animosity. Most had moved on or joined other white supremacy movements; the movements that inspired action.

It had been fifteen years since she had set foot in a courthouse, fifteen years since that guilty verdict, and she hated the idea of going back. She silently sobbed through her mother's killer's entire trial and cried even more when the man was found guilty of her mother's death.

Her father was due to take the stand tomorrow.

She wasn't looking forward to that; the media coverage, the reporters at their gates, the chance that her photo might make the paper. She had to make sure that she laid low until it all blew over.

She heard her uncle's truck rumble up the gravel driveway. Her father stormed into the house first, slamming the door behind him but coughing louder than usual. He didn't even greet her before he went to the nebulizer machine that helped him breathe.

His time was coming, they all knew that, and it wasn't far away now. He refused to go back to the doctors, preferring to spend his last months in the comfort of his home.

Her uncle didn't follow him into the house.

Not long after her father started wheezing into the machine, she heard her uncle pounding the boxing bag that hung outside. It wasn't training. The way he pounded the bag was pure aggression.

"What happened?" Caylee asked as her father turned off the machine, helped by the dose of medicine to ease his pain.

"A black guy hit Burt." Her father grunted.

"In court?"

"What?" He walked to the fridge, pulled out a beer, and cracked it open. "No. Not in court. On the street!"

"Is Burt okay?"

"He's fine, but that boy hit him! That stupid boy blindsided Burt. Burt wasn't even watching when that dog hit him! What a dirty act! I should report him to the police!"

There was such anger in the house. Such hatred.

She stepped back from her father, retreating back into the living room. She didn't like him when he was like this. It was hard to talk to either of them when they were like this.

Caylee had a decision to make.

She looked at the picture of her deceased mother sitting on the mantle and gave it a kiss before she went back to her bedroom.

This was it.

Her time.

Her time to make a change.

CHAPTER 40

THERE WAS a time for power and a time for patience. As a private investigator, Ray Jones understood that.

With his height, size, and strength, he much preferred using power to get the answers he wanted.

And that's what he did.

Most people crumbled when intimidated by Ray Jones. He could talk the talk and walk the walk.

Getting the information he wanted wasn't hard, nor was convincing people to turn on Chuck Johnson. Most people wanted nothing to do with the family. Jones started with Chuck's small neighborhood, at the cheapest bar—where the seats where sticky, the lighting broken in places, and the bathrooms vandalized.

It was there he met an accountant drinking beer, avoiding his home. The one-man drinking machine was also a one-man business; he didn't earn enough to employ a secretary. His cheap fees meant that he attracted cheap clients, and it soon became clear that the Johnson family was one of those. The man's shirt was untucked, his pants had stains on them, and the few strands of hair that he had left were brushed over his bald patch. Even though he was alone at the bar, slumped forward on his elbows, he preferred it to going home and being told how much of a loser he was by his wife.

The more drinks Jones bought him, the more the accountant opened up.

Jones knew he could drink most people under the table, and by the fourth pint of Goose Island IPA, the man was talking freely. Jones guided the conversation to the use of passwords, and the accountant let it slip that he used one password for everything—the name of his first pet.

Within an hour of talking to a drunk man about his dogs, Jones had the password to unlock the information.

Two hours later, after he helped the man into a cab, he was at the accountant's office in a small strip mall. There was a convenience store on one side, a used goods shop on the other. The only car in the lot looked abandoned, and the lights were turned out since it was after midnight. The accountant's office had less security than a ghost town. Even the back door, with the lock already broken, was left open. With the knowledge of the password, Jones sat at the lone computer in the office and searched through the database's files.

*****

Eight hours later, Jones waited at the defense table, still another hour before the court case was due to begin.

"Ray." Hunter greeted his friend as he walked into the courtroom. "You look like you haven't slept a wink."

"I haven't."

Hunter approached cautiously. "What have you been doing?"

"I've been looking into the White Alliance Coalition." There was hatred in Jones' eyes, venom in his voice.

"Why?"

"They rubbed me the wrong way, and I'm like a cat. If I'm rubbed the wrong way, I like to get revenge." He smiled. "And I did it."

"You did what?"

"I found what we were looking for." He handed Hunter a manila folder. "They have an accountant, and security wasn't tight in the office."

Hunter didn't open the folder. "I can't use this as evidence."

"I called Mrs. Nelson this morning. She called me two days ago to talk about the case. Nice lady. Proud of her heritage, which is the same as my family. She gave me the information that confirmed everything in that file." Ray indicated towards the folder. "Have a look at the information. Read it."

Hunter placed his briefcase down, confused as he opened the report that was at least fifty pages long. "Is there anything incriminating?"

"Nothing that proves Amos is innocent, but page four has information that you'll want to know."

Hunter opened the file to page four.

And then he smiled.

CHAPTER 41

HUNTER WAS still looking through the manila folder as the first witness of the morning walked in.

The information Jones had taken from the accountant's office was damning; it held secrets that certain people didn't want exposed. He was thinking of a way to use them—how to get the information into the court record without using the documents that Jones had printed—when Lucas Bauer walked past him.

Lucas Bauer was the first witness for the day. That was good for Hunter—just after his second coffee kicked in. He instructed Esther to bring him a constant supply of caffeine, delivered in between witnesses, as the prosecution had Bauer, Chuck Johnson, and Reverend Darcy coming to the stand.

The day was Hunter's Super Bowl.

Bauer's suit was bright enough to force people to look twice at the blue color, his hair slicked back to the left, and his accessories glittering in the lights. It almost seemed appropriate for Bauer to wink at the jurors as he passed them.

Bauer had woken up next to one of the dancers from his cabaret show—after he promised her the world the night before. He promised that she would be a star, that he would be the one holding her hand as she tackled the bright lights of Vegas. She fell for him; convinced by his smooth talking, flashy displays of wealth, and conviction in his own power.

But in the morning, after he had received what he wanted, he couldn't even remember her name.

Bauer was sworn in, and Law opened with her questions, fast and to the point.

"Thank you for talking with us today, Mr. Bauer. Can you please explain to the court your relationship with the defendant?"

"I'm the business manager for The Faith Healing Project. Amos is the main faith healer within the group. Actually, he's the only faith healer we have in the group at the moment."

Something didn't feel right. Law was too confident. The smirk across her face was too broad.

"Do you have a personal relationship with Mr. Anderson?"

"I do." Bauer turned and flashed his bright white smile to the jury. "We're friends, and we've been friends for many years. I would call him one of my closest friends."

Hunter didn't like the angle they were taking.

"Who were you with on the night of February 1st?"

"I was with Amos. We had attended the seminar on depression together, where Amos had given a speech, as had Reverend Green. Reverend Green's speech wasn't much of a speech; it was almost a debate against everything that Amos had said earlier. I came to the seminar with Amos, and we left the building together as well."

This was too rehearsed. Too clean. There was no thinking time between the questions and answers, and that could only mean that Law had spent a lot of time preparing Bauer for the testimony.

That was trouble.

Gripping his pen tightly, Hunter prepared for a new twist in the tale.

"Did you see Mr. Anderson and Reverend Green together that night?"

"Yes."

"Where did you see them?"

"The first time I saw them together that night was backstage at the seminar when they got into a physical altercation outside the waiting room."

"Did you break up this altercation?"

"That's correct."

Hunter felt the tension rise in the room. Bauer was going to make a play of his own.

"Did you see them anywhere else?"

"I did."

"Can you please tell the court where else you saw them?"

"I saw Amos in the alley behind the Congress Hotel, where he was talking to Reverend Green. Amos asked Reverend Green to meet him in the alley after the seminar. Amos said that he wanted to have a quiet discussion with Green, away from all the cameras and the crowds, to try and smooth things over between them."

Anderson's mouth dropped open.

"That's quite a revelation, Mr. Bauer," Law replied, but she wasn't surprised at all. "Mr. Bauer, I have a sworn police statement here, made two days after that night, that states you didn't see Mr. Anderson and Reverend Green together after leaving the function. In the statement, you declare that you saw Amos near the alley, but that was all. Are you now changing that statement?"

"I said that to the police because I was defending my friend. I was scared for Amos, and what he did and what might happen to him. He's my friend."

"Do you expect us to believe the change in your statement?"

"I'm only telling the truth. I saw them in the alley together. Amos asked to meet Reverend Green there." Bauer looked down, trying to pretend that he felt bad for what he had done. "The guilt was weighing heavily on my mind when I decided to tell the truth. It was too much of a cross to bear. I wanted to tell the truth, but I also wanted to protect my friend. In the end, after not sleeping well for a month, I decided to come forward and tell the facts about what I saw that night. I wasn't going to lie anymore."

Hunter threw his pen down. The disgust was clear on his face, as was the shock on Anderson's.

Bauer wanted Anderson out of the picture—he was holding back his business plans. Bauer wanted to expand, advance the business, bring on more faith healers. He wanted to franchise across the country and across the world, but as an equal business partner, Anderson wouldn't let that happen.

Bauer needed Anderson out of the business, and this was the perfect opportunity to make that happen.

"What did you see when you saw them together that night in the alley?"

"We had walked out of the seminar together, and Amos felt quite angry about the way that Reverend Green attacked him. I had never seen him so angry. We were walking down the street when we saw Reverend Green at the entrance to the alley. He was waiting for someone to come and pick him up. Amos went up to Reverend Green, but I told him not to go. He was so angry." Bauer shook his head. "He asked Reverend Green to have a quiet word with him, away from the cameras, so they could sort out their differences."

"What happened next?"

"It was dark, but I saw Reverend Green and Amos walk down the alley together. I waited at the entrance to the alley while they talked. I was checking emails on my phone while they went down the alley, so I didn't see what happened."

"Did you hear anything after they walked away together?"

"I heard a scream, but it sounded far away. It didn't sound like it was close by, so I wasn't too worried. I've heard screams before in the Loop, but I've never seen any trouble."

"When was the next time that you saw Mr. Anderson or Reverend Green?"

"Amos came out of the alley and said he needed to catch the train home. I told him that I could give him a ride, but he said he wanted to catch the train. He seemed quite nervous, so I left it at that. I asked him how the conversation with Reverend Green went, and he avoided the question."

"Did you see Reverend Green again that night?"

"No, I didn't." Bauer leaned forward to talk into the microphone. "I assumed he walked out the other end of the alley."

"Did you check the alley?"

"No." He shook his head.

"Do you have anything to gain by changing your testimony about Mr. Anderson?"

"I don't." He leaned forward. "In fact, it's the opposite—I have everything to lose. He's the star of my business and who knows what will happen if he's convicted of murder," Bauer lied. "I might lose everything."

"Are you aware of the penalties that you may face now that you have admitted to lying to the police?"

"I am."

"Thank you, Mr. Bauer, for your honesty. No further questions."

As he stared at the paper in front of him, the sweat built on Hunter's brow; it was quite the damning statement—Anderson's business partner, his friend, was testifying against him.

Not only was Hunter fighting for the freedom of Amos Anderson, fighting against an almost impossible case, but now, he was also fighting a lying manager.

Not the way Tex Hunter had expected the morning to start, not the way he planned things to go.

But he had a secret weapon in the folder.

CHAPTER 42

BAUER LOOKED supremely poised as he waited in the witness stand for the cross-examination. His hands were laid peacefully in his lap, his legs spread wide apart, and his shoulders were at ease. He felt like he was winning this game. He was invincible. Untouchable.

He had made a play, crossed his friend, and had planned to come out on top. In Vegas, it was commonplace, almost expected, to cross, double-cross, and triple-cross your friends. Using other people to get ahead was the way business was done, and Bauer was a master of convincing people to fall for his charms. It was only once he was unable to pay his debts to a casino boss, after three failed show ventures, that his life fell apart in Vegas. They took him for everything—even his pet goldfish was gone after they went through his house.

Moving back to Chicago was a new beginning, a fresh start, but a leopard doesn't change its spots.

He had the opportunity to push Anderson out of the picture, and he took it.

After he was called to begin his cross-examination, Tex Hunter contemplated the case at his desk, thinking over the opportunity that lay before him.

"Mr. Bauer," he began, questioning Bauer while still seated. "Can you please confirm where you were on the night of February 1st?"

Bauer had a growing smile. "Like I have stated previously, I was at the seminar on depression before I stood at the end of the alley behind the Congress Hotel, which is also where I saw Reverend Green and Amos interact. Are your ears painted on?"

"My ears function fine, Mr. Bauer," Hunter replied. "And you state that you have nothing to gain by changing your sworn police statement?"

"That's correct. In fact, I have everything to lose. My main income is from the Faith Healing Project."

"Do you have any plans to expand the business and employ more faith healers?"

"Amos and I have discussed that; however, nothing has been put into action."

"Is it true that you and Mr. Anderson were in disagreement about this—that you wanted to expand and Mr. Anderson didn't?"

"Like all business ventures, we were working through our differences. That's normal in business; it's how things work. There was nothing wrong with that."

"With Mr. Anderson out of the picture, you could expand, couldn't you?"

"I guess so."

"So, in fact, you do have something to gain from turning against Mr. Anderson, don't you?" Hunter stood. "You can expand the business as you wish, can't you?"

"That's not relevant." Bauer was flippant. "I won't turn on my friend for the sake of business. That man is my friend, I want to protect him, but I also have to tell the truth."

"Is it true that you were next to the men when the argument started between Reverend Green and Mr. Anderson in the hallway of the Congress Hotel?"

"That's correct."

"Did you begin that argument?"

"I'm sorry? No, no. I didn't begin that argument."

Hunter looked over the file that Jones had handed him earlier. He placed his palm on it, looked directly at Bauer and then back to the folder. Bauer squinted with confusion at the reference.

"Did it annoy you that an African American man had the right to speak at that function?"

"Pardon?"

"Let me repeat the question for you, Mr. Bauer." Hunter's voice rose. "Did it annoy you that an African American man had the right to speak at that function?"

"No." Bauer shook his head.

"Really?" Hunter tapped his finger on top of the file, making a clear enough statement for Bauer to see. "Do you consider yourself a racist?"

"What?"

"Objection," Law called out. "Immaterial. Not relevant to this case."

"Your Honor," Hunter argued. "I assure you this is very relevant to this case. I'm establishing this witness' credentials."

"Overruled, but get to the point quickly, Mr. Hunter." Judge Lockett turned to the witness. "Answer the question."

Bauer squirmed in his chair. "I don't consider myself a racist."

Hunter exaggerated his surprise. "But you were there that night? Did you also argue with Reverend Green?"

"Just because I argued with Reverend Green doesn't make me a racist."

"You also saw Reverend Green in the alley that night?"

"I'm not sure what you're implying."

"Mr. Anderson." Hunter stood tall. "Is it true that you make monthly donations to a group called the White Alliance Coalition?"

A gasp went through the courtroom.

The shock was clear on Bauer's face. He gripped the arms of his chair, breathing heavily through his nostrils. Hunter paused for a few long moments, creating an uncomfortable silence, and then continued.

"Mr. Anderson, can you please answer the question?"

"Objection," Law called out again, more so Bauer had time to think. "Immaterial. I fail to see how this is relevant."

"Overruled, again, but let's get to the point, Mr. Hunter," Judge Lockett said.

"That's where the money for the White Alliance Coalition comes from, isn't it?" Hunter tapped the file on the table with his finger. "And I will remind you that you're under oath, Mr. Bauer. Any lies here are subject to contempt of court and perjury."

Bauer looked to Law, but she avoided eye contact.

"I…" He shrugged.

Hunter tapped the folder on his desk, indicating to Bauer that he had the evidence.

"My company makes many donations to many different causes." He was fumbling his words. He turned away from Hunter and crossed one leg over the other.

"Can you name another organization that your company makes donations to?" Hunter knew that Bauer was not the helping type. Unless he was committed to something, unless he believed in it, then it was unlikely that he would help anyone.

"I can't remember any."

"If you made donations to other companies, you would have evidence of these donations, wouldn't you?"

"I don't think so. I don't track all my donations." His body shifted away from Hunter.

Hunter's response was quick. "Interesting. So, I'll ask you again. Do you directly deposit money from your personal account into the account of the White Alliance Coalition?"

"I'm not sure."

"Do you agree with the White Alliance Coalition's beliefs?"

"I don't know all of the White Alliance Coalition's beliefs." There was shaking in his voice.

"But you have attended some White Alliance Coalition meetings?"

He shrugged, unsure how to avoid answering the question. "I may have been at the same place at the same time when the meetings were held."

"Mr. Bauer." Hunter's fist slammed down onto the table. "I'll ask you again. Are you a racist?"

"I'm not a racist! I want what's best for this country! I want to protect our rights! That's not a crime!" Bauer jumped up in the witness stand, the aggression surging through his veins.

"Order." Judge Lockett was firm. "Sit down, Mr. Bauer."

Bauer composed himself, ran his hand down to smooth his tie, and then sat down.

Hunter closed the gap between Bauer and himself. "You hated Reverend Green, didn't you?"

"No."

"You were there in the alley with him, weren't you?!"

Bauer's voice rose as he became increasingly frustrated. "No!"

"You've testified that you saw them in the alley together. Are you now changing your statement, Mr. Bauer?"

"C'mon, man! Let it rest," Bauer fired back. "I don't have to answer this!"

Judge Lockett looked down at Bauer. "Please answer the questions asked of you, Mr. Bauer."

"No!" Bauer snapped. "I saw them together and they were arguing! I didn't go into the alley!"

"Did you hit Reverend Green?"

"What is this?" Bauer replied angrily, looking to the prosecution.

"Please answer the questions," Judge Lockett stated again.

"No!"

"Did you punch Reverend Green?"

"Objection. Inflammatory," Law stated.

"Sustained." Judge Lockett glared at Hunter. "You've overstepped the mark, Mr. Hunter."

"You killed him, didn't you? All because of his skin color!"

"No!"

"Objection! Argumentative! Inflammatory! Not relevant to this case! There's no established connection between the White Alliance Coalition and this case!" Law called out.

"Mr. Hunter!" Judge Lockett was not impressed by the defense's consecutive outbursts. "The objection is sustained! You will stop that line of questioning immediately!"

"Withdrawn, Your Honor." Hunter kept his stare locked on Bauer.

"Stick to the current case, Mr. Hunter!" The judge's eyes narrowed as he shouted at the defense attorney.

Hunter moved back to his desk to review his notes.

He didn't have enough to press forward. He knew

that.

All he had was a link, and that wasn't enough to break Bauer. He had played his trump card, he had played his perfect hand, and he was left with nothing more than the connection between the White Alliance Coalition and Bauer.

"At this point in time, we have no further questions for this witness." Hunter sat down. "However, we reserve the right to call this man as a defense witness."

He caught two jury members nodding.

And that was what he wanted.

CHAPTER 43

HUNTER SAT in the small meeting room on the second floor of the courthouse, rubbing his brow, looking over the files. The room was small, had no natural light, and smelled musty. The round table in the middle of the room was sticky, the chair wobbled every time he moved, and the ceiling felt too high compared to the width of the room.

Hunter had expected Bauer to crumble under the weight of the new accusations, crumble with the eyes of the court on him, and admit to everything, but Bauer was a man skilled in the art of evasion.

He had spent his whole life doing it.

Ray Jones stood in the back corner of the room, arms folded across his chest, and Esther Wright sat directly opposite Hunter. Esther chewed loudly on her gum, flicking through the files in front of her.

Hunter coughed. "Ahem."

"Oh." Esther lifted her gaze from the file. "Yep. Sorry." She took the gum out of her mouth and threw it in the wastepaper basket in the corner of the room.

"I'm sorry too, Tex," Jones stated. He pulled out the third wooden chair at the table, sitting down as he signed exasperatedly. "I really thought that it was going to be worth something. I really thought that it would be a tipping point for him. We had one big play, and it proved nothing."

"It exposed a racist. Everyone knows the truth now. That has to be worth something," Esther said.

"Worth what?" Hunter threw his hands up. "Worth putting an innocent man in prison? It's not worth that. We have to find a way to expose him. There has to be something."

"What about the necklace?" Jones asked. "Bauer must've taken it the night that Green was killed. That's the only way he would've had it. That has to prove he was there—he was with Green in the alley. What about the fingerprints on the necklace? Maybe there was something we missed?"

"Browne is too clean for that. The necklace was tested for fingerprints and DNA, and there was nothing. Not even Green's fingerprints or DNA was on it, which means it was wiped clean before it was placed in Anderson's bedroom. We've tried that play with Browne, and it got us nowhere." Hunter stood and began to pace the room. "And we have nothing to prove that he took it that night."

"So we find a picture of Green with the necklace that night?"

"That'll work against us." Hunter remarked.

"But the necklace proves Bauer was there," Esther said. "Now, all we have to do is prove it in court."

"Not quite. We know that Bauer was in the alley that night, but we don't know if he actually killed Green."

"Come on." This time, Jones threw his hands up. "It has to be him. He's a racist, he hated Green, and he wanted to stop Green from destroying his business. It had to be him."

"It certainly checks out that Bauer, not Anderson, could've met Green outside the hotel and asked him to go down the alley for a quiet word, away from the cameras. We can play that angle in court." Hunter stood and paced the room. "I imagine Bauer offered him a deal to discuss something, perhaps to get rid of Anderson, and Green was interested. He would've been cautious, but Green was a confident man. He wouldn't have been scared of walking down an alley with Bauer."

"So where does that leave us?"

"Nowhere. Absolutely nowhere." Hunter stopped pacing. "We've got nothing on Bauer except a theory."

Silence fell over the room, the two men staring into space as they contemplated their next move, while Esther scrolled through her phone. Hunter drew deep breaths as he tracked over the night in his head—what could have happened or how it took place. He was sure he was missing something, something that would tie the details together. In the courtroom, the doubt was building around Anderson's guilt, but it wasn't enough. Even with one juror on his side, possibly two, it wasn't enough to carry the case through the deliberations.

Jones broke the silence. "Come on. Bauer is full of hate. He must've killed Green. Green could've said the wrong thing, and then whack—Bauer hits him."

"Green didn't look like a man that went down easily," Hunter said. "And even though he was a minister, I bet Green could've taken Bauer in a fight. Green was punched head-on, which meant that he would've been outmuscled."

"Or maybe surprised."

Esther's phone pinged. She looked at the notification.

"Give me another day on Bauer. I'll be able to find something else. I'll ask Mrs. Nelson to help us. We've got Bauer as a racist, maybe we can find more information," Jones stated.

"This might help us." Esther placed her phone on the table.

"What is it?"

"I followed Caylee Johnson on YouTube, and I set it up to receive notifications any time she left a comment on a video. Look at the latest video that she has commented on."

She brought up the information on the screen.

"What does it say?" Jones squinted.

"'I've always watched these videos. They're so inspiring. Thank you for sharing.'"

"Are you sure this comment is from Caylee Johnson?" Hunter asked as he began to watch the video in question. The video was posted a year ago, with fifty thousand likes and five hundred comments.

"I'm absolutely sure that comment is from Caylee Johnson," Esther replied.

Hunter stood. "Then we still have a chance to win this."

CHAPTER 44

CHUCK JOHNSON limped to the stand. His walk was uneasy, the cancer finally taking its last shots at his body. It had been a slow process, one that had been happening for many months. He first felt ill over a year ago but refused to see a doctor for another six months. Denial was his way of dealing with mortality.

Even at the beginning, the illness didn't feel normal; it was like a heavy hangover that never went away. The doctors suggested surgery, but he refused; he knew his time was up, and he wanted to go out on his terms. He regretted the decades of smoking a pack a day, but there was nothing more he could do about it now.

After the murder of his wife, death became a long-term goal, a way out of his pain.

He coughed through his oath and was still coughing when Law began her questioning. He coughed into his handkerchief, sounding like half his lung was coming up with it.

"If you would like to take some time out—"

"No. Go on," he insisted, tucking his handkerchief away.

Michelle Law began her questioning sitting down, reading from the laptop in front of her. She had spent the last hour going through the testimony with Chuck Johnson—after the angle of the case changed with Bauer's testimony.

"Can you please tell the court where you were on the night of February 1st?"

"I was meeting with a person in the alley behind the Congress Hotel."

The comment caught the interest of the jury, who were all paying close attention to what was coming next.

"Who were you meeting that night?"

"Amos Anderson."

The courtroom erupted.

"Murderer!" Green's supporters shouted at Anderson. "Murderer!"

"Order!" Judge Lockett slammed down his gavel. "Order! Order! Remove those people!"

Law waited while Reverend Green's supporters were ushered out of the courtroom, continuing to yell as they were taken out.

Chuck smiled, Anderson shook his head repeatedly, and Hunter was sure that the testimony was nothing more than a lie; leverage to get him off the weapons charges.

It was too convenient, too perfect, to be anything more than a lie.

Hunter had established the connection between Bauer and the Johnson clan, and he was sure that a large amount of money would be transferred after this imaginary statement.

Once the commotion in the court had died down, Law looked back at the witness.

"Are you here because you've been given a deal to testify?" Law continued.

"That's correct."

Law wanted the information to come out in court before Hunter could use it to his advantage.

"What's the deal that you've accepted?"

"I was arrested last week for having unlicensed weapons in my truck," Chuck said as if he was proud of breaking the law. "I had two shotguns that were registered as stolen. I was given immunity for that charge if I made a testimony about what I saw that night."

A deal with the Devil.

It hurt Law to have to work with the Johnson clan, but she knew that the Unlawful Possession of Weapons charge, even though his second arrest for the offense meant a class 3 felony, was nothing compared to this case. Although she was working with a racist, although she was working with a convicted felon, she felt like she was still in the right.

Some wins come at a cost.

"Why haven't you come forward before?"

"Because I wanted nothing to do with this. I wanted nothing to do with this court case."

"What exactly did you see that night?"

Law swallowed hard as she read the notes, keeping her composure. She hated working with the scum that was Chuck Johnson; even without his racist ideals, she still would've hated working with the sleaze. His lingering eyes, his bad breath, and creepy smile didn't win her over.

But it was the racism that she hated most. She hated the fact that she was working with a man known to spread hate based on someone's skin color.

The State's Attorney was reluctant to give him a deal, knowing how it would look to the public, but the State's Attorney also knew that losing this case, letting Anderson go free, could cause a riot on the streets.

Doing any deal with a felon was a risk, let alone a vocal racist, but they signed off on the deal with thoughts of the greater good.

"I was alone, and I stood at the end of the alley, and I saw Amos Anderson walk into the alley next to Dural Green. When they were around thirty yards into the alley, I saw Anderson push Green to the ground and then hit him three times while he lay on the ground."

A jury member gasped. Another shook his head.

"Did you intervene?"

"No, I didn't. It was none of my business."

"What happened after you watched Mr. Anderson beat Reverend Green on the ground?"

"He began to walk away, and that's when I left. I didn't want Anderson to see me, even though he asked me to be there. I didn't see Green walk away, but I assumed that he did. I didn't know that he was dead at the time. I thought he would've gotten up and walked away, but it appears the black guy was weak—"

Law cut him off from speaking any further. "No further questions."

It was a risky play—the prosecution was already ahead in the courtroom, and if the testimony went wrong, then the potential consequences would be very damaging.

She had given a racist a soapbox, but she hoped that it was enough to convict a killer.

Chuck Johnson's revelations had shaken the courtroom, changed the balance of the case, but Hunter had his cross-examination to come.

He knew it was all a falsehood, a fabricated lie to try and take down Anderson.

And now was the time to make his play.

Time to use the leverage.

CHAPTER 45

CHUCK JOHNSON wheezed as he waited for Hunter to begin his questioning. Getting air into his lungs was getting harder and harder—not that it motivated him enough to give up the cigarettes. He figured that if he was going out anyway, he might as well go out his way.

He fumbled with the cigarette packet in his pocket, desperate to get outside for a hit of nicotine. Nicotine had been a comforting friend for him, an escape from the terrors of the world. He knew it was killing him, but without that escape, without that respite, he would have ended his life a long time ago.

"Mr. Johnson, are you currently ill?"

"I have lung cancer and emphysema. The doctors have given me only a few more months to live."

"Does this illness restrict you in any way?" Hunter had a distinct lack of sympathy in his tone.

"I can't do most things. I can't lift anything heavy, I can't work anymore, and I can't go for long walks without using a breathing machine."

"Can you drive for long periods, say anything over thirty minutes?"

"No." He shook his head. "The breathing problems don't allow me to do that."

"Mr. Johnson, can you please confirm to the court if you are the 'Grandmaster'—" Hunter used his fingers as quotation marks. "—of the White Alliance Coalition."

"I am." Chuck sat up proudly, with not one hint of embarrassment about his title. "I'm the founder and driver of the White Alliance Coalition. We believe in—"

"Thank you, Mr. Johnson." Hunter held up his hand. He had no interest in giving him a platform to preach. "How many members of the White Alliance Coalition are there?"

"At our peak, we had more than one hundred members, with around twenty attending our monthly meetings."

"And now?"

He shrugged. "Maybe ten."

"Mr. Johnson, what motivated you to start the White Alliance Coalition?"

"My wife and daughter." He grunted, but it sent him into another coughing fit. "They were shot by a black man when he broke into my house. A black man killed my wife and permanently injured my daughter. She's hobbled her whole life with a painful leg injury."

"And because of that event…" Hunter was flat in his tone. "… do you feel that it's your duty to protect your daughter?"

"Of course. She's my angel."

Caylee may've been Chuck's angel, but she was also about to become Hunter's leverage.

"How did it make you feel when she liked Reverend Green's videos on YouTube?"

Chuck's mouth dropped open, unsure of how to answer.

"Mr. Johnson?" Hunter raised his eyebrows. "How did it make you feel when your angel, your daughter, Caylee Johnson, watched and then liked Reverend Green's speeches on YouTube?"

"I didn't…" Chuck looked to the prosecution, but they couldn't help him. "I… I don't know how you know that."

"That's not an answer, Mr. Johnson."

"I…" He opened his hands. "I was shocked."

"You were shocked," Hunter agreed. "You were shocked that your daughter, who you raised to be a racist, liked a video from Reverend Green, an African American Baptist minister. Once that shock subsided, did it make you angry?"

"Yeah." Chuck tilted his head. "Of course it made me angry."

"Angry enough to kill?"

"Objection. Argumentative." Law called out.

"Withdrawn." Hunter was quick in his response. "When you were in the alley that night to allegedly meet someone, did you drive there?"

"Yes."

"And you testified that you were alone?"

"Yes."

"But you weren't, were you?"

"Pardon?"

"You weren't alone. You've testified that you can't drive for more than thirty minutes. How could you drive the truck in your current state when the

Congress Hotel is more than one and a half hours from your home?"

"I..." Chuck moved again, putting one hand on the smokes in his trouser pocket, his fingers rubbing the edge of the box. "I must've had rest stops along the way."

"Really?" Hunter's voice rose. "Is it not true that you were driven there by someone else?"

"No, I mean, yes. No. I don't understand the question."

Hunter stood. "You were driven to that alley by someone else, weren't you?"

His eyes looked to the back of the courtroom. Hunter caught the eye movement and turned. "Ah. Mr. Johnson, you were driven by your brother, Burt Johnson, weren't you?"

Again, Chuck was speechless.

"Or perhaps it was your daughter, Caylee, that drove you there?"

He was quick to respond, hands leaping out of his pocket "No. It was Burt. He drove, okay? We parked in the parking lot next door. Caylee had nothing to do with this. Leave her alone."

"Burt drove to the parking garage next to the

Congress Hotel." Hunter's voice became aggressive. "And when you and Burt walked down that alley, what did Reverend Green say to you?"

"Nothing!"

One of the jury members gasped.

Chuck looked confused for a moment. "No, No! I mean, he didn't say anything. We didn't talk to him!"

"Order!" Judge Lockett shouted.

"I said—"

"Mr. Johnson! I think that you were the one that killed Reverend Green!" Hunter shouted.

"I—"

"Mr. Johnson! You were there!"

"I—"

"Mr. Johnson, you're under oath!"

"Objection. Your Honor!" Law stood up. "Argumentative!"

"I didn't do it," Johnson argued.

"Mr. Johnson, you beat him to death!"

"Objection!"

"Sustained!" The gavel slammed, but Chuck didn't stop.

"So what if I talked with the black man that day! That doesn't prove anything!"

Hunter kept his eyes on Chuck.

"Mr. Hunter, I will not warn you again. Once an objection is sustained, you will stop that line of questioning." Judge Lockett pointed his finger at the defense table.

"Yes, Your Honor." He turned a page on his desk and then turned back to the witness. "You were angry, weren't you? You were angry that your daughter liked his speech?"

"No."

"And when you hit Green the first time, what did he say?"

"Shut your mouth, Chuck!" Burt Johnson yelled from the back of the courtroom. "Don't say another word!"

"Order!"

"What happened, Chuck?!" Hunter shouted.

"Order!"

Chuck looked around.

Hunter leaned forward.

He needed to push Chuck's buttons. He needed to get under his skin.

And he knew exactly how to do that.

"Or should I ask Caylee Johnson that question? Maybe she will tell us what she did that night?"

"Caylee?" There was desperation in Chuck's voice. "No. Not Caylee. Don't bring her into this."

"She was there, Chuck. She was with you," Hunter bluffed. "She loved Reverend Green's videos. She was turning against you, and Reverend Green was doing that!"

"Don't say anything!" Burt pointed his finger at his older brother as the bailiffs began to wrestle him out of court. "Say nothing!"

"Order in the court!" The gavel slammed again. "Get that man out of here!"

"It was Caylee, wasn't it?"

"No!" Chuck leaped up. "It wasn't Caylee, she wasn't there!"

"You've told us she was there."

"No!" He shook his head. "Leave her alone!"

"Caylee punched him. She punched Reverend Green!"

"No!" he shouted. "Leave Caylee alone! I did it all. It was only Burt and me there. That's all. I did it. I killed him!"

The court erupted—the supporters of Reverend Green yelled their hatred, the reporters jumped up, and the bailiffs struggled to maintain command.

"Order! Order!"

"Murderer!"

"Racist!"

"Killer!"

"Order!"

Hunter had a confession. He had that statement in court.

But he didn't have the killer.

"But you didn't punch him, did you?" Hunter shouted over the noise. "You aren't strong enough to kill a man with a punch. You're protecting someone!" Hunter slapped the table. "Was it Caylee?"

The crowd continued to shout.

"Order!" Judge Lockett stood. "Order!"

"It was me! It was me!"

Chuck glanced to the back of the room, where his brother was being held by the bailiffs.

"It was me!" Chuck Johnson repeated.

Hunter turned. There, at the back of the courtroom, was a boxer. A large man who would do anything he was told. A man that didn't know his own strength.

Against a defenseless pastor, he was a giant.

"Burt threw the punches, didn't he?" Hunter turned back to Chuck, his voice softer this time.

Chuck was overwhelmed. He broke down, sobbing.

"You were there to rough up Reverend Green for Lucas Bauer, tell him to back off, but Burt went too far, didn't he?"

"He didn't mean to," Chuck said, still sobbing. "He didn't know his own strength."

Hunter turned and saw the defeated look on Burt's face.

Standing at the door, being restrained by guards, he looked stunned.

"Burt Johnson is a trained boxer with a heavy

punch—certainly heavy enough to kill a man after three blows to the head."

Chuck Johnson shook his head again.

"Burt punched him, didn't he?"

"He didn't mean to kill him," he pleaded. "It was an accident. It was manslaughter. Lucas wanted us to rough him up, put the fear of God into Green. He didn't mean to kill him."

"Burt hit him too hard."

"It was an accident. He pushed him, and he fell over. And then it was only three punches. Nothing more." Chuck was begging. "Let Burt go. Take me to prison instead. It's all my fault. I shouldn't walk free. Take me to prison instead of Burt."

"The law doesn't work like that, Mr. Johnson." Hunter turned as police officers gathered around Burt. "But you'll see Burt in prison after they've charged you with being an accessory to murder."

CHAPTER 46

TEX HUNTER sat in his office, a smile stretched across his face. He had a hangover from celebrating the night before, but nothing could wipe this smile away. It was the smile of a winner; someone who had faced the challenges, overcome the odds, and somehow, walked out in front.

He hadn't planned on Chuck Johnson's confession, but thinking on his feet was part of his job.

Chuck thought he was strengthening the prosecution's case by admitting he was there, as did the prosecution, and they thought he was forcing the case closer to a guilty verdict. When he was arrested for the Unlawful Possession of Weapons charge, facing a class 3 felony for his second arrest, he tried to weasel his way out by offering information and a witness testimony.

But he was out of his depth in the courtroom.

When Lucas Bauer called him that day to 'rough up' Reverend Green, Chuck saw an opportunity. He knew his daughter had been listening to his sermons online, and it ate him up inside. He had to do something about it. He couldn't leave this world knowing that his daughter was being influenced by an African American preacher.

Bauer had enticed Reverend Green into the alley, under the guise of doing a quiet deal that would end Anderson's practices in Chicago. Bauer was threatened by Green's attacks, scared that his business profits would suffer. He offered a deal that they would move the business to Los Angeles if Green agreed to stop his public attacks on their business.

Under Bauer's instructions, Burt Johnson was waiting in the alley and sprang into action. Bauer didn't want Green dead, but Chuck Johnson did. Burt landed three punches, and the damage was done. Heavy bleeding in the brain caused his death.

"Could you look any happier with yourself?" Esther laughed as she stood in the doorway to Hunter's office. "Look at you, sitting there, staring out the window, smiling to yourself."

"It's a beautiful day, Esther. I have every reason to be happy." Hunter's smile widened. "Not only did we find a killer, but we also took the heart out of a racist organization. That's a reason to smile."

"Always the hero." Esther grinned, her slight figure leaning on the doorframe. With her arms folded, and her hair flowing free, she was the picture of good health and good will. "I know Chuck and Burt are going to prison for the rest of their lives—"

"Which, in Chuck's case, is only a few months."

"Right." She came into his office and sat on the chair opposite his desk. "But what about Lucas Bauer?"

"He's an accessory to murder too, and his reputation is destroyed. It's out in the open court that he supported the White Alliance Coalition. The papers printed that this morning." Hunter grabbed the Chicago Tribune off his desk and handed it to Esther. "Page three details it all. Bauer is included in their rundown."

Hunter's mobile phone buzzed on his desk. He picked it up, read the number, shrugged, and put the phone down again.

"Who is it?" Esther asked.

"Detective Jemma Knowles," he replied as the phone stopped buzzing. "She's an old friend, but she's still a cop. I'd prefer to bathe in this victory a little longer before someone else throws new stresses at me. Let me enjoy this glow."

Esther continued to read the paper, but the phone buzzed a second time. Hunter squinted, saw that it was Detective Knowles again, but pressed the button to send the call straight to voicemail.

"Last night Amos said that he's going to leave the Faith Healing Project and start something on his own. He's going to continue to practice," he said.

"Amos was very happy last night. I've never seen a man drink a bottle of champagne that quickly." Esther smiled. "I wouldn't want to have his hangover this morning."

The phone buzzed once. It was a text this time.

'Urgent. Answer the phone.'

The phone rang again.

Hunter answered his phone. "Jemma, what a pleasure to hear from you."

"Lock your doors, Tex. This isn't a friendly call." Her voice was firm.

"What's going on?" Hunter stood.

"Where are you?"

"In my office."

"We're sending a car straight there."

"Jemma?" He walked out of his office to the reception area, shut the office door, and locked it. "What's happening? What's going on?"

"We're at the White Alliance Coalition residence, Chuck Johnson's home. We came to talk with Caylee Johnson, but she's not here."

"And?"

"Last night, Chuck told us everything. He told us where all his guns are, and where he kept the explosives he owned. He spilled everything he knew in the hope of getting into a nice prison hospital to spend his last days. We offered him that deal, and he spent hours talking about what they had. He admitted to the church shooting and then two other unsolved crimes."

"What's that got to do with me?"

"It's all gone, Tex. Everything. The guns, the explosives, and the van that was used in the church shooting." Her voice was panicked. "Everything has been cleared out, and it's going to be used in an attack."

"Caylee."

"She's going to lead an attack. We have the SWAT response team heading to Northeastern Illinois University right now."

"And you think that we're a possible target?"

"Yes." Jemma's voice was firmer. "Don't leave that office building, Tex. You're in lockdown. We have a car on the way to your house and one to your office."

"And Amos?"

"We don't think he's a target."

"Of course he's the target! Get the car to his house, not my office!"

"We have limited resources, Tex. Right now, we think the university and your office are her main targets. We're searching for the van, but we've got nothing yet. This is where we're sending our resources."

"No, get to Anderson's house. That's where she's heading. She'll blame him for everything."

"Tex, don't do anything stupid. We have a car on the way to you. You can call Amos, but don't leave that office. We—"

Hunter hung up the phone. There was no use arguing with Jemma Knowles. He knew that.

"Tex? What's going on?" Esther asked.

"The building is in lockdown. Don't leave this

office, and lock the door after me."

"Where are you going?"

"I'm going to stop Caylee Johnson."

CHAPTER 47

SHE HAD a choice.

She always had a choice.

Caylee Johnson drove down the road in the white van that had sat in the garage for more than three months.

She hadn't been able to drive it, not after the church shooting. The last time she was in the van, her Uncle Burt was driving, and her father was in the front seat. She sat in the spare seat in the back, scared of the anger in their voices. They hadn't told her where they were going that day.

They hadn't told her what they were doing.

When they got to the church on that Sunday morning, she pleaded with Burt to drive away.

But the more she'd pleaded, the more hatred had grown inside her father. When he wound down the window and fired three shots at the church, she screamed over and over.

She sobbed the entire drive home, and they told her not to say a word.

That was her punishment for watching Reverend Green's videos on YouTube. She shouldn't have liked one of his sermons. That was her mistake. When Chuck found out, he went into a psychotic rage. How could his own daughter betray everything he had taught her?

Her Uncle Burt hit her so hard the day he found out. They wouldn't even give her the chance to explain why she was doing it. They wanted to hear nothing about it.

That day wasn't the first time he hit her, but it was the hardest.

After the church shooting, the van wasn't supposed to leave the garage, but now she didn't care.

This was the end.

The choice had been made.

She had spent the night crying in bed, not sleeping a wink after hearing about her uncle's arrest. She couldn't avoid the story; it was the lead news on every station, the lead talking point for every chat show.

The police took her father and uncle into custody immediately after her father's statements. It was the first night that she had spent alone in the house, ever.

It felt so cold. So alone.

She thought that it might happen. Her father wasn't smart enough to outwit those educated lawyers. When her father told her the plan, she begged him not to take the stand; she knew what they could do. Although he had been coached many times, he wasn't smart enough to hold onto the lie.

She had to do it now.

It took thirty minutes to reach her destination in the suburb of Bucktown. When she arrived, Caylee Johnson sat in the van, watching the outside of the suburban home.

It looked like a pleasant residence; close enough to the city to be part of the action, but far enough into the suburbs so that it felt like an escape.

She watched the latest news bulletin on her phone. Someone had taken footage of Amos Anderson celebrating with friends, supporters, his lawyer, and his lawyer's team.

Of course, Anderson looked so happy. He had been cleared of murder; a murder that her uncle committed and her father was an accomplice to.

In the first video, Anderson looked joyous. In the second video, he looked like a drunken mess. She was sure that he would be inside his house, probably nursing a very large hangover.

A middle-aged woman with a stroller walked past the van. The woman was bundled up, keeping the cold out with her goose-down jacket, but soaking up the weak winter sunshine.

A man, walking his dog, said hello to the woman and then waited for his dog to use the tree next to the van. Caylee made eye contact, and he smiled a friendly hello.

The suburb was nice.

Something she wasn't used to.

Everyone in her neighborhood hated the Johnsons. That was all she had ever felt directed towards her family—hate. People had spat at them when she walked with her father to the post office. People often destroyed the fences around their home or threw rubbish over their hedge from the street. Three of her teachers at high school wouldn't even look at her—not because of anything she did, but because of her father, her family.

Growing up, the only place she had ever felt welcome was in her home.

And now that home was about to be taken away from her.

Her father was driven by anger. All of his rage was born from a place of hatred for what happened to his wife. Caylee understood but didn't feel the same hate inside of her.

She was more level-headed, less emotional than her father.

Her style was more planned, less impulsive.

She still felt hate; it was always part of her life.

She couldn't understand the people that avoided anger—it was an emotion, a feeling. She had always been taught to embrace her hatred, let it flow out like a river of rage.

To her, hate was a part of life; as common as sunshine.

To reject it would be to reject herself.

"I can do this." She said aloud, biting her fingernails. "I can do this."

Inside the van was every gun that the White Alliance Coalition owned.

And every explosive.

She drew a deep breath.

"I can do this."

She stepped out of the van.

It was time.

CHAPTER 48

ANDERSON'S HOUSE was a fifteen-minute drive from Hunter's office, and he wanted to make it in under eight. He raced through the streets, screeching his tires around every corner, pushing through the red lights. He sped around the quiet streets, only slowing down when he turned onto the street that Anderson lived on.

He wasn't sure what he would find, he wasn't sure what Caylee was capable of, but he knew that she was in a position with nothing to lose. Everything had already been taken away from her; her life had already been turned upside down by the court case.

He had no idea how dangerous she was, no idea how much hate she harbored.

As he came closer to Anderson's house, he saw it.

The white van.

The same van that he saw on the day when his

shoulder was shot.

He slowed his car, looking for any sign of activity, any sign of danger. Cautiously, he rolled the car forward until it was next to the van.

And there, in front of the van, was Caylee Johnson, dressed in a black sweater and jeans, biting her fingernails, staring at Anderson's house.

"Caylee." Hunter slowly stepped out of the car, palms open to her. "Don't do anything stupid."

"Tex Hunter?" She turned to look at him, confused. "How did you know that I'd be here?"

"Everyone is looking for you, Caylee. The police, the firefighters, and the SWAT teams. They know what's in the van."

She looked confused. "How? How could they know that?"

"The police are at your house, Caylee. Your father told them everything. They know what's missing. They know there are explosives in that van." He stepped closer to her, keeping his arms wide.

She turned and looked towards Anderson's house, biting her fingernails again.

"You don't have to do anything, Caylee. You don't have to do this."

"My uncle and father are in prison."

Anderson stepped out of his house, rubbing his sore head. He hadn't bothered to answer Hunter's calls; he needed a dose of fresh air first.

He saw Hunter, guardedly stepping across the street, and then he spotted Caylee Johnson at his front gate, only ten yards away from him.

He almost fell over backwards.

"Don't move." Caylee said to Anderson. "I want to talk to you."

Anderson didn't respond; he couldn't. He was struck by fear. The attacks from the public over the past few months had almost broken him and he was sure that it was over now, he was sure that part of his life was finished. To be confronted with his worst threat, one of the people he feared the most, was almost too much.

"Caylee." Hunter moved onto the sidewalk. "Don't take another step towards him."

She was still biting her nails, still staring at Anderson.

"I'm not going anywhere, Caylee." Hunter came within five yards of her. "I won't allow you to do this. Not now."

She stared at Anderson, who was still in shock, and then turned to Hunter.

"That van has every gun, weapon, and explosive that belongs to my family. Everything that the White Alliance Coalition owns. There's enough pain in that truck to sink an army." She took a step towards Anderson, who was on the other side of the small fence. "I have to know, this faith healing, does it really work?"

"It works." Anderson mumbled. "If you believe it works."

"But how can you be so sure that it works?"

"The results speak for themselves." Anderson took a step back, onto the first of the stairs that led to his front door. "We've cured hundreds of people from their issues."

Caylee paused and bit her lip, then turned back to Hunter.

"Caylee. Don't do anything stupid." Hunter was ready to dive at her.

"I had a choice to make—one road or the other. Do I continue with the generational hatred, or do I end it? It's something I've wrestled with for a long time." She bit her nails again. "In the van is everything that keeps the White Alliance Coalition going. I don't want it anymore. I want it gone. If I left it at home, one of the other men would've taken it. I don't want it, and I don't want the White Alliance Coalition to have it. It ends here. Today."

She reached into her pocket, and then threw the van's keys to Hunter.

She turned back to Anderson. "Can you cure hatred? I don't want it anymore. I don't want to hold onto this hatred any longer. I want to be one of these people that can let go of the past. Can you cure me?"

"Do you believe I can?" Anderson stepped towards her.

"I do." She pulled a strand of hair behind her ear. "I believe you can cure me. That's why I came to you, that's why I'm here. I want all this to be over. I don't want this hate. I don't want this racism. I want to leave it all in the past and be friends with whoever I want to be friends with. I want to be free of this pain."

"Then, yes, faith healing can cure you of your hate." Anderson's smile was nervous. "We can leave it in the past. We can use this moment to turn over a new leaf, create a new chance, a new spring; but you have to believe."

Anderson looked at Hunter.

Caylee Johnson turned as well and offered him a smile. "I believe."

Amos Anderson walked up the four steps to the door of his home, opened it wide, and gestured for Caylee to follow him.

"Then, please, Caylee Johnson, come inside."

CHAPTER 49

"YOU'RE OUTTA here!"

Maxwell Hunter jumped up and punched the air, the crowd erupting around him. The sea of blue was engulfed in the contest, engrossed by the game they weren't supposed to win. The Chicago Cubs were playing well, better than they had in a month, and were about to deliver the greatest upset victory for the year.

The crowd had packed in on the Saturday afternoon, and the smiles couldn't be wiped off any of the Hunters' faces. Patrick and his son, Maxwell, sat next to each other in the fourth row from the front, with Tex next to them. It was the first time Patrick and his son had seen each other in over a year, and Patrick hid his first tears under his sunglasses. It was also the first time that Hunter and Patrick had been to a baseball game together.

Alfred Hunter's actions had stolen his sons'

youths, stolen any chance to spend time together in public, but the brothers were beginning to make amends for the past.

"Mr. Hunter?" The voice came over the back of the aisle, and all three Hunter men turned around. "Tex Hunter?"

The African American male came down the concrete steps and offered his hand. Tex Hunter stood and shook it. The man looked familiar, but Hunter couldn't quite place him.

"I'm sorry, I don't know if we've met."

The man pointed to the top of the stairs where a girl sat at the end of the row, happily dressed in Cubs colors, but distracted by the hotdog she was eating. Her mother sat proudly next to her, equally decked out in Cubs colors, and Hunter recognized the woman.

"Derrick West. We met in the hospital." The man drew a breath. "Today is our first weekend out of there. Eva's recovered, she's doing well, and this is the first place she wanted to go when she got out. The Cubs heard about Eva getting out, and made sure we had good seats." The man gave a broad smile. "We're so lucky that she pulled through, all those prayers worked. And Mr. Hunter, I wanted to apologize for—"

"Wait. Don't apologize. I would've reacted the same way. You were under a lot of stress in that hospital."

"At least let me say thank you."

Hunter nodded.

"Thank you, Mr. Hunter. You saved her life. Without you, Eva would be dead." Jackson looked to his daughter. "Come up and say hello."

"Not today." Hunter shook his head. "Let Eva forget about it all for a while. Let her have her moment of joy here with the Cubs and be a child again."

"Thank you." The man smiled. "You know; my wife cooks the best lamb shanks in Chicago. We could never thank you enough for what you did, but let that be an offer of our gratitude sometime soon."

"Well, I do love lamb shanks."

The man patted him on the shoulder. Hunter grimaced.

"Oh, sorry. That must be your sore shoulder."

"That'll have to be two lamb shanks now."

"I guarantee they're the best in the city." The man laughed, removed his phone, and took down Hunter's number. He sent him a text with an address, a date and time. Hunter shook Derrick's hand again before the man sprang back up the stairs to his family.

He took a moment before he sat back down next to his brother. The break in play had people pushing everywhere in a rush for food, beer, or the bathroom, but the mood was fun, jovial, and happy on the early spring afternoon.

"Max." Patrick Hunter smiled at his son and handed him a twenty. "Can you grab us a hotdog? I can't move these old legs to get up the steps like I used to."

"Sure thing." Max grinned and leaped to his feet. "I've got you covered, Dad."

As Max made it to the end of the aisle of people and began walking up to the hotdog seller, Patrick turned to his brother and rubbed his brow.

"Tex, now that it's all over, when are you going to release that information about the faith healing? When is Amos going to make that statement?"

"He's not." Hunter sat up straight. "The faith healing works. It worked for Max, it worked for hundreds of others, and hopefully, it works for Caylee Johnson. I can't deny that. I can't suggest that science trumps truth, no matter how relative that truth is. The fact is that if someone has faith in Anderson, then the healing works, no matter how many trials say that it doesn't."

"Does this mean that your sense of truth and justice has changed?" Patrick looked at him, confused.

"Everyone needs faith; whether it's in religion, science, or the powers of the universe. My faith isn't in a church or in scripture, or in magical powers. My faith is in people, in their innate sense of justice." Hunter looked to the field in front of them. "And a wise man once told me that everything is relative. Even truth."

THE END

AUTHOR'S NOTE:

Thanks so much for reading Faith and Justice. I hope you enjoyed the twists and turns of this story.

I wrote the bulk of this story while in Chicago, working out of various co-working offices; my favorite space was Ampersand in Logan Square. And a few of the ideas in this story were born after a night at The Burke's Web Pub in Bucktown—what a fabulous place full of fabulous people. Thanks to those places for the creative spaces they provide; and a special thank you to Parliament Co-working.

To all my amazing family and friends, thank you for your inspiration... and your patience!

Extra thanks has to go out to my editor Lara; to my proofreader Jessica, and to Bel, my cover designer.

Whether I'm traveling, in a co-working office, or on a tour, I always come across fascinating people. I believe that everyone has a story, and I love to hear them all. To all the people I've met along the way, thank you. You've inspired these characters.

If you enjoyed this book, please leave a positive review. Reviews mean the world to authors.

I've already started the next book in the Tex Hunter series, so keep an eye out for it…

You can find my website at: peteromahoney.com

And if you wish, you can contact me at: peter@peteromahoney.com

Thank you!

Peter O'Mahoney

(level)

② de /zov

level ①

Flat
← Flat → ← Flat →

Also by Peter O'Mahoney:

In the Tex Hunter series:

Power and Justice

*****

In the Bill Harvey Legal Thriller Series:

Redeeming Justice

Will of Justice

Fire and Justice

A Time for Justice

Truth and Justice

*****

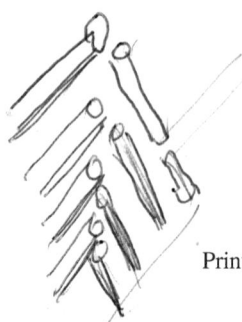

Printed in Great Britain
by Amazon